**Praise for Julie Smith and the Edgar-winning
SKIP LANGDON SERIES:**

"In choosing a tour guide to crime and corruption in New
Orleans, you want to know where the authors will send you
for a good time. Julie Smith will stroll you through the
Garden District, and treat you to a muffuletta at Napoleon
House...Not a nuance of the city's byzantine social politics
escapes [her]."
—*The New York Times Book Review*

"Smith catches New Orleans from blues in the night to
beignets at dawn ..."
—*Los Angeles Times Book Review*

"Gritty, witty, and mesmerizing! Langdon is a splendid
female heroine."
—*People*

"BRILLIANT."
—*San Francisco Examiner & Chronicle*

"With *The Axeman's Jazz*, Julie Smith not only firmly estab-
lishes her claim to the New Orleans crime scene, but she
explores an intriguing new franchise for the serial killer.
Well-researched, engaging, with solid psychological insight,
this novel is the perfect follow-up to Skip Langdon's *New
Orleans Mourning* debut."
— *Sue Grafton, author of* "H" Is for Homicide

"Julie Smith's New Orleans is a subterranean Mardi Gras where the masks cover smiling sociopaths and even Deadly Nightshade comes sheathed in silk."
—*Andrew Vachss, author of* Sacrifice

"Marvelous...If Tennessee Williams wore a trench coat, he'd feel right at home here."
— *Chicago Tribune*

"Smith is a gifted writer and she tells her story on many levels, through many dimensions."
— *The Washington Post Book World*

"Julie Smith writes like jazz should sound—cool, complex, and penetrating right to the heart."
— *Val McDermid, author of* The Last Temptation

"If you haven't read Smith before, it's time to start. If you're a fan, you're in for yet another treat."
— *Marcia Muller*

"Julie Smith resurrects New Orleans' historic, never-caught Axeman in this stunning tale of a serial killer loose in the city's self-help groups. In her incisive characterizations of Policewoman Skip Langdon and of New Orleans itself, Julie Smith proves herself to be a wise and wonderful novelist."
— *Sharyn McCrumb*

"Skip knows her city, from the down-and-out dives to the conspicuous consumption mansions, and has access to all the gossip, history and outright fantasies of New Orleans power structure."
— *Dallas Morning News*

"Langdon is as captivating a character as the city in which she lives and works. This is a series that gets stronger with each book."
—*The Denver Post*

"Like a good Grisham: taut, fast, and thrilling, but with a lot more heart and soul ... Whether she's concocting delectable murder and mayhem in the Golden City or stirring it up Cajun style in the City that Care Forgot, Julie Smith is still the best tour guide going."
— *The Clarion-Ledger (Jackson, MS)*

"If you haven't discovered Smith yet, now is the time to do so... Move over, Sara Paretsky."
—*KPFA-FM (Berkeley, CA)*

"In *Jazz Funeral*, Smith writes from multiple viewpoints, creating a kind of literary chorus with contrasting voices that interweave and form a pattern....Welcome back, Skip Langdon."
— *The New Orleans Times-Picayune*

"Suspenseful and moving...Full of authentic New Orleans atmosphere, *Jazz Funeral* is every bit as good as her Edgar Award-winning novel *New Orleans Mourning*."
— *Mostly Murder*

"A genuinely moving mystery...It's always a pleasure to spend time with Skip, a non-nonsense, level-headed heroine in a wild and reckless city."
— *The Baltimore Sun*

BOOKS BY JULIE SMITH

The Skip Langdon Series

NEW ORLEANS MOURNING

THE AXEMAN'S JAZZ

JAZZ FUNERAL

DEATH BEFORE FACEBOOK

(*formerly NEW ORLEANS BEAT*)

HOUSE OF BLUES

THE KINDNESS OF STRANGERS

CRESCENT CITY CONNECTION

(*formerly CRESCENT CITY KILL*)

82 DESIRE

MEAN WOMAN BLUES

MURDER ON MAGAZINE

THE BIG CRAZY

The Rebecca Schwartz Series

DEATH TURNS A TRICK

THE SOURDOUGH WARS

TOURIST TRAP

DEAD IN THE WATER

OTHER PEOPLE'S SKELETONS

THE BIG CRAZY

A SKIP LANGDON MYSTERY

JULIE SMITH

booksBnimble Publishing
New Orleans, La.

The Big Crazy

ISBN 978-0-9998131-6-4
Also available as an eBook

www.booksnimble.com

First booksBnimble publication: October 2019

To Nevada, my treasured friend and comrade in crime

SATURDAY, AUGUST 27, 2005

THE DAY BEFORE DOOMSDAY

1

Hurricane Katrina was the monster we all knew would get us—the genuine article, no messing around this time—and it was coming in twenty-four hours give or take. It was Saturday night, August, 27, and everybody who had any sense and enough money for gas was loading the car to get out of Dodge if they hadn't already.

That is, everyone but those with relatives who couldn't go (or wouldn't go), everyone with animals they didn't want to put through the trauma (although many with kids didn't balk), everyone who didn't have a car, the very very stubborn who'd never left for a goddam storm and weren't going to start now, the odd thrill seeker, and anyone who had to work.

Detective Skip Langdon fell in the last category. She was still in New Orleans because if you were a cop, the mandatory evacuation order didn't apply. You had to go to work as soon as the wind subsided. This was because thousands of people wouldn't heed the order, and there'd be crime as usual, not to mention out-of-control traffic due to impass-able streets. All with a side of looting.

She had the weekend off, but first thing Monday, she had to be out on the streets fighting crime.

So despite dark messages of near-immediate doom, for Skip, it was just another Saturday night barbecue in the courtyard, only with an undertone of fear and excitement that kept flaring up and putting everyone on edge. They were definitely losing power sometime late Sunday night—Katrina was at least *that* big and deadly—so her neighbor and landlord Jimmy Dee Scoggin had grilled a redfish he'd recently caught, so it wouldn't go bad. It was just about the only thing in his refrigerator he'd miss, although, as he pointed out to Skip, there was some good stuff in there and she should eat it while he was gone.

He was leaving for Shreveport first thing in the morning with Sheila and Kenny, his two adopted teen-age kids, and his partner, Layne. Layne's extended family had a house there big enough for everybody except Angel, the kids' little black and white dog, to whom Layne was violently allergic. No house was big enough for both Layne and Angel, and certainly no car, so Angel was staying home with Auntie Skip. Since it was too hot to eat outside, Layne wasn't even having dinner with them, due to his allergy, and Skip had been invited instead.

She lived in the slave quarters out behind Jimmy Dee's French Quarter townhouse, but for the next few days, until the storm blew over, she'd been elected mistress of the manor and Angel's babysitter. The first part was fine—she was happy to take care of Jimmy Dee's house—but she wasn't sure at all about Angel.

"How's she going to pee?" she protested. "I could be gone 12 or 14 hours at a time. Longer, maybe."

"Don't worry, she's trained to puppy pads," Kenny advised, "and anyway, there's no choice. Who else is going to take her? Vets aren't boarding animals right now—we know, we tried. But we should have known—what if a vet's roof blew off and she was stuck with twenty-five dogs? And we can't leave her with anyone who's staying and has their own pets to take care of."

"Like Ollie," Jimmy Dee said, throwing a dark look around the dining room. "My darling keeper of the peace, is there no way you can talk some sense into her?"

Skip sighed. "I've tried, Dee-Dee. But you know how she is."

Ollie—aka Olivia Brown—was a neighbor who also lived in a "dependency unit" a block or two away, but it was nothing like Skip's sturdy slave quarters. It was a flimsy cottage Jimmy Dee was pretty sure was going to literally blow away in the storm, taking Ollie with it along with her half-feral cat, Ignatius. She was a neighborhood character who worked as a housekeeper for Jimmy Dee and others in the hood. And because Jimmy Dee had the two kids, she was at their house twice a week, thus pretty much a fixture. Skip knew he felt responsible for her. That was who he was. (Along with being the most fun of anyone she knew.) When his widowed sister was dying, he'd never questioned whether to become a father of two on a moment's notice.

How Ollie "was" was large, raw-boned, New England bred, and stubborn. She thought she could do anything, including, apparently, go up against a Category Five hurricane. Mostly she was right about being able to do anything that required strength and perseverance, but this was a whole other thing. Both Skip and Jimmy Dee thought she was nuts to even consider it. Jimmy Dee'd begged her to evacuate with his family, but she wasn't having it:

It would be too hard on Ignatius.

He'd never been in a carrier.

He couldn't eat when he was upset.

And Ollie'd never ridden out a hurricane.

She did love the cat, but given her indomitable outlook, Skip thought the last reason was probably the main one. She promised Dee-Dee she'd try again.

"She's just a few blocks away," Kenny said. "Can't she just call you to come get her if it gets too rough?"

Everyone laughed but Sheila, who'd never seen a hurricane either.

"What?" Kenny blurted, his sweet face stricken. He was far the more sensitive of the two kids.

Skip stepped in quickly. "Sorry, I know you don't know what it's like, but she probably can't. That's why everyone's evacuating. We'll lose power and phone towers, so she may not be able to call. And it'll be blowing too hard for me to go get her anyway. That kind of wind can literally blow a person down. Or up against a building."

"It couldn't blow away a car," he said with a sneer. He was embarrassed and a bit pissed off as a result.

"Maybe not, but the roads wouldn't be clear. The storm will take down tree limbs and power lines and turn patio furniture into UFOs that can come through your windshield..."

"Okay, okay, we get the picture," Sheila said. She turned to Jimmy Dee. "Uncle Jimmy, it sounds so cool! Can't I stay?"

"No, you may not, young lady! Are you out of your Princess Diaries Pretty In Pink Clueless mind?"

This time the two kids laughed. "It's so easy to get you going," Sheila said to her uncle.

And Kenny said, "Are those movies out of the Flint-stones or something?"

Skip took a sip of pinot grigio and a bite of redfish. She was on her second glass of wine and reveling in every good thing life had brought her. Sure, they'd heard the warnings about how it could all blow away tomorrow night, but like half the town, she didn't believe it.

"You know what?" she said. "That storm's not gonna hit us. Hurricanes always turn East. It's gonna hit Biloxi."

Jimmy raised his glass to that. "Hear, hear."

2

Lieutenant Adam Abasolo was busy kicking himself around the lakefront, planning to cancel his Saturday night date so he could wallow properly. He was so furious with himself he was thinking how nice it would be to get drunk—and *that* thought sobered him up. He was a recovering alcoholic who hadn't had a drink in years.

Should he try to find an emergency meeting? he wondered, but before he could figure it out, Kathy Bordelon called, the woman he'd been dating for the past two months. "I have to be at work at 7 am." she said. "You?"

"It's pretty much all hands on deck after this thing blows over. I was just thinking..."

"That we should forget about tonight? I was afraid of that."

He had been, but suddenly his bad mood dissipated, transformed into something hopeful. He suddenly realized how much he wanted to see this woman, how he'd cherish a few hours with her before he lost everything he loved— well, everything except his job. And Crevette, the pint-sized cat that slept on his head at night. Although maybe he wouldn't miss Crevette so much. It would be good to have his pillow to himself again.

"You kidding me?" he said. "You would have been a real downer on the Titanic. We're supposed to have a hurricane party. Dance on the decks and all. But you're right, let's not go out. This could be my last night in my house—come spend it with me."

And then he was mortified that he'd said that. Their relationship hadn't reached that point yet—her choice. "Oh sorry, I didn't mean that. I meant..." he had a sudden inspiration... "let me grill you a steak."

"How soon they forget," she said. "Tell you what. I'll bring over some vegan gumbo I've got in the freezer."

Right. She was a vegetarian. But she ate fish, and he had a nice one. "Oops, forgot about the meat thing. But don't bring anything. I've got a nice speckled trout I caught awhile back. We should really try to eat everything frozen before the power goes out."

She arrived without the gumbo, but with salad makings, ice cream, and a bottle of wine for herself. He'd already made a salad and he had an open bottle ready for her, and he even had some shrimp for hors'd'oeuvres. "So I win the thoughtfulness sweepstakes," he said, kissing her and feeling a small flutter. "The shrimp put me over the top."

This woman had stopped him in his tracks the first time he saw her. He'd brought a psychotic into the Charity Hospital emergency room and the man had quickly been assigned to a doctor. He was handcuffed, raving out of his mind, and struggling to get away. They couldn't get him out of their waiting room fast enough.

The doctor waiting for him was a tall broad-shouldered woman who reminded him immediately of his favorite partner, Skip Langdon, although she wasn't *that* tall. But with the same sturdy strength and air of authority. He was pretty sure nobody would mess with her, not even this nutcase. She had a nurse with her, a big bald black guy.

Abasolo expected a quick injection of something, but the guy was too fast and too agitated to hold still long enough. "Give him to me," the doctor said and, very gingerly, Abasolo began to uncuff the patient.

"What's your name?" she asked him.

"Robert. Robert. Robert." He repeated it about ten times, but she spoke over him.

"Okay, Robert Robert. I'm Dr. Bordelon and this is nurse Norm. Give me your hand. You want to get a little more comfortable?"

"We're old friends," Norm said. "Robert, you been here before, right?"

"Faggot," he spat at the nurse.

Abasolo released one of his hands.

She took it, her hand small in Robert's bear paw. "How about you lie down on that gurney?" She nodded at Abasolo to let him know she could use help. Together, they wrestled him into place, the doctor cooing to him, making little maternal sounds, as Norm downloaded his medical history to determine what they could safely give him. And then she nodded to Norm, all the while holding Robert's hand as if he were a child. Norm struck, aiming at Robert's bare arm. Robert sat straight up, and Abasolo flew to her rescue, but she said, "I got this," and talked him back down. In about thirty seconds he was out cold.

She turned to Abasolo. "He'll feel better later. Or not. I'm Kathy Bordelon." She offered her hand.

"Adam Abasolo," he said, and for some reason couldn't think of a single other thing to say.

"Let me walk you out."

She thanked him and as he was about to go, he just blurted the thing on his mind. "Hey, can I call you?" And then, embarrassed, added, "About Robert."

She laughed. "It's okay. I'm single. Are you?"

She'd succeeded in thoroughly intimidating him, but he felt such a rush of joy at her reaction that his easy bantering self returned instantly. Even so, his face felt a little hot. "Single and lonesome," he said, which wasn't quite true. "Let's skip the phone call. Want to do something this weekend?"

"Lonesome" was the part that wasn't quite true. Abasolo dated a lot, and had a terrific on-again-off-again relationship with Cindy Lou Wootten, the department's consulting psychologist. Each of them was always there for the other, but he knew that was never going to be a permanent thing —Cindy Lou had some issues he didn't understand, which Skip described as "horrible taste in men—present company excepted of course."

He knew he had a bad-boy vibe and wasn't the world's most eager to settle down, but he probably wasn't nearly bad enough for Cindy Lou, and it was also doubtful whether either of their families would accept their interracial relationship.

Cindy Lou was as serious as it got for him. Yet he'd been friends with her long before they started dating. She hadn't hit him like Dr. Kathy Bordelon. Kathy was sort of beautiful, he was pretty sure of that, although he pretty much thought all women were. He certainly liked her statuesque, sturdy quality, and long wavy dark hair and big brown eyes. But it couldn't be said that he had a type— blonde and blue would have been just as good. And Cindy Lou was African-American. Maybe it was that strong, authoritative quality combined with the sweetness he associated with Cajuns—she had plenty of that. Whatever it was, she flattened him; absolutely rendered him helpless.

He didn't try to impress her on their first date—in fact, didn't even ask her to dinner. Instead, they went to the beach. It turned out she'd never been to some of his favorite tiny museums on the Gulf Coast, so they popped down to Biloxi and Ocean Springs. He hadn't even thought about it at first—it just seemed like a fun thing to do—but then he realized this was the perfect jaunt for a psychiatrist.

"These guys are totally up your alley," he'd told her. "You know who George Ohr was? They called him 'the mad potter of Biloxi.' And Walter Anderson—besides being a great artist—was the most famous schizophrenic Mississippi ever produced."

She laughed. "So long as I don't have to wrestle them."

The beauty of this trip, for him, was the hour-and-a half car ride—not enough time to get bored, but just right for loosening up a conversation. Something about sitting next to someone, but not having to look into their eyes made people more comfortable than a couple of margaritas.

She was from Houma, had gone to, as she put it, "LSU— went in dumb, came out dumb too," and arrived in New Orleans six months ago, to work in emergency psychiatry.

"Why psychiatry?" he asked, and she said, "I don't like blood."

"I don't either," he said. "Why'd I become a cop? Go on, psychoanalyze me."

She didn't let a beat pass. "You like the excitement," she said.

"Nailed it."

"Naaah, There's more. Why'd you bring that patient in

the other day? Perry, his name was. I've been curious about that."

"You kidding? It's my job."

"Yeah? First time I've seen it. Usually, it's paramedics who bring them in. He was pretty violent—did he bust something up?"

"A lot of things. Went roaring down the street, turning over restaurant tables and scaring the hell out of people. He even grabbed their packages and threw them at other people."

"So why didn't you arrest him? Or call the paramedics?"

Abasolo shrugged. "He was going to wind up with you anyhow. Just seemed more efficient to eliminate the middle man."

"And it got him here a lot more quickly and safely too."

"That's what you call good policing." He risked turning sideways and winking, to show he wasn't bragging.

She smiled. "Not all cops would have seen it that way. More hassle for you, less for him."

Hey, he thought, *she likes me!*

So here they were eating shrimp and trout on what he'd decided to nickname the eve of destruction—because he was believing the weather reports. He'd always felt the inevitability of this, of possible wipeout, even as he made the questionable decision to move into a boathouse at the West End.

Well, it had been a good few years. He was living the dream —marina, both sunrise and sunset views, deck, open floor plan, boat hoist, and slip. He didn't have the boat yet, but he sure had a nice peaceful place to live, right on the lake. He'd known it was too good to last. You didn't live right *on* the water without understanding the risk. But what he hadn't realized was how much he was going to come to love this—this casual, nautical existence that was urban and close to nature at the same time.

That was why he'd been kicking himself to hell and back. He'd set himself up for a nasty fall and he was pretty sure it was coming tomorrow night.

But with Kathy here, he was looking at it differently. The idea had come to him even as they'd spoken on the phone —*might as well go out in style*. Wring every delicious minute out of what might well be his last night here. If that storm didn't veer east—and no one thought it would—he sure as hell couldn't stay here tomorrow night.

It was hot, but there was a breeze off the lake and they were up too high for mosquitoes. So it was nice on the deck, so nice he settled into the beauty of the evening, and of Kathy, and hardly thought about conversation, which was usually one of his great pleasures. Eventually, he was so overcome with contentment and good feeling—the earlier anger and panic completely dissipated—that he said, half-jokingly, "Want to make out?"

They'd kissed, but not a lot. He didn't think she was ready to take it further.

"Tell you what," she said. "Let me stay with you."

"You're kidding me! That easy? Hey, did I word it wrong before?"

"Actually, I don't remember any words. It was more like... ummm... actions speaking louder if you know what I mean."

"Well..." He was confused. "Seriously, what's different tonight?"

"You know. The end of the world as we know it? Something like that? The Titanic, like you said."

"Hope you're not allergic to cats."

They took it slow and easy. Oddly, he didn't feel any urgency, any of the usual desperate need to just rip off clothes and let fly before someone changed their mind. Sex with Kathy felt almost relaxed. But insanely hot at the same time. He wanted her like crazy, but something about her gave him permission to treat the experience more like a relaxed swim in the ocean than an Olympic 100m freestyle event. He was pretty much hallucinating by the time it was over.

"I think," he said, "I just had an out-of-body experience."

She laughed. "I was wondering where you'd gotten to."

He sat up, shaking his head to regain his equilibrium. "What *was* that?"

"A success, I think."

This line of patter wasn't working for him. It had been something so much larger, so much deeper than these kinds of words implied. He pinned her hands on each side of her flowing hair. "Stop. That was... really powerful for me."

He looked right into her eyes, hoping to see his own feelings reflected, but instead she closed them. A tear slid down her face.

"That bad, huh?"

She shook her head. "I just can't talk, that's all."

He made a pretense of recovering. "Okay then. How about that ice cream?"

"Sure. And then we have to sleep. I have to be out of here by about five to be at work for seven."

He brought her the ice cream in bed and as they ate it, she said, as if it had just occurred to her, "Aren't you worried about your house?"

He nodded. "Not gonna lie. Crazy worried."

She touched his cheek. "I don't blame you. Where are you going to stay?"

"I think the department's setting something up."

"But you don't know for sure?"

He shrugged. "I can always stay with a friend."

"You can have my house," she said. "I'll be at work."

"What? No, I couldn't do that."

"You'd be doing me a favor. I need someone to watch it."

"What about...?"

"Of course bring Crevette. You know you can't leave her here."

Come to think of it, he couldn't.

"I don't know what to say..."

"My mama always said, 'just say thank you.' Could we go to sleep now? I've got about 100 crazy people depending on me to get them through this."

He was horrified. "Seriously? That many? You gonna be okay?"

"Oh, sure. I'm not the only doctor. Hubie Julian's working with me. He's terrific in a crisis—almost like a partner."

Like Langdon, Abasolo thought. They'd gotten each other out of many a tight spot. But she was back in the Eighth district and he was in the Sixth. He sighed, glad Kathy had a partner and wishing he did.

3

Billy knew what had to be wrong the second he saw his aunt's car come barreling down the street and screech to an abrupt halt in front of the house. Aunt Makayla flung her good-sized self out of her car, leaving her door open, racing up the walk and then up the steps, skirts flying, hands flailing.

He locked himself in his room and stuck in his ear buds and cranked up the sound. Aunt Makayla didn't act like that for no reason. Somebody was dead.

He knew who it had to be—either his brother or his semi-stepdad. One of them had disappointed him so badly he could barely think of him without his throat closing up, and he never could stand the other one.

Even so, he was surprised he felt so little except dread. Either way, he knew what was going to happen to his mama. Despite his inept attempt at soundproofing, he heard her keening. "My baby! Oh noooooo! My *baby!*"

His brother Ivory then, who wasn't even her baby. Billy was. To his amazement, all the years of careful detachment peeled away. Tears sprang to his eyes. He couldn't keep pretending. He ripped out his earbuds and charged into the living room, where he found his well-padded, nicely dressed aunt holding his skinny, unkempt, shorts-clad mama.

As usual, Mama looked like all the devils of hell were after her and Makayla looked like she was ready to take them on. The thing was, his impression wasn't wrong— Mama had enough demons inside her to populate a horror movie, and her sister was always trying to exorcise them. But failing. The only thing that did any good were the meds the doctors prescribed, and half the time Mama wouldn't take them. Even if she was on them now, this was going to knock her straight into Crazyland.

"He's gon' be all right," his aunt said, holding onto her sister, but now pushing her a little bit away. "Come on now, let's go see him." Without looking in his direction, she said, "Billy, I got bad news. Ivory's been shot."

Billy felt as if somebody'd punched him and let all the air out. Even though he'd known. Even though this was good news, compared to what he imagined. "He's alive?"

"Course he's alive! Why wouldn't he be alive? We gotta get on over to Charity Hospital. Come on, y'all, get in the goddam car!"

Makayla was the only person in the world who could do a thing with Mama. She didn't waste another second, just got in the goddam car, Billy trailing like a baby duck.

Mama sobbed loudly all the way over, but that didn't stop Billy from grilling his aunt. "How come you know about this before we did?"

"Happened right near where I stay." His aunt grimaced. "I heard the shots. Ain't no mistakin' that sound, you know?"

That made Billy wince. He knew all too well, the kind of world Ivory lived in. And he lived in too, there was no denying it. It was all over the hood. Danger. Gunshots when you least expected them. Crazy people shooting each other up for no reason.

"I went out to see who got shot and lo and behold, it was my own nephew!"

And then she said, barely loud enough for him to hear, "*Couldn't* have been Kaynard, goddammit!"

He didn't know if his mama heard that or not, but he knew his aunt didn't care and neither did he. Life would be a lot easier for everyone without Kaynard in it, including his mama.

She was sobbing, "Why somebody do a fool thing like that? Ivory wouldn't harm a hair on nobody's head. He ain't like Billy—I'm not gon' say that—but he's a *good* boy. He shore is good to his ol' mama."

Ha! Billy thought. The only part that was true was that Ivory wasn't a thing like him. Last thing Ivory was was a good boy, he'd never been kind to his mama a day in his life, and to top it off, his mama wasn't even a little bit old. She wasn't but thirty-seven.

The most deluded part, though, was the idea that Ivory wouldn't harm another person. He damn sure would, Billy knew that. Nobody could live the life he did and remain innocent. Gangs existed for violence and crime—that's who Ivory was now. A gang member who got shot had very likely done some kind of harm to somebody.

He hoped like hell Ivory wouldn't die before they got to the hospital. His mama would go nuts and not come out of it if she didn't get to see her baby at least one more time. As it was, he had no idea how he was going to get the little house ready for a hurricane. He sure as hell couldn't depend on Kaynard to help—and they couldn't go to his aunt's. She had a real sick husband and didn't need any more grief.

Billy was going to have to figure out a way to nail the shutters shut all by himself, and see if he could lay in some food and candles and flashlight batteries... and keep his mama calm.

How was he going to do that now?

SUNDAY NIGHT

THE FIRST BANDS

lthough Code Gray, Charity's hurricane protocol, required her to report at a ridiculous hour Sunday morning, Kathy was pretty sure she could coast on caffeine, no matter what happened. She hadn't had a lot of sleep, but it wouldn't be the first time—after all, she'd once been a resident. And the storm wasn't even supposed to hit till that night, or more properly, the wee hours of Monday.

She had violent patients, and suicidal patients, and plenty of just plain difficult patients, but she'd have plenty of help. Her partner Hubie Julian was one of the best, and Norm Alexander, her favorite nurse—for sense of humor as well as competence—would be with her along with Brenda Keene, younger but great with the patients.

The building itself was about as sturdy as you could get. It was an imposing twenty-story Art Deco duchess in much reduced circumstances still called Big Charity by some of its habitués. Though it might have one of the best trauma units in the country, it was a duchess whose make-up had smeared and whose wig had slipped. Kathy fervently hoped her imperfections were only cosmetic. Truth to tell, she loved the old girl. It was a truly beautiful building, for one thing, and for another, they did great work here.

Charity had been founded to serve the poor and it served them well. Anybody who'd ever worked in the emergency room was proud of it. Doctors trained there had the edge on those who'd opted for places where what they called The Saturday Night Knife And Gun Club wasn't quite as active. You worked here, you better move fast and be on your toes.

It was a damn fine hospital and she'd have been proud to be here even if it was the only one in the state where she'd been able to find a job after her own personal traumas. She'd trained there herself, that was why they took her. One of her LSU mentors came to her rescue.

She arrived that Sunday alive with the optimism of the freshly fucked and the newly in love, finding her patients weirdly excited—in a good way—about the challenge of riding out the storm. Some of them had family members with them. This was one of Charity's traditions—families of patients and staff could come here to ride out a hurricane. There would probably even be animals in kennels and cages somewhere in the hospital, although she hoped not in her world—the humans were enough to wrangle. Whether it was true or not, it felt like safety in numbers. When people sought shelter in hotels, which seemed pretty similar to her, they called it "vertical evacuation." Great unless the power failed. But of course Charity—and all hotels and hospitals for that matter—had back-up generators, so they should be okay.

She and Hubie had talked a little about how all this was going to work, but they still had a lot more to work out. She focused on getting her caffeine level up and, since she had a few minutes, also thinking about the luxurious feeling of having someone care about her—and wondering if she'd been wise to take her relationship to the next level.

Abasolo was the first man she'd been with in any way at all for the last year and a half. She hadn't even had a date in that time. But something about the kind way he treated that patient he brought her—the way he stayed and made sure he was all squared away; and of course the shy way he'd asked if he could call her—had flipped her right out of lonesome cowgirl mode.

Even Norm had noticed the chemistry between them. His exact comment had been, "Baby, if you don't get off your fine white ass and go after that gorgeous man, I'm gon' pluck him right up for myself." That was the other thing—Adam looked like a movie star. He was by far the handsomest man she'd ever dated. And there was something about dating a cop that made you feel safe. She could use a little of that. She'd thought a lot about whether to have sex with him— whether that road would just lead to a broken heart in the end. She wasn't at all sure she was strong enough for that, but something about the doomsday quality of the approaching hurricane made it suddenly seem important to put her feelings on the line.

She'd thought less hard about lending him her house. That she'd done completely on impulse, and she was starting to regret it. She was basking in new love and unfamiliar sex and had thrown caution to the wind when she should have been very cautious indeed. There were things in that house she didn't want Adam to see, and they weren't all in her medicine cabinet.

Nurse Brenda dropped by looking for advice. "Alonzo Thurgood's mom's here and she's got her cat. What's our feline policy?"

She was a serious girl, the antithesis of Norm. He'd been around; she'd barely been out of Kenner. She was a skinny young redhead from a Catholic family, and he was a middle-aged, rotund, shaven-headed, gay-as-pink-ink sybarite. If it felt good, Norm would probably just up and do it; whereas Brenda would need to pray on it. But Kathy had a feeling Norm was rubbing off a little—Brenda's lips were definitely curving up as she said the words "feline policy."

"Oh, hell!" Kathy said. "Is she a nice lady?"

"Seems like it."

"Is he a nice kitty?"

"She. She has her kittens with her."

"Jesus, Mary and Joseph, what kind of person turns away kittens? Tell me they're at least in a carrier."

"Two. Madonna in one, Bonnie and Clyde in the other. They're six months old."

"You tricked me!"

Brenda laughed. "Wait'll you see 'em. They're the prettiest kittens in the world." She raised an eyebrow. "Hey, have you seen Dr. Julian around?"

"Not yet. Why?"

"Have you noticed it's getting close to eight?"

"Good grief! He lives in the city, right?"

Brenda nodded. "Uptown."

"So... not caught in traffic. And he hasn't called." She was trying to take in the fact that no one is ever an hour late without calling in...

He wasn't coming.

He was leaving her alone with 100 psychotics. "I don't believe this!" she blurted. But she was talking to herself. Nurse Brenda had discreetly slipped out of the office.

Furious, she called from her cell rather the hospital phone, which she didn't think he'd answer. He picked up on the first ring, his soothing voice, the voice that had talked so many hundreds of people off the ledge, speaking before she could. "Kathy, I'm sorry as hell about this. Bottom line is, it's my marriage or my job."

Okay, that was a good excuse. She supposed. "We've got three boys and a dog. And no family to help Tina with the boys, nobody to evacuate with her—spell her on driving and... um... child care. Can you imagine that kind of nightmare? She was going to have to leave the dog behind and the boys pitched every kind of fit, up to and including throwing Legos at her."

"I'm trying. To imagine it." She was. It was a pretty grim scenario.

"She didn't think she could do it—and to be honest, I finally had to admit I didn't even think I could if the roles were reversed."

"Okay. Good luck to you." She flicked her phone off before she gave in to the rage that had bubbled up inside her. She held the phone in front of her face and shook it; and yelled at it: "You couldn't have let somebody know? You couldn't have found a substitute? You couldn't have had the decency to..."

Plan ahead, she was going to say, but before she could, Norm poked his shiny head in. "Heard you might need a psychiatric nurse. And sure enough, here you are, cussin' at inanimate objects."

"I just don't understand why he couldn't have given us a heads-up."

Norm shrugged. "Sure you do. Ashamed to."

"What kind of psychiatrist raises kids who throw things at their parents?"

"Oooh, I could tell you some stories." He laughed.

And, finally, so did she. "Yeah. Psychiatrists are probably

the least sane people in the hospital."

"Well, normally, I'd just keep my mouth shut and look wise, but I do know one who thinks her phone is Yorick."

"Yeah. I gotta get a grip. This could be a long day. And night. You know we've got cats in here?"

"Oh, so that's why I'm sniffling."

"Sorry about that. We better figure out if anyone else is allergic. Do we have any new customers?"

"Not since about 3 a.m. But Maxine Polite was here, multi-tasking—trying to wheedle a pain script while visiting her son in ICU."

Kathy froze. "Her kid's barely in high school! What on earth happened to him?"

He shook his head. "She's got two. This one's a fully baked grown-up gangster."

"Damn! Gunshot wound?"

"Sad to say, yes. He might not make it."

"Must be making her crazy. Surprised she hasn't been back here before this."

"Seems like she was handling it pretty well..." He gave her an ironic grin.

"Hence the need for more meds. What did we give her? I need some of those."

"I hear you."

"Let's call a meeting for after lunch. Make sure everybody's cool."

He sneezed. "And not allergic to cats."

She had patients to see before that—without Hubie, anyone who was in the waiting room was hers and hers alone.

First up was Lisa, a seventeen-year-old dancer on Bourbon Street. She was a runaway and a sometime hooker, Kathy suspected, and she was holding onto a teddy bear like it was her last dollar. She was a regular, a desperately damaged girl who had no idea how to manage her emotions and often chose to just start yelling to see if that would help. She was forever fighting with the other dancers, drumming up rivalries and forming temporary alliances.

This time she'd gotten herself slugged by her best friend, although she wasn't here for a black eye. The fight had thrown her into such a depression she couldn't go to work, couldn't eat, couldn't get out of bed even to eat or drink. After a couple of days, her neighbor, Eileen Fisk, 80 and another regular, had poured her into a taxi and delivered her to the emergency room, where she'd announced that she, Eileen, was from Venus and they couldn't make her go back. She was awaiting her turn.

Lisa's problem today was that she was worthless, she'd never get her life together, she didn't have any friends, nobody loved her, nobody ever would, and her laundry needed doing. It was all Kathy could do not to hug her, but that would have been unprofessional. Still... if anyone ever needed a hug, she was sitting there crying all over her teddy bear. Kathy couldn't see sending her back out there to ride out the hurricane by herself. She admitted her.

She was just getting ready for Eileen when Norm appeared. "You gotta come see this."

"What?"

"Just come."

He led her out to the hall behind the admitting desk, where Bridget Young, who was indeed very young and who'd been there only a few weeks, was cringing from a patient who was holding a bloody handkerchief on his arm and trying to define his emergency.

"Motherfucker Tourette's," he was explaining. "Goddam

can opener cut my—blow me, bitch, Tourette's. I'm bleeding so bad fuck you Tourette's..."

Bridget was shrinking further and further into the shadows, obviously having never heard of Tourette's. Norm was laughing so hard he was shaking. Kathy poked him with her elbow. "Do something, you idiot, before that poor man bleeds to death."

He moved forward and took over, affording Kathy a moment of watching him try to straighten it out, which was actually much funnier than the previous tableau, especially since it was destined to end better. She hoped it wasn't going to be her last laugh of the day.

WEIRDLY, the post-lunch meeting went smoothly—so much so that the adage about calm and storms came to mind. "Everybody knows the building's going to shake, right?"

"Now it's an earthquake?"

That got laughs. A good sign. The speaker was Rafe Joseph, a reasonably intimidating substance abuser who did construction around town. He was a regular customer who'd come in yesterday worrying about bugs that were eating him alive. He'd had fantasies like that before, the danger being that he could decide anyone in his immediate area was probably a bug or bug ally, and attack without mercy.

When he was off his drugs of choice and on meds, he was something of a hoot.

"Okay, I have something else to bring up. We're lucky to have Mrs. Danielle Thurlow with us tonight—you all know Alonzo, right?" Alonzo was an affable young rapper coming off a manic episode that had once involved daily escalations of his tales of Hollywood success alternating with his gory gangland tales. "Hi y'all. Everybody call me Ti Meanness," he said, waving as if from the stage at the House of Blues. "My mama's came down to pray with us tonight."

Danielle stood up, ready to lead the prayers, but Norm cut in: "Maybe later, when the storm gets going good. That'll be very comforting, Miz Danielle. For right now, we need to ask y'all a question. Miz Danielle has three feline friends with her. Is anyone here allergic to cats?"

"Cats? Oh, God!" Lisa shrieked. "I can't even be in a building with cats!"

"Do you have asthma or something?" someone asked.

"I have ailurophobia."

"You got *what*?" someone else said. "Is it catching?"

Kathy was relieved. At least they wouldn't have to worry about her breathing. "Ok. We'll deal with that."

"What if we lose power?" Eileen asked. Kathy had admitted her too, although she knew perfectly well Eileen didn't think she was a Venusian. But she was anxious enough—probably about the storm—to pretend she was, so Kathy reasoned that made her vulnerable enough to require hospitalization.

"We're all gonna get pretty warm," Rafe Joseph said. That was everyone's fear—losing air conditioning. In Eileen's reasonably delicate state of health, the summer heat could be life-threatening.

"Don't worry," Kathy replied confidently. "We have generators."

5

It was odd for Adam, being alone in Kathy's house. He'd picked her up there, sometimes had dinner or pizza there, but that was about it. He didn't feel as if he knew the place well enough to make himself at home.

It was a smallish house, a perfectly restored Victorian camelback, the kind with a squared-off roof and square skinny columns—no gingerbread, very clean. Italianate, he thought it was called. Kathy kept it in as perfect condition as a museum, but it didn't have that cold don't-touch-me quality. It was actually quite welcoming. She'd created a lovely nest for herself, one that Adam, afraid of what was about to happen to his own home, envied her.

He took Crevette's carrier into the kitchen and opened it. The tiny calico stared at him, unmoving. Adam spoke for her. "Dad, whatehell are we doing here?" When he did his Crevette imitation, she had a robust whiskey voice, completely unsuited to an animal whose English name was synonymous with "miniature."

"We're escaping certain death, Babycakes," he told her.

"How would you like to be a six-pound furball caught in a Category 5 storm?"

"I would loathe that, Daddycakes; but what, may I ask, is wrong with the Windsor Court?"

He ignored that one. "Go ahead and make yourself at home while I get you some nice hospitable litter." He went out to the car to get her cat box, food, and other supplies, plus the duffel he'd brought for himself, containing more clothes, he suspected, than most people who'd evacuated—because he was pretty sure he was going to wake up homeless.

Almost the second he'd managed to grab and balance everything, his phone sounded off. "Goddammit, can you wait?" he said, aware that he was talking to himself a lot more than he usually did, and he wondered what that was about.

Probably a little anxiety, but a lot more anticipation, he imagined. He loved a challenge, especially a physical challenge. You had to, to be a cop. By the time he'd gotten back to the kitchen and unburdened himself, Crevette was nowhere in sight. It was Kathy calling, a rather delightful prospect.

He punched in her number, hoping for a little billing and cooing, but she got right to the point. "Hi, Handsome. Listen, do me a favor?"

Well, at least he'd gotten a compliment. "Sure. You need another night of rapturous passion?"

Her voice softened ever so slightly. "Probably. Now that I think of it, almost certainly. But one tiny other thing? My neighbor already evacuated. I told him I'd feed his dog and stuff."

Uh-oh. "And what stuff?"

"Oh, you know. Little walk now and then?" Her voice

had become a pleading little purr. "Just a tiny little walk?"

"Your neighbor's got some nerve, asking you to do that."

"You mean I do, asking you?"

He thought about it. "Naaah. No other choice, really."

"See, that's how it was with him. His parents in Baton Rouge are allergic. You know what? I should have brought him. Did you know plenty of people did bring their pets? As well as their relatives."

"To the *hospital*?"

"It's a tradition. In our department we've got two insanely beautiful long-haired white kittens. And their mom."

"So in that case, okay if I bring Fido over to your house?"

"Darth."

"*Darth*? I'm taking care of a dog named Darth?"

"Count yourself lucky. They were thinking of 'Voldemort'. But don't worry, Darth only bites package thieves. You'll be fine."

"I'm taking that as a yes."

"Sure. Crevette could use a buddy."

"She hates dogs."

"Tell her it's another frigging opportunity for growth." She suddenly seemed distracted. "Oops, gotta run. It's the yellow house on the right. I left the key on my vanity."

He took the larger of the two guest rooms, the one painted a soothing sage and hung with Audubon prints, which Skip always mocked as the go-to Uptown wall decoration. But he noticed she didn't make fun of JazzFest posters, and everyone who didn't have Audubon prints had those. Kathy had both, plus some very nice original art.

Adam needed birds right now. The resident kingfisher and brown pelican perfectly matched his mood, which was... oddly tranquil. Despite their business-like phone call, he was still savoring his night with Kathy, but not in a riding high kind of way. He was just feeling quietly peaceful.

As he dropped off his duffel, he realized this was a room he'd never been in. Actually, he'd never even been in Kathy's bedroom. He went there now, feeling a little like a burglar, although Crevette had no such compunctions. She was relaxing in Sphinx Pose, deep in a nest of luxurious-looking pillows arranged on the pile of downy clouds Kathy used for a bed. *Whoo!* The woman sure had a knack.

He didn't know whether she'd meant the key was on her bathroom vanity or whether there was one in the bedroom, but the latter proved to be true; sure enough, there were a couple of keys attached to a yellow plastic tag. There were also a number of framed pictures that puzzled him. And, it must be admitted, that also disturbed him. He picked up one and studied it, trying to figure out what it meant, yet knowing it was none of his business.

Unless it was.

The whole concept left too big a question mark on his current universe to deal with now. He headed next door, having no idea what to expect, but even from the porch he could tell Darth had quite a voice on him.

He was in no way prepared for the ball of white fluff that flew at him. "What *are* you?" he marveled. "A snack for Crevette? Shouldn't a Darth at least be black?"

Unlike Crevette, Darth didn't answer, just barked his tiny tail off till Adam sat down on the floor and let the dog take a layer of skin off his face with its tongue. When that was done, and he'd gathered up dog food, food dish, and leash, he took Darth home to an outraged Crevette, and went to work, still wondering why Kathy had so many pictures of herself with a small child, the most disturbing of which was one of her in a hospital bed, being handed a newborn.

6

B efore the phones went dead, Skip made one last attempt at talking sense to the world's most stubborn individual. This time making it a demand: "Ollie, get Iggy in his carrier. Don't argue, I'm coming to get you. *In a district car,* you hear me? You need to get out before that tree in your yard comes down on your house."

Everybody'd left hours ago. It was early evening and she was holed up in Jimmy Dee's palatial French Quarter digs with Angel, trying to batten down whatever hatches she could at the last minute. Katrina was already dumping barrels of rain.

Although Dee-Dee'd made Skip promise to drag Ollie over by whatever means necessary, she couldn't believe she'd just threatened a district car. That was probably a bridge too far.

"You're too late," Ollie answered.

"What, you're already dead?"

"I'm already here," she said, "and I'm not alone." The doorbell rang, prompting Angel to come barreling down the stairs.

"Here," Ollie said, handing Skip a carrier full of wet, yowling cat. "Okay if I bring some friends? These guys don't have anywhere else to go."

Although it was bucketing down rain, she stood aside for a short plump woman, a short, beer-bellied man with a beard, and a sodden golden retriever, who shook himself all over Jimmy Dee's Oriental carpet the second he lumbered inside. "Oooohhh, Breesy," crooned the woman, laughing, not even slightly apologetic. "You might have a Saint's name, but a saint you ain't." It sounded like a line she used a lot. To Skip she said, "Hey, I know you. Where do I know you from?"

Skip sighed. "Delta Dawn. We meet again. Come on in."

"Hey, how do I know you?"

"Is that Dickie you've got there? Dickie, you too, before you drown."

She tossed Ollie a look.

"They're my neighbors," Ollie said, skulking in with a guilty look. She seemed the only one who minded dripping all over the carpet. "Their shutters don't work and they already lost a window. I knew Jimmy Dee'd want me to bring 'em."

He would, of course, Skip thought. *But it would be less awkward if I hadn't handcuffed Dawn that time she threw a beer bottle at Dickie at The Tin Roof.* They were Dickie and Dawn Horvath, neighborhood characters in their fifties, half Boho music fanatics, and the other half routine New Orleans nutballs. Everyone knew them, but it was the rare person who wanted to know them better. Ollie, who had to put up with them living next door, was usually pretty vocal on that subject.

Skip put the cat carrier on the floor, causing Breesy to stick his nose through the wire cage part and Iggy to whack the hell out of it. Breesy proceeded to squeal like a mating skunk, and Dawn shot Ollie a look of pure hatred. "Look what your goddam cat did to my baby!"

Angel, wagging innocently, stuck her nose in Dawn's crotch, eager to make friends.

Dawn screeched like the small black and white dog was a gator. "EEEEEEEEE! Who the fuck are you? Get your rudeass nose out of my pussy!"

Oh, boy, Skip was thinking, *gonna be a long night,* but Ollie laughed. Maybe she was getting hysterical. "Good thing we didn't bring along that drenched kid we found."

"Kid?" This was the last thing Skip needed. But if there was a juvenile out in a hurricane, she had no choice but to get them inside.

Ollie shrugged. "He wouldn't come. But we did kind of give him our address. I think he might have followed us."

Sighing, Skip opened the door again. She knew Ollie was lying. She'd brought the kid. She just didn't want to spring the whole package on Skip at once.

Sure enough, a short, skinny figure, possibly a male teen-ager, was standing against a building across the street, looking straight at the house as if he expected something— like an invitation. He was hugging his chest against the rain and Skip could have sworn she saw him shivering, even from that distance.

She beckoned him, yelling, "Come on in!" and hoping he wouldn't resist. Chasing a kid down the street was her absolute last choice for a way to spend the next part of the evening.

The kid didn't have to be asked twice. Without even looking for oncoming cars, he ran straight for the door. The wind had picked up and was now hurling small objects through the sheets of rain. No question it was miserable out

there, and starting to get scary. He must have already made
the decision to accept any shelter he could find.

He hurtled through the door, the wind at his back, dripping more water, it seemed, than the other three and the
dog combined. "Wet out there," he said.

"Well, you're welcome to stay here."

Angel and Breesy barked in disagreement.

"What's your name and how old are you?"

The kid straightened up and looked Skip right in the
eye. It showed a lot of self-possession under the circumstances—he had to look up to do it; she was six feet tall to
his five-six or so and two dogs were barking at him. He was
African-American, light brown, skinny as a stake, as blue-
eyed as Ollie was. And those piercing eyes said it all—*I've
got more nerve in my little finger than you Billy Bob Bubbas do in
all four of your giant bodies. Mess with me at your own risk.*

"Name's Billy," he said. "You got a mop? Lemme clean up
this mess."

"I'm Skip," she answered. She held out her hand and he
responded with a jiveshake meant to intimidate, but she
could tell he was surprised she could anticipate and follow
each intricate move. Such was life as a cop. "Dickie here's
gonna clean up the mess. You've got to warm up. Go get in
the shower while we still have hot water. Angel, you and
Breesy shut up."

Which caused both Dickie and Dawn to set up a whine.

"You can't talk to my dog like that."

"Hey, I need the first shower. I got a condition."

"He's got a condition."

Ollie broke in, "Okay, new plan. You guys can share
Sheila's bathroom—it's got a bathtub *and* a shower. Billy, off
to Kenny's—I'll show everybody where everything is, and
collect your clothes for the dryer."

"Whothehell are Sheila and Kenny?"

"Jimmy Dee's niece and nephew. Sheila's sweats will fit Dawn and I'll round up something for everybody else. Skip, can you mop?"

"Sure, but one thing first. This is gonna be a long night. If anybody brought weapons, hand them over."

"You kidding me?" Dickie said.

Billy snorted. "What kinda racist shit is this?"

Ollie didn't say a word, just opened her backpack and laid a Ruger LCR in Skip's open palm.

"Ohhh, nice," Skip said, before she realized she shouldn't.

"Shee-it," Dickie said, and opened his own backpack, extracting a .38 and a hunting knife in a sheath, but not before Skip caught a glimpse of a green box labeled "Depends." *Oh, boy*. The aforementioned condition. Talk about a long night.

"I don't gotta give you nothin'," Billy said, and turned toward the door, as if to brave the storm again, giving a clear view of the bulge in the back of his jeans. Whip-quick, Skip threw him against the wall, and grabbed the gun.

The kid's eyes dilated. "Who the hell *are* you? You a cop or something?"

"I'm somebody who's trying to help you out, okay? You could be killed out there. But you're a stranger in this house and so are those two with the dog. No guests here are going to be armed tonight, especially those under twenty-one. You okay with that?"

"Yeah, okay."

She let him go. "Glad to hear it." More glad than he knew—she'd have really hated to cuff him. "Okay, Ollie, show them where to go. I'm going to put the guns in the safe."

She didn't know the combination of Jimmy Dee's safe, but they didn't know that. One of his desk drawers had a key —that was good enough.

She cleaned up the hall, tried to soothe Ignatius, who howled intermittently, and examined Breesy for any serious nose damage, deciding he mostly had his feelings hurt.

Earlier, she'd set out the remaining spoils of Jimmy Dee's last fishing trip and a very nice beef tenderloin to thaw. They were going to lose electricity soon and she'd need to salvage whatever was in the refrigerator.

There was also some deli ham and cheese, so she made a tray of sandwiches and some iced tea. Dickie was the first one back, wearing a seersucker robe of Jimmy Dee's that gapped just enough so she could see all kinds of things she wished she couldn't—chest hair, a watermelon where his stomach should have been, the bulging incontinence briefs. It was hard not to avert her eyes.

Dickie eyed the iced tea. "Got anything stronger?"

"Sorry, no."

"Well, I do." He retreated and came back with a bottle of bourbon.

She thought about confiscating it. The neighborhood didn't call the Horvaths the Drunkersons for nothing, and she'd personally broken up a bar fight between them. She could do it again if she had to. She decided to bet on the delightful proposition that tonight they'd pass out instead of fighting.

Gradually, everyone else filtered in for sandwiches, clad in whatever sweats, shorts, and T-shirts Ollie had managed to dredge up.

"How about a drop of that bourbon?" Ollie asked timidly.

"I'm in," Billy said.

"The hell you are," Skip told him.

Dawn clutched the bottle to her pillowy bosom, as if she thought she could hide it between her breasts. "Get your own."

That incensed Skip, not to mention Ollie, whose eyes flashed like a furious cat's. Ollie was a take-no-prisoners New Englander. Skip had seen her in bar fights too. She patted air to keep her quiet and spoke softly to Dawn. "Give her a drink."

"Why should we?"

The voice of justice turned out to be so young it had barely changed. Billy spoke up. "'Cause she rescued you from the fuckin' storm, assholes. Are you kiddin' me? How cold can you be?"

Sulkily, Dawn poured Ollie a short one, and that set the tone for the night. Ollie's good deed had backfired on her. Although she was going to get a couple of drinks out of it, they were all going to have to go through the hurricane with hostility snatching at them like claws. Skip regretted not confiscating the booze, but not for long.

Pretty soon Katrina really got to rocking and rolling, terrifying Breesy, who peed on the rug and then stood shaking in a corner as Dawn and Dickie proceeded to get more and more annihilated, prompting Skip to decide the hooch was a great little babysitter.

Let the Drunkersons drink while she and Ollie raced about, inspecting, making sure the windows were tight, fetching pots to catch the leaks, fussing over a banging shutter it was too late to fix, and otherwise obsessing.

Billy and Angel both tried to comfort Breesy but that— or possibly the general vibe—infuriated the cat, who set up a caterwauling that drove Ollie to his side to be Cat Mom. That was okay with Skip. She'd told Jimmy Dee she'd take

care of his house, and she could do it by herself. But help
came anyway, from an unexpected source. Without being
asked, Billy cleaned up the dog puddle and then went on
leak patrol, helping Skip shove furniture and rugs to safety,
emptying the pots as they filled up, and replacing them. He
didn't talk a lot, just threw himself into the job. Skip found
herself liking him.

When they lost electricity, the two of them sat in the
room with the screwed-up shutter so they could watch the
storm, and sipped some of the tea Skip had made. Angel
curled up at Skip's feet. "Thanks for the help."

The kid gave her a crooked smile. "Guess I was raised
right."

Skip thought about the contradictions that brought up
in her mind. "Hey, you never said how old you are."

"Going on seventeen."

That meant fifteen, she figured. "Mind if I ask what you
were doing out in the rain?"

"Oh." He had guts, but he was still young enough to
squirm at that one. "Well, I had to get something for
my mama."

"In a *hurricane*?"

"It was something medical, you know? She's got a... a...."

"A condition?"

They both burst out laughing. "Yeah... a condition."

It was funny because the Drunkersons' whining begged
to be mocked, but the unfunny part was that Skip could
think of lots of conditions Billy's mom might have that could
make her so callous she'd send her young son out in the
storm of the century. They were medical, all right, and they
all had cures that could have rendered Mom too helpless to
go out herself. None of them involved prescriptions. Not
alcohol, she thought, because nothing was open. But every-

body's dealer would be home, because where else would you be in a hurricane? Billy's mom had to have sent him out for drugs.

So who had raised him right, she wondered? "Is your daddy at home?" she asked.

And Billy asked again, "You a cop or what?"

"So what if I am? You know I'm not going to hurt you, right? Let's be friends."

He crossed his arms and gave her a hostile side-eye. "I ain't gon' be friends with no white po-lice."

It just about broke her heart, knowing all the toxic ingredients that had gone into producing a kid who felt that way and wasn't embarrassed to say so.

And then he said, "What's your name again?"

Somehow in the traffic jam at the door, she hadn't introduced herself. "Skip," she said, and held out her hand. "Detective Skip Langdon, at your service."

"At your service, my ass." He still wasn't looking at her, but she could tell he was testing, trying to see if there might be the tiniest grain of truth in what she said.

"Believe it," she said, and stood up. "Come on, I'll take you to Kenny's room. You better get some sleep."

She found Dawn and Dickie asleep on matching sofas, and Ollie dozing in Sheila's room. "Ollie, wake up. Can you take leak duty for a while?"

And then she sacked out in Jimmy Dee's room.

While she slept, Ollie rigged up some garbage cans and plastic bags to catch the leaks, and it went on like that for the next several hours—they spelled each other while the storm raged. The eyewall—the nastiest bands—hit in the wee hours, ripping a chunk out of the roof, but fortunately it was a chunk covering a bathroom, which could be easily closed off.

The ripping shingles evidently woke Dickie, who staggered upstairs in the dark, looking for, of all things, a bathroom—that bathroom. "Hey, I gotta get in there." He pointed at his adult diaper. "My condition! Ya know?"

"Dickie. You know there's a bathroom downstairs, right?"

"Oops! Too late," he said, and ran for Kenny's bathroom.

Maybe he'd just been looking for company. Katrina was clutching and tearing at the house. The screwed-up shutter banged incessantly, and now and again something hit the house—who knew what? Maybe flower pots someone hadn't taken off their balcony, maybe branches or even electric wires.

She wanted to talk to someone herself, in particular her boy friend, Steve Steinman. But it was also the dead of night in California, where he'd gone on a film editing job. She couldn't even justify calling Jimmy Dee. What was she going to say? Sheila's bathroom's flooding? Who wanted to hear that? Besides, it wasn't so bad—a lot of the rain was ending up in the bathtub.

She went back to bed, curled up with Angel, and slept a few more precious hours.

7

"Big Pharma, I thank you," Kathy said aloud when Miss Danielle had prayed for everyone who'd listen and all the patients had been medicated for the night. She was at last able to catch a nap on the air mattress she'd set up on her office floor. "Damn, look at that!" she murmured, noticing a line of ants making for crumbs under her desk.

After that, nothing. It had been a heavy day preceded by a night of hormones and adrenaline, to say nothing of dopamine. She was an empty sack.

It was a blissful three hours—or maybe thirty minutes (things started running together) before Nurse Brenda came in and woke her. "Maxine's back!"

Kathy was groggy. "Who?"

"Maxine Polite, your favorite schizophrenic. Remember, we mentioned she was here earlier?"

"Oh, yeah, something happened to her son."

"Well, now she's got something else going on."

Kathy got up and pulled herself together.

Maxine was in the waiting room screaming and pacing,

her hair wild, her face contorted. She was drenched, clothes clinging to her contours and dripping on the floor. "Y'all don' let me in here I'ma shoot this place up! Swear to God there ain't gon' be a one a ya left standing. Out of my way," she said, pushing a patient who looked terrified—and also pretty sick.

Oh, lord, we're gonna have to wrestle, Kathy thought, but a guard—one of the hospital police—was approaching from another entrance. She slowed a little to let him get there first. Norm came up behind her. "I'm here, Doc."

"Take your hands off me!" Maxine hollered at the guard. "Who you think you is, put your hands all over me? I'ma file a complaint. Where's Dr. Ken? I gotta see Dr. Ken!"

Kathy saw blood spattered all the way down her soaked t-shirt, some on her face as well. Once the guard had her secured, Kathy approached gingerly. "Hi, Maxine. It's just me today. Dr. Ken's on vacation."

"Don't wanna see you. Wanna see Dr. Ken."

"You don't have a weapon on you, do you? Norm's just going to check."

Shooting her a dark look, Norm checked Maxine's pockets as if there might be scorpions in them, but stopped short of a pat-down. Finally he said to the hospital cop, "You know how to do this? I could hold her."

The cop recoiled.

Maxine started laughing, the low guffaw of a madwoman. "I ain't got nothin', you pussies! I'm gon' jack *his* gun and shoot y'all up." She lunged at the guard, who tightened his grip on her.

Kathy said, "Okay, let's go," and they wrangled her into a treatment room. "We're going to have to restrain you."

"No! I'll be good! Don't do that. I got problems. I got stuff to tell y'all. Watch me." She went limp.

"What drugs you been doin'?"

"A little rock. Not much."

Kathy was willing to bet it *was* much, but as long as Maxine was calming down, she was willing to listen. "All right, get up. Let's get your vital signs."

Norm took her blood pressure while Kathy examined her face. "Maxine, what happened to you? What's that blood from?"

All of a sudden she seemed to remember something. "He hit me! Oh, shit! Shit! He hit me."

"Mmm. Looks like you have a split lip." Kathy touched the woman's face. "Might need a stitch or two. Is it bleeding from the inside?"

Maxine made a face and evidently tested with her tongue. "No, I think it's okay."

Kathy had a look. "Let's leave it alone for now."

"I gotta see my boy."

"Your boy?"

"My boy Ivory, in the ICU. He's all shot up. I gotta say good-bye to him."

Kathy began to clean up the woman's face. "He's that bad off? You're afraid he's going to die?"

"Who, Ivory? Hell, no. Y'all gon' take good care of him. I'm the one leavin'."

"Where you going?"

"Jail."

Brenda handed Maxine a hospital gown and a towel. "Let's get you out of those wet clothes." Kathy wasn't about to leave her alone to undress, so she let Brenda help the patient while she busied herself with Maxine's chart.

"Why are you going to jail?" Kathy asked nonchalantly. "Did you get in a fight?"

"No, ma'am. I killed somebody."

Brenda sucked in her breath. "Dr. Kathy? Take a look at this."

Kathy turned around, but before she could look, Maxine said in a low growly voice, "Come one step closer and I'm gon' blow your head off."

A young man in thug clothes stood in the door—baggy jeans so low they were about to fall off, turned-around ball cap, fancy sneakers. Kathy said, "Can I help you?"

"She can." He pointed to Maxine.

For a moment the room went dead quiet, while Maxine apparently gathered her thoughts.

And then she began squawking like a flock of crows. Even for the psych unit it was pretty impressive.

"You leave my baby alone, you come one step closer, I'ma take you apart with my bare hands, snatch every hair ya got out ya head, you gon' wish you never been born..." all in a voice you could probably hear in Jefferson Parish. She was drawing a crowd, too. Kathy could hear running footsteps, those of hospital cops she hoped, coming to their aid.

Before anyone could get there, Maxine swooped off the table and dived at the thug, who let one instant of terror cross his face and took off running. Despite all, Kathy felt her lips turning up, almost involuntarily. She cherished that tiny flash of fear. *Go, Maxine,* she said silently. But nonetheless, she couldn't suppress a tiny shiver of her own fear. Nothing like that had ever happened here before.

The kid was running, pushing crash carts at his pursuers, dumping one over, grabbing at anything he could to make a mess, put things between himself and the various guards and nurses who were trying to stop him.

But what were they going to do with him once they stopped him? "Let him go!" Kathy screeched and, apparently seeing the wisdom of it, everyone stepped out of his way, then began chasing him—hopefully right out the emergency doors.

Kathy's cell phone beeped that she had a call. Her heart speeded up. She couldn't help it, she sneaked a peek. It was Adam.

Brenda was speaking soothingly to Miss Maxine, which, against all odds, was working, but such was the power of Brenda's personality. Taking advantage of the moment, Kathy ducked into the ladies' room and answered her phone. She just needed to hear his voice. But she wasn't prepared for what it was conveying, slightly off-color news about his sad condition of loneliness during the storm, touching on how much he missed her, and coming around to how delightful it would be if she were there with him and where that could lead. All in a witty, but slightly unprintable way that would have melted her if she hadn't just gotten a scare.

But she wasn't remotely ready for that right now. She was trying to take it in, to pull together some sort of affectionate but non-sexy answer that would hide her fear, yet not drag her down a path she couldn't deal with, when he said, "What is it? What's wrong?"

"What makes you think..."

He cut her off. "You're not breathing right. What is it?"

Someone knocked on the ladies' room door, loudly, like a police knock. "Dr. Kathy, you in there?" Norm's voice, sounding urgent.

She opened the door on the uncharacteristically agitated nurse. "Just a heads-up. There's some guys in the waiting room. If you know what I mean."

"Guys?" she said, and held up a finger while she said to Adam, "I've gotta go..."

"I heard. Keep your phone on. I'll be there in ten." And he was gone before she could say another word.

ABASOLO KNEW HE WAS AN IDIOT. Who calls a doctor at work in the middle of a hurricane? But he couldn't help it. He kept thinking about her, wishing she was with him. Anyhow, he didn't expect her to answer. He was just going to leave a message that she'd find when she had a minute.

He aimed for slightly sexy, a little bit lazy, funny if he was lucky—and the truth was, everyone knew he was funny. Just a fun, funny message to cheer her up while she worked. He'd pictured her finding it. She'd bust out laughing and it would give her a warm glow, and she'd smile about it in between crises tomorrow.

But she'd said, "Hello," and, startled, he'd gone right into his funny spiel, but he was kicking himself now. It couldn't have been more inappropriate. He'd caught onto that the minute he'd heard her startled intake of breath, and realized she was having trouble reacting.

But he'd only realized she might be in danger—that something scary might be going in at Charity—when he'd overheard the heads-up.

He thought about calling for back-up, but that was stupid. The first bands were already breaking off limbs and airlifting porch furniture. Rain was pelting against his windshield, making visibility more a concept than a reality. The wind was pummeling and jolting his car, so brutally it was impossible to stay in a lane. Not that it mattered—he had the streets to himself, give or take a few tree limbs. Any police unlucky enough to be scheduled to work would be dealing with emergencies, and he didn't know if he was walking into one. Maybe a "bunch of guys" were somebody's grandsons fleeing to higher ground.

Adam didn't think so, though. There were all kinds of desirable drugs at Charity and his guess was they weren't well protected. Maybe half the gangbangers in New Orleans had also come to that conclusion.

He screeched to a stop at the emergency room door and called Kathy to let him in. She was there in about thirty seconds, evidently awaiting his call. "They're in there," she said unnecessarily. Adam could hear them perfectly well, along with mostly male voices that may have belonged to guards, or perhaps nurses and doctors.

"You gon' take us there or we gon' whip yo' ass?

"Listen, there's a hurricane out there..."

"Show us, goddammit!"

"You just need to leave."

"*Ain't leavin'*, don't you get that? You goddam gon' take us where we want to go!"

At least it sounded as if nobody'd pulled a gun yet, but Adam figured it was only a matter of time—and not too much time, either. "Stay here," he said to Kathy, knowing she wasn't about to. She followed him like a shadow into the waiting room proper, where most of the still-waiting patients had bunched up in a corner, scrunching down to make themselves invisible. Nobody wanted to be noticed by these dudes. They all wore three-hundred-dollar athletic shoes (some of them untied) butt-crack jeans so baggy you could have cut a matching jacket out of every pair, and enough attitude to intimidate a platoon.

They were surrounded by a little ring of timid-looking hospital employees trying ineffectually to keep them at bay.

Adam, in contrast, wore butt-hugging jeans, a jacket that said "police" on the back, his badge around his neck, riot gear, and more attitude than the whole brigade of them. He spoke in a loud, authoritative voice, sounding like someone used to being obeyed: "Police, assholes! Shut the fuck up and listen."

The room went still. "What the hell's going on here?"

Dead silence. "One of you gangbangers want to tell me what you're doing in a hospital in a hurricane? Y'all come down to volunteer? Hey, somebody put a muzzle on y'all? You sure were noisy a minute ago."

He shut up and let the silence shout for a while, watching them tense up, not sure what do to with themselves. One of them kept looking wildly around in a skittish way that made Adam think if one of them was dumb enough to pull anything, it was going to be him. "Hey, Bozo! Yeah, you! Get outta here!" He jerked his chin towards the exit. The bozo gave one last wild look around, saw Adam rest his hand on his gun, and started to move. "All'a y'all. OUT! Get the FUCK outta this hospital. Now!"

The first ones slunk sulkily, not wanting to seem cowed, but the rest of them practically ran. Adam strode past Kathy, marching on their heels, a human broom sweeping them out.

"Lock the doors," he said to the guards, as if he owned the place.

Kathy followed. "My... hero?" she said, and even given the ironic way she said it, to Adam it was like the sun coming out.

But he said, "Hey, what's up with the question mark? You have doubts?"

She laughed. "Nope, none." And as they strolled back from the entrance into the emergency room proper, applause broke out from staff and patients alike. He noticed with pleasure that Kathy joined in. "See? You're everybody's hero. You want to come back to my office a minute? I've got a bottle of... oh, wait! Forgot you don't drink."

"I'll have some water."

When the door was safely closed, she fell against him. "I need a hug. Bad."

He squeezed back. "Me too."

"I don't know how to thank you for this."

"It's my job, ma'am."

"I happen to know you're off-duty. I know I'm supposed to say it wasn't necessary, but really, I can't thank you enough. Who *knows* where that might have gone?"

"No biggie. They'd probably just have taken all your drugs and left."

"I don't know. Seemed like they were interested in one of my patients. A lady named Maxine Polite. Know her?"

"I don't know a Maxine. There's a pretty big gangster named Ivory Polite."

She smacked her forehead. "That's gotta be her son! He's here. With a gunshot wound."

Adam felt a sudden coldness in his belly. "Where? I'm going to just make sure he's all right."

"I'll show you."

He wasn't crazy to have her go with him, but then again, the gangsters were gone. And as it turned out, all was peaceful. Ivory was deep in morphine slumber, breathing regularly and looking undisturbed.

"I better get going," he said, "before it's too messed up out there to drive."

"I'm sure Crevette misses you."

"You kidding me? That cat's cool as a crustacean..."

"...which she happens to be named after."

"Yeah, she's shrimpy in more than one way. *She's* cool, but Darth is going out of his mind."

She smiled slyly. "You're worried about *Darth*? Ha! That pooch gets to everybody. You've fallen in love, haven't you?"

He couldn't help cracking a smile. "There could be something to that." It didn't seem the time to ask her about the baby pictures.

KATRINA MONDAY

8

The eye, if the forecasts had been correct, had passed around six a.m., but the wind was still howling when Skip awoke sometime around nine and went down to make coffee, grateful Jimmy Dee had a gas stove and hadn't obeyed the instruction to turn off the gas. The house felt as if it was being shaken by Godzilla.

As she puttered, her phone rang. Her lieutenant, Sylvia Cappello, addressed her as Skip, which wasn't good at all. She was only Skip when things were going so badly Cappello couldn't bother being formal.

"Skip, it's hell out there. The Superdome's got a hole in the roof. The 911 lines are down... and there's flooding. I think some of the pumping stations got knocked out."

Of course there was flooding. There was always flooding. That was why thousands of people had left their cars parked on the neutral grounds and sidewalks. It was a way of life.

"We've had reports," Cappello said tentatively, apparently not wanting to speak the words, "that people are in their attics."

Skip's scalp prickled at the ever-so-careful phrase, the

way it did when she ran into a perp who was going to be dangerous. She could feel it before he even gave her a sign. People had had to go to their attics in Hurricane Betsy—and many of them had died.

"Where? In the Lower Nine?"

Cappello was barely able to keep her voice steady. "You know Detective Little? He's still got cell service—and he's in his attic. Also, we've talked to the Coast Guard. Since the 911 lines are out, people are calling them instead of us. People are on roofs."

"Oh, Jesus! Should I..."

"No, there's nothing you can do. Are you kidding me? There's still a hurricane out there. And even when it stops, you won't be able to drive with all the trees down. If the levee's overtopped..."

"I'd need a duck boat."

"Uh... you don't happen to have one, do you?"

And that was when Skip knew how bad it was. Or thought she did. Nobody really had any idea.

She answered tentatively. "You almost sound as if you're serious."

"Serious as hell. I had a call from Adam Abasolo ..."

"God, I miss A.A." He'd been assigned to the Sixth.

"Yeah. Me too. He's on search and rescue, calling all over for boats."

Oh, hell! "My brother's got one. He lives uptown and he's stubborn as hell. I'm pretty sure he rode out the storm."

"You don't even know?" In a city where family meant weekly get-togethers if not daily drop-bys, this was just about unthinkable.

Skip felt sheepish. "We're not close. But my parents told me he was planning to stay."

"They didn't stay, I hope."

"Oh, no, they went to Jackson." One less thing to worry about, but she'd better check on their house. "Can you have Abasolo call me if you hear from him again? I'll give him a call as well."

"Will do."

Perhaps lured by the coffee smell, or awakened by the elements, Ollie and Billy filtered in, the Horvaths remaining peacefully sacked out.

Ollie rustled up some eggs and bacon—there was no way to make toast—while Skip sipped and listened to her police radio, trying to figure out what to do.

The news on the radio made her antsy to get going. Looters were out in force. All officers had been ordered to report in. She had, and had been told to stay where she was till the wind was below 50 mph. How was she supposed to measure that? She interpreted the order this way: "Get out there and act like a cop as soon as you can walk without getting blown against a building."

Driving would probably be out of the question, due to debris. And there was still the question of what to do with a loose-cannon juvenile.

"Whathehell?" Billy said. "Did you hear that?"

"Hear what?"

"On the radio. The IBoys."

"Huh?"

"That's a gang. From where I stay. They out lootin' right in the storm."

Skip knew who the IBoys were. They weren't just any gang. They were as lethal as you got. She would have thought looting was beneath them. "You live in the Iberville?"

He shook his head. "I stay in Treme. Henriette de Lille St."

"You know those guys?"

She thought she saw his eyes flash fear before he turned away, but she couldn't be sure. "Wish I didn't," he muttered.

She excused herself to make a call.

"Skip! You okay?" It was good to hear Abasolo's voice.

"Fine, thanks. Rode out the storm at Jimmy Dee's with four neighbors, one of whom I once handcuffed in a bar fight."

"That could be awkward."

"Nope. Wasn't at all. She was too drunk at the time to remember. How're *you* doing?"

"That is a very fraught question." She felt her scalp prickle once again, the way it had when Cappello reported flooding. She paused to let him explain, but he only said, "I actually don't think I can talk about it right now."

He sounded so subdued she was alarmed.

"That bad?"

"Oh, way worse. It's so goddam frustrating! We know what's happening, but the goddam storm's still here!"

"And what's happening is..."

"Well, let's work with the part I know about. As soon as I can get out there, I gotta spend the day trying to save people from drowning. Is that a little on the apocalyptic side? And there's something really bothering me."

She waited.

"At roll call yesterday, they said come in at two or three a.m."

She tried to take that in. "At the height of the storm?"

"Yeah. Till somebody mentioned that was impossible. And then they said six, when the eye was supposed to pass."

"Oh, Jesus."

"What does that tell you?"

She considered that. "Nobody thought anything out. There isn't really a plan in place."

"Yeah."

She shivered, but didn't answer.

Finally, he said, "Know where I can find some boats?"

"One, anyway. That's why I'm calling."

She could have called her brother herself, but she knew he'd get a kick out of getting the request from Abasolo himself. She gave him Conrad's cell number and went back to her own unaccustomed set of dilemmas.

With no AC, it was getting hotter and hotter in the house. And the wind raged on.

She thought she was going to go nuts with no electricity and no idea what was expected of her. She had to get out there—people needed help, lots of them, she suspected. The problem was, she already had a houseful of people who also did. She could leave Ollie in charge of the Drunkersons, but Billy was a real complication. He seemed like a nice enough kid and he'd been a big help. But he'd been on the street when he shouldn't have been and he'd arrived with a loaded gun tucked into his jeans. And however helpful or dangerous he was, he was also a juvenile who'd as good as admitted he had an unsavory home life.

Yet she had to get him home before she did another thing. Fortunately, he lived within walking distance. As soon as she could open the door—admittedly with Ollie on the inside pushing it—she stepped out and tested. It was wet and windy, but she was pretty sure she could walk.

"Billy, I gotta get out there. Come on. I'm going to walk you home."

"You crazy? I can't go home with those assholes out there."

"What assholes?" And then she got it. "The gangs? You're afraid of the gangs?"

"I got my reasons."

"You're afraid to walk on the street with a cop?"

"Not if you give me my piece."

"I'll return it to your mom, but not today. Today, you're going to put on Jimmy Dee's rain gear and accept a police escort."

"'Aight," he said, barely audible. *All right.*

She put on Sheila's gear, which thankfully included a pair of Wellies, and went for a walk in the hurricane. With a sulky teen-ager.

The house Billy lived in was tiny and beat up, yet an architectural gem, she was pretty sure. At any rate, it was old and beautiful—to her, anyway. Tiny as it was, it looked as if generations had raised rowdy, lively families in it. "This is us," Billy said. "I be okay now."

"Let's make sure your mama's home."

"You don't need to come in." Anxiety twisted his young face. He no more wanted her coming in than he wanted to run into the IBoys.

"I do. It's kind of my job. You got a key?"

"Yeah. I got a key." He unlocked the door and opened it.

Skip knew immediately something was wrong. It didn't smell right in there; it reeked of rot, as if nobody lived there —or had recently died there. There was a dark puddle on the floor. And another one across the room from the first, as if two idiots had been dueling with pistols. But there were no bodies.

"Mama!" Billy cried. She could hear the panic in his voice. "Mama! Mama, you here?"

Before Skip could say don't, he ran into the other two

downstairs rooms, a bedroom and a tiny kitchen, and up the stairs, with Skip on his heels. "Mama, Mama!"

He ran downstairs again and, before she even knew what was happening, out the door and down the block. She chased him until she lost him. He knew the neighborhood and he'd ducked in somewhere, in some hidey-hole he'd probably known about since he played here as a pre-schooler.

9

W hat had *happened* in that house? If his mama
was dead, it was almost certainly Billy's fault.
When she hollered, "Git out of this house and
don't come back," he'd left without so much as a jacket. Just
run out the door like she was chasing him with a frying pan.

What was wrong with him? He knew better than that,
but he'd been so confused. So much had happened the day
before, with Ivory getting shot, and then last night before
Mama had kicked him out. He was all messed up inside, so
he just did what she said.

And he'd run right into the arms of the cops. Or at least
a cop. A homicide cop. He had no idea what to make of
Detective Skip Langdon except that he had to get away from
her and stay away. He couldn't believe he'd let her in the
house. He never should have done that. But he'd never
expected his mama not to be there either.

If she'd left on her own—and he hoped to God she had
—she'd have gone to her sister's house. His Aunt Makayla.
She stayed close, close enough for his Mama to have run

there—over in the Iberville. The problem was, Billy couldn't go into the Iberville.

He tried calling her, but that didn't work. Okay, he was going. He hated leaving his hiding place without even talking to his elderly neighbor about the new thing he'd just discovered. He wasn't at all sure Elmo'd be safe. But what could he do? Nothing but warn him, and that would probably backfire anyhow. Elmo was an ornery old cuss.

He rolled out from under Elmo's house and stood up. The wind was dying down, big-time. Katrina had come and gone and Billy's house still stood and so did Billy. It wasn't that bad after all. Although other things might be. He sure wished he had his piece back.

He was hardly across the street when along came the Dark Knight. Half the Iboys had names like that—Dark Knight, Black Knight, Jedi Knight, even Christmas Knight and Twelfth Knight. They didn't have a single spark of originality. Wasn't funny after *Dark Knight*, didn't they get that? That's who everyone was sucking up to, with those names. Dark was the first Knight, and the meanest. His name was really Petey.

Well, Billy had a street name too. Only bad thing, his mama gave it to him when he was a little bitty thing 'cause she thought it was cute. Now they used it against him.

"Hey, Toast," hollered Dark Knight.

"What *you* want, Darkie?"

Billy didn't wait for an answer, he just took off running deeper into Treme to throw the Knight off the track. He knew damn well what Petey wanted, and he knew he better move his ass if he wanted to keep it attached to his body.

The older boy—man really—Petey must be nineteen or twenty by now—was heavier and probably loaded as well. Billy just ran at a normal, easy pace, and pretty soon he no longer heard the Knight's footsteps behind him. He doubled back across his own neighborhood and into the Iberville Project, slinking around the buildings, being careful to stay out of the open courtyards.

Almost as soon as he knocked, his aunt opened the door and pulled him into a hug. "Hey, baby, we dodged a bullet didn't we? This was just a l'il ol' baby storm."

"Hi, Aunt Kayla. Well, it sure was noisy where I was." He grinned as she pulled him inside. Aunt Kayla was definitely a glass half-full kind of person.

"You looking for ya mama, aren't you?"

"She here? She threw me out the house last night and when I got back home she wasn't there. I don't know where else she'd go but here."

"Lord, lord." Kayla sighed. "That woman's got some serious mental health issues."

"Yeah, well..." They all knew that. "You got her?"

"She did come here. She came here last night, all bloodied up..."

Billy winced.

"... and talking crazy. And *wet!* Woman was soaked. Dripped all over my nice rugs."

"She ain't here?" He was nearly frantic. "Where'd she go?"

"Now you take it easy, baby. She all right. You come in and let me make you a sandwich."

He blew out his breath. Now that she mentioned it, he could use a sandwich. If his mama was okay, he might as well stay and let Kayla tell her story. She wasn't the kind of person who could be hurried.

"You want ham or tuna fish?"

"Ham, please. With a whole lot of mustard."

She laughed. "Hell, I knew that. I been knowin' you all

your life! I don't even have any tuna fish. I was just playin'
with ya."

He grinned up at her. There were times when he wished
his aunt had been his mama. She had a good job and had
raised three children of her own and never for a moment got
involved with drugs or violent men. Why couldn't everybody's mama be like that? He pushed down the disloyal
thoughts and sat down in Kayla's cheery kitchen. Without
electricity, she had candles going, even though it was
daytime. That was just like her.

"When did you get home?" she asked.

"Just a few minutes ago. Met some people who took me
in. White people."

"You kiddin' me? White people took care of your skinny
black ass? Now I know you crazy as ya mama."

"It was... *different*, all right." He wasn't about to tell her
he'd been befriended by a homicide cop.

"Why'd Maxine throw you out anyway?" She placed the
completed sandwich in front of him, along with a glass of
lukewarm iced tea. "Sorry, ain't got no ice left."

He shrugged. "You know how she is."

"What I know is she was all beat up. That crazy man of
hers do that?"

"Yeah." He spoke almost in a whisper. "She was afraid he
was gon' start in on me."

She sat down across from him, nodding. "That's what
she said, all right. But, you know... it was kind of mixed up
'cause that wasn't all she said."

He took a bite so he wouldn't have to speak.

"She said she had to go see Ivory 'cause she was going to
jail this morning."

Billy jerked his attention away from the food. He hadn't
seen that one coming. "Why she say a thing like that?"

Kayla was watching him like a cat at a bird-feeder. "Say she killed him."

She didn't take her eyes off Billy's face. "That the real reason she threw yo' ass out?"

"Kaynard ain't dead."

"How you know that?"

"'Cause when I got home neither one of 'em was there. Somebody *should* kill him, though." He rubbed his midsection. In fact, Kaynard *had* started in on him, and he had a pretty nasty bruise to show for it.

Kayla nodded, looking satisfied. "Man just needs killin'."

"Mama spend the night with you?"

"Hay-ull no! She wasn't havin' no part of that."

Billy waited.

"I had to haul her scanty ass over to Big Charity in the middle of the storm. You believe that?"

Billy sucked in his breath. If Maxine was at Charity, he had to book it over there before she started talking crazy. But Kayla's outrage kind of made him grin.

"You *drove* her?"

"Yeah, I drove her. Limbs flyin' off a trees, stuff in the road, the car shakin' and swervin', every kind of thing."

"You did that? For my mom?"

"Well, she is my sister." She paused. "Actually it was kinda selfish. She was about to have a psychotic episode, I'm pretty sure, and I sure didn't want that with... you know..." She pointed at the ceiling, meaning the second floor, where her diabetic, 400-pound husband spent most of his time. "Last thing Paul needs."

Billy'd seen his mama's "episodes." That was one of the reasons he freaked out when he didn't find her at home. When she went off the rails, she might do anything. He was pretty sure she wouldn't hurt Ivory, though. He just needed to shut her up or she really would end up imprisoned.

He pushed back his chair and stood up. "You know what? I think I better get on over there and see her."

"What? You going to Charity?"

"Yeah. May be time to bring her home."

"You want me to ride you over?"

"Naaah. If you thought there was stuff in the road yesterday, think what it's like out there now."

"Well, okay then."

That wasn't the main thing. If he ran into any Iboys, he didn't want his aunt to get busted up.

They were waiting for him. He saw the Dark Knight almost the minute he closed the front door. Too late, it dawned on him that Petey'd figured out where he'd be. He knew Kayla. He might know everyone in the Iberville. All he had to do was wait for Billy to come out.

Billy took off running—straight into an ambush. But he was fast, and he changed direction, quickly losing the new guys. And then they started coming on bicycles—Petey and another guy. They'd finally gotten smart. He couldn't outrun bicycles.

Instead, he stepped off the sidewalk and grabbed a fallen branch, swinging it as hard as he could across the first one's chest, knocking him off-balance and causing him to lose control and crash. Petey, following too close to stop, hit the fallen bike and went down as well, but Billy only heard it, didn't have time to turn around for a look. He just beat feet, and the sounds he heard were pretty hopeful—thunderous cussin' and moaning like they were fucked up as hell. *Goddam,* he hoped they were! With luck, maybe one of them broke something.

He kept running, hoping for some kind of cover,

someone to help him if they got up and tried again. One thing, this time they couldn't guess where he was going. It wasn't far, actually a little less than a mile.

He was pretty sure he'd outrun the Dark Knight and his buddies when he heard the gunshots. Could they be *shooting* at him? He suddenly felt something the size of a golf ball in his throat, but he tried not to panic. It didn't make sense—they needed him to give up what they wanted, so why would they kill him? Then he realized logic needn't apply, they might just do it in a fit of rage. These thugs were always doing stuff like that, stuff that worked against their own interests. His mama had schooled him on all that street stuff, which was one reason it was so wrong for her to be with Kaynard. He knew she knew better. But he also knew she had the kind of mental problems that made her addictive and needy as well as crazy. Wasn't much she could do about it.

Two more gunshots. Okay, they *must* be shooting at him. Panicked, he picked up the pace and pretty soon the shots stopped. But he was still running on adrenaline and fear, and he was nearly exhausted.

He was almost to Tulane Avenue when he tripped on a curb. Instinctively, he broke the fall with his hands, hearing a very distinct crunch followed by sharp pain in his left wrist.

10

Skip put her hands on her knees and took a few noisy, painful breaths before facing whatever bad news the little house held. First, she retraced Billy's footsteps, making sure no one was hiding in it. Then she made a more thorough search, improvising gloves with a pair of socks she found in a drawer. She touched the puddles on the floor with a paper towel. They were sticky and dark red. Blood for sure. And something else, she thought, gagging—a piece of organic matter. Brains? She found a baggie to put it in, along with a bit of the blood.

She went through the few drawers she found upstairs— there were none in the living room and those in the kitchen held nothing but kitchen equipment. Curiously, she found no weapons. She went through any papers she found lying about, including a bill from the Sewerage and Water Department, addressed to Kaynard Cochon. So someone lived there besides Mom and Billy.

Kaynard had only a few pairs of jeans and half a dozen t-shirts, but he did own an expensive leather jacket. There were women's clothes in the same closet as his. A second bedroom, with kind of a combination hip-hop, sports, and piles-of-clothes theme, was obviously Billy's.

The kid had a laptop, but Skip couldn't see trying to figure out the password when she was supposed to be out on the streets.

She tried the usual hiding places, like shoes, shoeboxes, and under the mattress. But, ironically, it was almost in plain sight, in a bathroom cabinet, that she found a Walmart plastic tub full of crack—the biggest stash she'd ever seen. Obviously Kaynard was a dealer. So Billy hadn't been sent out for drugs.

In that case, why had he left the house?

It had to be because of violence therein. Blood had clearly been shed. But where was everybody?

She thought of confiscating the crack, but couldn't see walking the streets with a tub of crack. In the end, she left with only the baggie of whatever dark matter she'd found on the floor, the haunting sensation that whatever had happened here had happened after Billy left, and the bad feeling that something serious had happened to his mom.

She felt as if her brain was scrambled. She shouldn't have disturbed what was probably a crime scene. But she felt as if all rules might be suspended today. On the other hand, she was a homicide detective and this might very well be a homicide.

She tried Cappello. "Back!" the lieutenant said. "Had to charge the phone in the car. There's a lot of flooding out there. Everything's haywire everywhere. There's no 911, there's looting, there's all kinds of crap in the street, trees down all over the city—oh, yeah, and get this—OPP's flooded." Orleans Parish Prison. "So do this... walk down St. Claude and do what you can."

Skip was flabbergasted. "Huh? What's that supposed to mean?"

"It means we don't know what the hell's going on out there. Half the police who were scheduled didn't even report in. Phones are down, people are on roofs. You want to know the truth? It's chaos around here. And out there. So I repeat: Just get out there and keep the peace."

Somehow, Skip had felt that no matter what happened elsewhere, at least it would be business as usual in the police department. But Abasolo had said there was no plan. It looked like he was right. She tried to adjust her attitude.

"On it. But I need to report a crime scene. Maybe."

She quickly described what she'd seen, and Cappello said, "I'll make a note of it. But if you didn't see anyone bleeding and you didn't see any bodies, that's Priority Z today."

"I did see crack. More crack than I've ever seen."

"Langdon, I just don't think you're getting it. You've got bigger fish to fry today. We all do."

Skip tried to lighten the mood. "Okay, then. Off to sauté some poissons."

Cappello, never one to joke around, didn't let it pass. "Skip. While I appreciate your upbeat attitude, there's something you should know—I think this is a lot worse than a few looters and a little flooding."

"I kind of thought so. I saw some smoke. Is there a fire somewhere?"

"That's the least of it. The levees have broken."

Skip's stomach fluttered. So, she could have sworn, did her heart. Everything inside her did a double-take, trying to take in what she'd just heard. The city's drainage system was antiquated and inefficient—and so, when she'd heard the word "flooding," she didn't understand it was something she hadn't seen before. Flooding was normal in New Orleans when there were heavy rains. But now she understood exactly what Cappello meant. A levee breach would mean The Big One—the thing meteorologists and scientists had been warning about for years. The geographic bowl in which New Orleans was built would fill up.

"Okay, I'm outta here." It was all she could trust herself to say. She felt a surge of energy, a physical need to do something.

Later, she'd barely be able to remember anything she did that day. She found parades of wet, panicked, disheveled people straggling down the neutral ground on St. Claude, headed vaguely towards the Superdome, which was being used as a makeshift shelter. *What was happening here?*

But she couldn't find out from the rag-tag army. Most of its members were incoherent.

"The water. It just... came."

"I can't find my mama! She stay just down the block. Her house gone. My mama ain't nowhere I can find."

"My baby! My *baby!*"

This last one she heard over and over. Sometimes it meant a young child was missing or injured, sometimes a grown one.

She managed to piece together that these were refugees from the flooding in the Ninth Ward. Every one of them had lost their homes and many had lost family members or neighbors. Sadness and misery oozed from them like sweat. Some openly wailed. Some just looked at her with hopeless, unbelieving eyes, unable to speak.

She tried to organize transportation or temporary shelter—even an umbrella and a blanket!—for those who'd run out of steam or fallen apart emotionally. For the sick and hurt, she called for help and crossed her fingers that it would come.

She broke up fights, but she didn't go out of her way to stop looting—unless it was senseless looting of non-essentials. She didn't have the heart to stop people taking supplies like food, water, and baby diapers.

Technically, she should have arrested every looter, but with the jail flooded, where was she going to put them? And how was she going to get them there? It was raining, the streets were blocked by fallen trees, and not only was she running out of juice on her phone, she was finding fewer and fewer people were answering theirs. Cell towers were out for some and others just had to find a place to recharge. She understood without anyone telling her that she was going to have to make her own rules today—and probably for the next few days. And, also, with a sick feeling she knew she had to swallow, that what she was seeing was chaos on a scale that wasn't going to be controllable for a long time.

She worked as late as she could, but when it got dark, there wasn't much she could do with only a flashlight, and not much the most determined thugs could do either, but those were in short supply, it seemed. Even criminals had lost their homes and their relatives and, momentarily, their minds.

Back at Jimmy Dee's, she found everyone gone, including Breesy the dog and Iggy the cat. Angel was thrilled to see her, though. And starving, although, thanks to puppy pads, otherwise apparently quite comfortable. Ollie'd done her usual stellar job of cleaning up, even in the flooded bathroom and the rooms with leaks. That was a relief, but she badly wanted to go home, to her slave quarters in the courtyard. Well, tomorrow, maybe. It just didn't feel right to desert the Big House.

11

L angdon didn't talk much about her brother, but Adam could remember a few choice descriptions of him. The phrase "Uptown twit" came to mind. He gathered they didn't get along. She'd dismissed it when he asked: "Different values, you know?"

"Different how?"

"He's a big ol' conformist, that's all. Into the social scene. Totally disapproves of my job."

The address he'd given A.A. was Uptown. So, check. He was in his yard, trying to load his flat-bottomed boat onto its car trailer. From the back, you could see he had short brown hair and wore baggy khaki shorts, a faded-out HowAhYa shirt from JazzFest, and flip-flops. Nothing there to dispel the stereotype.

"Give you a hand with that?"

The other man turned around. He was nearly a foot shorter than Adam, and had the soft jowls and pinkish skin of the drinking classes, but also the warm smile of his favorite partner. Adam decided to like him.

Conrad greeted him warmly. "A.A.? Conrad Langdon. Skippy talks about you all the time."

Skippy?

"She's told you my nickname, I see. You can call me Adam if that's too cumbersome."

"Naaah. Skippy never does. You're A.A. to me. And boy, do I know some A.A. stories. Got a feeling more are going to come out of today."

They started wrestling the boat onto the trailer. "How's your house?" Adam said.

Conrad shrugged. "Lost some shingles, sprung a few leaks. About 5K worth, I guess. Could have been worse. Yours?"

"I don't know. Haven't been home yet." But he did know. It had to be trashed.

"Where we goin?" Conrad asked.

"Well, the Ninth Ward's real hard hit—we have a couple of officers out there in their attics. But I'm not too sure how to get the boat there. You need a chainsaw just to drive a block."

Conrad brightened. "Got one of those! Let's put it in the car. I got an idea. Let's go on the river."

"Hey, it's still blowing a gale. You sure about that?"

"Excuse me? Are you the famous A.A. or not?"

Uh-oh, Adam thought. He hoped this wasn't going to turn into some kind of machismo contest. In the first place he shouldn't put a civilian in danger—meaning he should kick Conrad out of his own boat—but it was evident Conrad intended to join him. Short of commandeering the vessel, such as it was, he didn't see a way to tell him no.

Besides, he'd never in his life been on the river in a tiny boat. He needed the guy, who was fast proving not nearly so worthless as his sister obviously thought him. They drove to an Uptown boat ramp, eased the tiny vessel into the very very Big Muddy, and prayed. At least in Abasolo's case. If they didn't die in that killer current, he figured they might survive the day.

At first they couldn't see much due to levees and wharves—and then they saw water. Water where houses ought to be. Blocks and blocks of them.

"Holy shit," A.A. said.

Conrad said nothing, just stopped the boat and stared.

A.A. had addresses for the stranded officers, but no streets were visible, only rooftops, many of which had people on them, sometimes whole families, all shouting for help. People were in the water too, struggling to swim, to get to relatives, sometimes just to stay alive. What the hell were they supposed to do here?

Almost immediately, that question answered itself. A woman shouted, "Help us! We've been here five hours!" The man with her looked as if he was in acute pain. He hollered, "Can y'all help? I can't hold on much longer."

He was holding onto a porch post with one hand and held a small girl with the other, but not that small. She was six or seven and had to weigh forty-five pounds or so. Standing with him, also grasping posts, but with two hands, were two older women, maybe a mother and daughter, a teen-age boy, and another man holding a baby.

"We're coming," Conrad yelled, and that was that. They just started hauling people into the boat, beginning with the first man and child, then the rest of his family. "We thought we wuz dead," the older of the women said, rubbing her bare feet. "My feet killin' me, standin' on that rail."

Adam did a double-take. "Wait a minute. You weren't standing on the floor of the porch?"

"No sir. Water come up and we had to climb on the rail.

Even then, it was above Laila's head." She pointed to the girl, whose father now sat stretching out his arms, then rubbing his temples, clearly trying to make himself believe the ordeal was over. The girl was curled in the lap of the younger woman, sucking her thumb. The boy stared straight ahead, his face blank, like the faces of children in photos of war zones. Adam wondered how long it would take these people to recover.

They were the first. He and Conrad took them to dry land—having no better destination than anywhere that wasn't wet—and the best they could do right now was the levee on the river side, the one that had held. Adam called for help, but, in his heart, he knew their fate now depended on the luck of the draw. Their best hope was that someone would spot them from the river and pick them up. *And take them where?* he wondered. Maybe there was a designated pick-up spot. He tried to call again, but got no answers.

And that was when he knew for sure: No one was in charge. No one at all. As he'd suspected, there was very definitely no plan.

After that, they worked fast, almost as if they'd been trained, grabbing anybody who was close enough, and as soon as they had a load, taking them to dry land anywhere they could find.

What had happened was obvious. This part of New Orleans was separated from the rest of the city by the Industrial Canal, which connects Lake Pontchartrain with the river. The levee just on the other side of the St. Claude St. Bridge, the one that protected the neighborhood from the lake, had to be the one that broke, releasing a vast tidal wave into the neighborhood, a fast-moving one driven by hurricane winds. The neighborhood must have been swamped almost instantly.

Imagining what that had to be like was mind-bending. And way too horrible for Adam to hold the thought for long. The other A.A., the organization of which he was a faithful member, was famous for its "one day at a time" philosophy. In his head, Adam amended it to mean he had to forget the big picture, focusing only on what—and mostly who—was right in front of him. He surveyed the scene with this question in his mind: What good could he do here?

He was still in contact with his lieutenant, who kept asking about the stranded officers. He tried to explain that there were no landmarks, no streets signs, no streets even. In fact, he hated to say it, but right near the bridge, there was pretty much nothing at all.

Everything was flooded except the Mississippi river levee by the Holy Cross neighborhood, where they'd dropped the porch post family. Holy Cross was underwater, but nothing like the blocks further inland. The closer you got to Lake Pontchartrain, the deeper the floodwaters were. The currents were fierce. You had to go where you saw immediate need. That was really all there was to do.

He was absolutely unable to make anyone who wasn't in the boat understand.

And after a while he gave up. There just wasn't time for that crap. There were children in that filthy water. And elderly and sick people. Maybe most dangerous of all, extremely fat people, who needed several people to help them into the boat. You just couldn't stop and argue.

Adam and Conrad barely talked at all, except about logistics, like whether there was drinking water. Conrad had thought to bring some. But there wasn't much. They had to hoard it in order to keep going.

But they rationed carefully and finally ended up giving most of it to three men they found swimming with a bucket of babies. The bucket was a knee-high plastic tub that looked like something you'd buy at Walmart to store toys in, but now it held five live dolls—four boys and a girl, all, he'd guess, under two years old. Two of the men held each of the tub's handles with one hand, while using the other arm to swim. The third held onto the back rim, kicking to propel the whole makeshift mechanism.

Once they had them in the boat, Conrad tried kidding around with the kids. "Rub-a dub-dub, five men in a tub...", but the babies were not amused. He chucked one under the chin, producing instant tears.

"Shit!" one of the men said. "Leave my kid alone."

Conrad blushed, looking at Adam. "Guess I'm not as funny as I think I am."

For once in his life, Adam didn't have an answer. He just clasped the other man on the shoulder.

"I didn't mean nothing," the dad said. "Just havin' a bad day."

One of the other men snickered at that. "Yeah, you could call it that."

And then they all laughed, even with misery all around them—for a moment they could laugh. All except the babies, who were inconsolable.

"They're hot," Conrad said, and poured a bottle of their precious water on them. He gave a bottle to each of the men before they dropped them off.

It was late afternoon when they spotted a blue plastic wading pool, headed straight for them. It was a kid's pool, nothing meant to float, and it was full of people, including a baby in a car seat. Two people, a man and a woman, were paddling with oars from some small vessel, a kayak, maybe.

"They're not gonna make it," Conrad warned, his voice slightly panicked.

Adam shouted for their attention. "We're coming! Wait for us, okay?"

Someone stood halfway up to yell back and before Adam, seeing a recipe for disaster, could stop them, the entire improvised craft flipped abruptly over.

Conrad handed him the tiller and slid overboard, nearly capsizing their own boat as well. Adam extended one of the flatboat's oars to a woman who clearly couldn't swim and was about to have hysterics and go under again. A man was tending to another man who was splashing helplessly, and a second woman was trying to push the one with the oar into the boat, which Adam was trying his best to hold steady. At least one woman was yelling, "My baby! My baby!" and several people were yelling, "Nathan! Save Nathan."

The baby, Adam thought.

With a huge sploosh, the car seat breached, in Conrad's arms, and landed in the boat. The baby was lifeless. Everyone was screaming now, the woman holding the oar, apparently the mother, wasn't even forming words, just emitting terrified shrieking sounds.

For a moment, Adam hesitated, trying to figure out how to keep the boat afloat *and* help the baby. Finally he settled on guiding one of the mother's hands to the boat and hoping for the best. "Hold on!"

Conrad, gasping for breath, held the boat steady from the water, while Adam tried to get the kid out of the damn car seat. The straps were too soaked to work properly, so finally he turned the whole thing on its side, and tried to clear the baby's airway. Water poured out of his mouth, and Conrad, grasping the situation, produced a Swiss army knife.

Quickly, Adam cut the straps and began compressions,

with the baby in his lap, completely unmoving. "Mouth-to-mouth," Conrad shouted. "Let me."

"I've got it," Adam said, and tried that, thinking at least he couldn't break a chestful of ribs this way. Still, he had to be careful not to blow too hard into the tiny mouth. The adults around him were now quiet, all eyes on the baby. Some were obviously praying.

Adam kept breathing, for minutes on end, it seemed like, beginning to give up hope. And then... a gurgle. The baby began to twist and squirm in his arms. He held him upright and Nathan produced a squeal to rival his mom's.

Applause broke out from another rescue boat that had stopped to help.

Then the mom started up again, yelling and reaching out her arms for the baby, which pitched her back in the water. Conrad said, "We've got to get this kid to the hospital."

"Yeah." He yelled to the other boat. "Can y'all get everybody? We're taking Nathan to the hospital."

"Sure can," was the answer. "Where you taking him?"

"Charity. What's his last name?"

"Watts." One of the men said, "He's Nathan Watts. His mama's Serena Thompson."

"I'm taking him to Dr. Bordelon. Can you remember that? Kathy Bordelon."

He made the man say it back to him and promise to write it down for Serena. It was horrible to have to leave without her.

Conrad eased the boat to open water and then let it go full throttle. "I don't think I did that right," Adam said. "Aren't you supposed to do breaths and compressions both?"

"Well, he's breathing. But what makes you think Charity'll take him?"

"It's our best bet," Adam said grimly. "But how do we get there?"

He wrapped the baby in his shirt and held him the whole way, unable to call Kathy till they'd reached land, sure they were going to lose Nathan any second.

Charity wasn't really near anywhere they could navigate to. Adam got on his radio and finally got an agreement for an officer to meet them on Tchoupitoulas near Walmart. Someone who owed Adam a favor.

12

"Y ou're bringing me a... *what?*"

The thought of Adam Abasolo bringing her a baby stirred up such a roiling stew in Kathy's chest she could hardly breathe. A baby he had rescued from drowning. She didn't know what to say, on either a professional or emotional level.

"Oh, come on. I'm all the little guy's got. He drowned. I brought him back."

She was impressed—but also beset by a lot of other emotions she tried like hell to tamp down. "Okay, but hurry."

"Well, you don't exactly know what you're asking, but I'll do the best I can."

She didn't know if she could handle this. Even the word made her want to cry: *Baby*. The most precious thing that had ever happened to her, and then...

...and then the worst had happened. Not just the worst, but the worst version of the worst. She couldn't think about it, she didn't want to think about it, she couldn't stand to think about anyone else's baby. She just couldn't.

She alerted the trauma team, hoping they'd whisk the baby away before she could see it, but it didn't work that way. The sight of Adam holding the tiny wet bundle just about did her in—a child that had almost *drowned*, but that Adam had saved. No one could possibly understand the kind of emotional weight all that held for her. Every bit of it —Adam, the baby, the near-death, the rescue... it was as if everything raw and miserable and ironic that had ever existed in her life had come together at this moment. She blinked a few times and clenched her jaw purposefully, hoping she could hold it together.

Oblivious, Adam ignored the waiting team and brought the baby right to her. "Nathan," he said, "this is Kathy. Kathy, Nathan."

He expected her to take him, she thought, and wondered if she could, just because she was supposed to, but the instant the baby saw her, he opened his mouth and set up a caterwauling worthy of Crevette herself. It wasn't the sort of thing a dying baby did, thus it was an incredibly welcome sound. Delighted, everyone laughed, even Kathy. Perhaps especially Kathy.

All of a sudden she was herself again. She hadn't fallen apart, in fact in that milli-second had fallen a little bit for the tiny fighter, had felt the sort of universal need to protect and pet every human does in the presence of a baby.

"I think we're bonding," she said, hardly believing she'd found the resources to make a joke.

Snickers all around.

`Adam said, "He's tough. I think he'll make it. I could swear he smiled at me."

"Gas," she said, thinking, *Another joke. I did it again!*

"Uh-uh. That only holds up for a few months, right? This kid's about a year old."

She showed him teeth. Smiling was hard right now, just as an all-around thing, but Nathan was alive and yelling. That was something to be happy about. "Well, here's me smiling at you. Good thing you did there, Lieutenant Abasolo!" She even moved forward to give him a hug, but he side-stepped her.

"You don't know the half of it."

"Bragging? Hard morning of heroics?"

"Listen. I've got some things to tell you."

He sat her down and told her what was going on in the city, causing an entirely new set of roiling emotions. "Surely the worst is over," she said. "I'm sorry to hear about the Lower Ninth, but this happened after Betsy too..."

"I dunno. I wasn't here then. But this is the closest thing to hell I've seen."

"Well, at least we're dry here. Crevette and Darth getting along okay?"

"I'll probably get to find out in a few hours," he said, and got up to leave.

She leaned forward to kiss him, but he stepped back. "I'm pretty disgusting," he said. She wasn't sure what that was about, but there wasn't much time to think about it.

Someone was banging on the emergency room door, a teen-age kid, it turned out, holding his wrist as if it was broken. Officially, Charity was "locked down"—taking only the most desperate cases—but the kid looked so distressed she debated making an exception. Before she could even make up her mind, someone else slammed out the door, someone young, African-American, and moving fast. The kid stared briefly at the fleeing man, then, relief flooding his face, slipped in the door and bent over, breathing hard.

She touched his back. "What's going on? Something chasing you?"

He stood up and looked her in the eye. "You could say that."

She pointed with her chin at his wrist. "Somebody beat you up?"

"Naah. Tripped."

She wondered if that was true. "Okay, go check in; let's get that wrist X-rayed while we've still got power."

She had no reason to think that would change. The generators were working. Why had she said that? Adam's story must have gotten to her.

A couple of hours later a nurse brought the kid back to her, wrist splinted and in a sling. "Can you talk to Billy, please? He's looking for his mama."

The nurse made sure she was gone before Kathy answered.

"I heard she was here," the kid said. "Maxine Polite?"

Kathy stared at him. "You're *that* Billy." If this boy had been raised by Maxine Polite, he'd already had a hard life, and he couldn't be more than sixteen. He was probably younger. "Your mama talks about you."

"Is she... uhhh... is she here? Is she okay?"

Define okay, she wanted to say, and then she caught on that he was frightened. He thought she might be hurt... or maybe dead.

She smiled at him, trying to help if she could. "Maxine's fine," Kathy said. "A little banged up, but basically okay. She checked herself in last night." Once again, she saw the relief in his face. Something most definitely was chasing this kid —probably lots of somethings.

Kathy'd finally gotten a look at the bruises Nurse Brenda'd been trying to point out when the excitement started. Something besides her demons had been torturing Maxine as well. She had a scalp wound too. "She have a fight with somebody?"

"Oh, yeah. She was fightin' with Kaynard last night. Boy friend, I guess you could call him." He spat out the words.

"Did Kaynard break your wrist?"

He looked annoyed. "I told you. I fell. I knew it was broken. Heard the crunch."

Involuntarily, she winced. "Ouch."

He laughed. "Thought doctors were tough." He'd loosened up the moment he knew his mother was safe.

"You want to see your mama?"

"Uh-huh. My brother too. He's in ICU."

"Oh, yes. Ivory." Maxine had come to see him too. "He got shot, right?

"Yes, ma'am. On Saturday."

Suddenly she realized the stress this kid lived with. Billy'd seen his mother beaten last night, and his brother was fighting for his life after suffering a gunshot wound the day before.

"What's the matter?" he asked.

"It's... a lot for one family."

He shrugged, impatient. "Could I see my mama now?"

13

Billy wondered which mama he was going to get—the nice one or the crazy one—but at this point he didn't much care. He was just going to be glad to see her again. Except for Aunt Kayla and her husband Uncle Paul, his mama was really all he had, ever since Ivory had left home and started hanging with the IBoys. He couldn't lose her too.

The truth was, he'd gone a little berserk in front of the cop when they went home and his mama wasn't there. He had no idea it was even possible to be so scared. No way in hell to tell what had happened—because if Kaynard was gone, he didn't think it was because he'd gotten up and walked out. Somebody'd carried him out, whatever kind of shape he was in. What in hell had happened?

Maxine had a room all to herself, and in it were three cats, two little ones chasing dust bunnies, the other in Maxine's lap. At the sight of Billy, his mama jumped up, not giving a thought to the huge white cat, which protested with a loud yowl. "My baby!"

She held her arms outstretched, even as she swore, "Fuckin' cat! Shut the fuck up!"

Billy hugged her like it was his last chance, hampered only slightly by his arm sling. "Mama, you okay?"

"Better than you. What happen to your arm?"

He shrugged. "Fell down. They splinted it. Can't set it for a few days."

She gave him the stink-eye. "You lyin' to me?"

"You mean about fallin' down? No, I did. But I'm not gonna lie. IBoys chased me all the way over here from Aunt Kayla's. I outrun 'em."

She swatted him. "That's my boy."

"Mama, what's goin' on here? Thought you hated cats."

She smiled. "They got me on some new medication. I pretty much like everything right now."

"That's good." It was. She was her old self when she was on her meds. Only thing was, for whatever reason she didn't like the meds. Said they made her sleepy. Seemed to him sleepy was a lot better than mad as hell and terrified, which was the way she often was when she got off them. He sure as hell hoped he hadn't inherited whatever she had, because no way were the Polites ever getting to the next level if he had to battle that monster.

And that was what he wanted to do—raise the family up. Get to that next level, whatever it was. He didn't think it would be so hard, long as he went to school and didn't get killed before he could grow up and move away from the world Ivory and Kaynard had created. He would take Maxine with him, and Makayla if she wanted to come, but he didn't know about Ivory. He knew Ivory'd made a different choice and Billy was trying to live with that. This was Ivory's third time getting shot.

Third time, his mama had wailed. He didn't want to write

his brother off, but he'd long ago admitted to himself that even if Ivory survived the current round of thug feuds, he was lost to Billy as a brother—a real brother he could look up to. He wasn't that person any more. That was already gone.

"I might have some good news for you, Mama."

"I almost forgot what that is." She smiled and looked at him like a little girl, face shining in anticipation. Whatever they had her on, he thought, it was working. "Hit me with some good news."

"Okay. Kaynard's gone. I don't know where, but he ain't home. That's good, right?"

Her face fell. "You sayin' he ain't dead? And that's a *good* thing?"

"Aunt Kayla said you thought you was goin' to jail."

She looked confused. "Well, I don' know. I don't rule it out. You seen Ivory yet? I wanted to see him one more time before they took me away."

"Nobody's takin' you anywhere. Come on, let's go see him." He said it even though he didn't want to see his brother. Try as he might to understand that Ivory wasn't his beloved big brother any more, that he might very likely die soon, he didn't want to have to look reality in the face. This was going to hurt.

They had to get Dr. Kathy to take them—Maxine didn't exactly have the run of the hospital—but even then, they couldn't get on Ivory's floor. It was completely closed off.

Billy had a bad feeling. Because when they let him in the door downstairs, clutching his broken wrist and thinking only about how narrowly he'd gotten away from the IBoys and that he was lucky to be alive, even if slightly busted up, someone had run out as he was running in. It happened too fast to be sure. He'd put it out of his head, but now it came back to him. It was someone he knew and wished he didn't.

ADAM WISHED he could go immediately to an AA meeting. He didn't even want to drink, he just wanted a place to talk. To tell someone what he'd just been through, someone who couldn't answer him, couldn't get out of hearing his share because that was the deal; someone he'd have no guilt unloading on. Because he couldn't see sticking anyone else with it.

It wasn't the morning's horrific toll that unnerved him, but what he'd experienced in the brief ride over to Charity. His buddy Jake, the friend who owed him a favor, wasn't alone in the car.

The first thing Adam noticed was the smell.

And then he saw that someone was lying in the back seat, someone covered with a tarp that had slipped a little, revealing her face. Since it had clearly been meant to cover her completely, she had to be dead. Probably been dead for quite a few hours, judging by the odor. He needed to tread carefully.

He held Nathan close, protecting him from whatever was going on here. "Jake? What happened here?" He jerked his chin towards the dead woman.

"You think they might take her at Charity? I can't get nobody else to."

"Who is she?"

"She's Mrs. Laura Roberts, thirty-two years old. I found her purse with her, on Felicity St., literally in the gutter. Right on the curb. I don't know what happened, maybe she had a heart attack, or a car hit her. I know she wasn't robbed. Forty-five dollars right there in that purse."

"Well, uh... is she someone you know? How did she come to be in the car with you?"

"I called the coroner to come get her, and he didn't come. And then I called again, and finally somebody told me it just wasn't gon' happen." He beat the steering wheel with his fist, and his voice rose to a near-scream. "Nobody'd pick her up, you get that, A.A.? I waited a couple hours and then I just picked her up myself. Not *decent*, her lying on the street like that, nobody to even care enough to come get her. Just not *right*.

"And now I'm just driving around, funeral home to funeral home, trying to get somebody to take her."

Adam tried to make sense of the story—both parts, what had happened to Mrs. Laura Roberts and what had happened to his friend Jake, who seemed on the verge of falling apart. He wondered if there was any way to get Kathy to take a look at him, maybe slip him something for nerves.

Naaah, probably not. If Charity was getting any of the casualties he'd seen in his travels, both on dry land and in the flood, they'd already have their hands full.

The thing Adam was grappling with was that Jake had grasped the situation in a way he hadn't, and most people hadn't, he thought. He'd come face-to-face almost immediately with the breakdown of systems, of normality, the world everyone knew, and he was mourning it, trying to deal with it.

Adam clutched the baby tighter.

In the end, once he was out of that death-smelling car and in a functioning hospital, he wasn't about to ask Kathy if they'd take a day-old corpse, or give his buddy a Valium. It felt warm and safe and normal in there, words he didn't often apply to Charity Hospital. Despite its stellar trauma unit, it was still a hospital, a place where people suffered and sometimes died. Right now, it seemed like a haven, and Kathy seemed like salvation itself, mystery woman that she'd suddenly become.

He didn't want her to know any of this, he wanted to protect her. And to give her that baby, as some sort of symbol of life, he guessed. Something like that. Life in the midst of tragedy. He was glad they'd had that moment with Nathan. He wanted to hold Kathy too, and kiss her, but the last thing he wanted was to get any of that death-stink on her. He felt as if he'd slunk out of there, and felt bad about it.

But now he had to do something about Laura Roberts. Jake had waited patiently while he did his business in the hospital. All he'd done all day was wait patiently. "Sorry, they won't take her," Adam said by way of greeting.

"I knew they wouldn't. Nobody will."

"Jake, you know what we've gotta do? We've got to take her and put her back exactly where you found her. Purse and all."

"I don't want to do that."

"I know."

That was all he said, but he noticed that Jake drove in the direction of Felicity St. He made a quick call to Conrad. "Got a little errand to run. You okay to wait?"

"I'm fine, man. I'm trying to track us down some food. You hungry?"

"Good god, yes!" He hadn't even thought about it, but he hadn't had a bite since breakfast.

They laid Laura Roberts out as carefully as if they were a couple of funeral directors, right on the sidewalk, with half the neighborhood looking on. Those who were left.

"They were here when I found her," Jake said. "They know what's going on. They saw me take her."

Nobody spoke to anyone, though. It seemed disrespectful. She had people to watch over her, and that was good. Like an outdoor wake, Adam thought, and hoped, for their sakes, that they were able to find some whiskey to make it official.

ATLANTIS

14

Skip was already asleep when A.A. called. "Adam. Sheesh. What a day, huh? How'd it go for you?"

"You sound tired."

"Naaah. Tired is when you work a double shift on Mardi Gras. This is more like when you run up Mt. Everest in fifteen minutes."

"Tell me about it. I could barely feed Crevette... not to mention me. Just got home. Too damn exhausted to eat."

"Yeah." She'd gone to bed without dinner as well. "You ever get my no-good brother?"

"That's what I'm calling about. Wanted to thank you. Your no-good brother's a hero."

"Huh? That's a different Conrad Langdon. The one I know acts like he thinks he's Captain of Comus. Although they'd never let him in."

"Right. That's a different guy. The one I spent the day with dived into filthy floodwater and rescued a baby in a car seat. Know how far that thing must have sunk? He was down there about ten minutes, seemed like."

"You kiddin' me! Conrad *Langdon* did that?"

"Maybe he gave me a fake name. You know what? You need to meet this guy. I'm bringing him over for breakfast."

"Breakfast? I'm a little out of your way, right?"

"You have drip coffee technology, right?"

"Yeah. Yeah, I do. I'm at Jimmy Dee's and it's at my house, but... yeah. Good thought."

"Well, I'd wade through floodwater for some coffee. And fortunately, we have a boat. I got eggs and mushrooms— what you got?"

Skip sighed. "Well, the good news is, I've still got natural gas, for one thing. Jimmy Dee defied all advice and didn't turn it off. So we could make an omelet. No way to make toast, though. Well, we could do it in the oven, but that would take till lunch. Let me think. Hey, you know what? I think I saw some tortillas in the fridge."

"Yaay! Breakfast burritos. See you at six."

"Six. Are you kiddin' me?"

"Think about it, Langdon. You were already asleep when I called, right? You're not gonna sleep past six."

"Come to the Big House. I'm taking care of it."

She hung up realizing two things—that it was remarkable both she and Adam had cell service; and that she'd forgotten to ask how the baby was.

And then she fell into a sleep so deep it was as if the call had never happened.

Adam and Conrad didn't make it till nearly six-thirty, but that was okay—it gave her some time to organize breakfast and tidy herself as much as she could. The water wasn't off so she figured it was okay to take a shower. *Hope I'm not kidding myself,* she thought. But it sure couldn't be worse than the water in the streets, and she'd waded in that.

She went out to her apartment to get the coffee materials. By the time the others arrived, she'd boiled water and had some credible coffee in the Chemex.

Abasolo squeezed her so hard she thought he was going to deflate her lungs. "*What* is that scent from heaven?"

She smiled at her brother, over A.A.'s shoulder. "Hey, Conrad."

"Hey, Skippy."

Abasolo let her go and she hugged her brother much more gingerly. "Now, see, that's why I don't like to have you meet my friends. Whoever heard of a tough cop called Skippy?"

Abasolo said, "Skippy Skippy Skippy Skippy," and Conrad said, "You're not so tough."

"I could kick your Uptown butt."

"She could too," A.A. said. "You two don't know each other at all. Conrad, meet the woman who took down Errol Jacomine. Skip, meet the guy who'll probably die from infections contracted saving a baby."

"The kid's okay?" Skip asked.

Abasolo set down a paper bag and began unpacking his scrambled egg kit, Conrad grabbing mushrooms and slicing them without being asked, as if they were a team that could almost read each other's minds. Skip was momentarily jealous. A.A. was supposed to be *her* partner.

"We got him to Charity, anyhow. And thereon hangs a tale."

"Huh?" Conrad stopped slicing and stared at him in surprise. "You didn't mention it when you got back."

"Yeah, well. I wasn't ready to talk about it. Skip, did you say something about some tortillas?"

"Already in the oven."

Over breakfast, he told them about Mrs. Laura Roberts.

They all left without even tidying up. The story of the

dead woman in the district car had disconcerted everyone. Nothing felt normal.

They all knew that for the next few days, this would be their life: sleep a few hours, then hit the streets and work until it got so dark they couldn't see. The days would run together, and there'd never be a break, never time to grieve for the thousands of people who were lost, the neighborhoods destroyed, maybe even a way of life wiped out. How did you take in a loss like this?

They'd be too tired at night, too wired in the daytime, even to come close. It would probably take months, maybe years, and many long nights of tears to process it, but it couldn't happen now. There was too much work to do.

And they didn't want to. At least Skip didn't. It was too much to handle.

All she wanted to do was get out there on the streets and put Mrs. Laura Roberts out of her head—not only Mrs. R., but also the possible death of the town she grew up in.

With her cell phone freshly charged in her car (it proved to be one of the phones that worked), she got her orders from Cappello. As best she could interpret them, the plan was "stay downtown and work with any officers you find." She left messages for Jimmy Dee and Steve Steinman, and hit the streets.

It was 7 a.m., early on a blazing day in New Orleans, never the earliest rising city in the world. Anybody who had a home would be in it. It was a perfect time, she figured, to check on Billy. She was able to walk right in—nobody had locked the house, nor, apparently, returned to it. Two things were different, though. The crack stash was missing. And she had to wade to get there. The flooding had spread to Rampart, which became St. Claude further downriver, the same street where she'd spent most of yesterday, the route people were using to get out of the Ninth Ward.

She was leaving when Cappello called again. "Oh, God, Skip, are you in the middle of anything?" She had a mental image of the lieutenant, in a gesture of frustration and fatigue, sweeping her dark hair from her face. "I need you for something special. Hostage situation at Charity."

"*What?*" Skip couldn't quite take it in. "But I don't... I'm not..."

"I know. You're not trained for it. But this isn't your average everyday domestic deal. All kinds of things going on here—and they asked for you. Don't worry, I'll get you some back-up."

"Who asked for me?"

"Two different people. That's why it's got to be you. Adam Abasolo..."

"A.A.? I just had breakfast with him. How's he involved?"

"Oh, he's *involved*. But he's on search-and-rescue. They can't spare him. He recommended you."

"Okay, and who else did?"

"The hostage-taker."

GETTING THERE WAS TRICKY. Some of the fallen tree limbs and other debris had been removed, but driving was only possible in certain areas. Skip had to wade for part of the short journey. Her back-up team beat her there. They met her at the emergency room entrance, two surprisingly eager-looking rookies who actually had on uniforms, though a little the worse for wear. They were accompanied by a phalanx of Charity officers and a young nurse named Brenda, who proved as commanding as she was young.

"Could everybody stay here but Detective Langdon? Just till we get her briefed. Here, come on in the waiting room and get comfortable."

What a concept, Skip thought. *Not a place you associate with comfort.* "Let me take one of these guys," she said, and picked the one who stood up the fastest. Peele, according to his nametag. "Come on, Peele."

Nurse Brenda led them into a small office and left to trade places with the doctor, who presumably, was standing in as a hostage negotiator. But the first person through the door was no doctor—it was her surprise houseguest from the night of the storm.

"Hey," he said shyly.

"Billy! What are you doing here? What happened to your wrist?" She stood and walked toward him. He backed up a step.

He glanced briefly at his sling, having obviously forgotten his injury. "Oh. Broke it falling down. Hey, I found out where my mama was." He gave her a half-grin.

A tall, striking, very stressed-out woman in pink scrubs followed him into the office. "Detective Langdon? I'm Dr. Kathy Bordelon. You come well recommended."

She was still confused. "Billy asked for me?"

Billy said, "My mama did. I told her about you."

"Your *mama's* the hostage-taker?"

"Her name's Maxine Polite," the doctor said. "Let's go talk to her. She's got everyone pretty freaked out."

Bordelon led her into some kind of meeting room with a dozen people Skip supposed were patients sitting in chairs arranged in a circle, in the center of which Maxine, a skinny, wild-haired woman, had her arm wrapped around the neck of another woman, someone about Maxine's age, and the other hand stuck somewhere around her ribs, probably, Skip surmised, holding a sharp object.

Billy said, "Mama, this my friend Skip."

"Ain' no white po-lice any friend of yours."

"She came, didn't she? Didn't I tell you she'd come?"

Skip was starting to get the hang of things. She could see why she was there, but she couldn't figure out how Abasolo figured into it. Well, never mind for now. "Billy, remember how I introduced myself?"

"Yes, ma'am, I do. You said, 'Detective Skip Langdon, *at your service.*'"

"Well, I meant that. I came down here to help you and your mama out. How you, Ms. Polite?"

"They killed my *baby*," she wailed.

But Billy was her baby. Wasn't he? She shot him a look that she hoped he'd interpret as a question. "She mean my brother Ivory," he said. "He died last night, right in this hospital."

"Oh, Billy! I'm so sorry to hear that. Ms. Maxine, I can't even imagine how sad you must be. I know I sure would be."

"This lady baby's fine," she said, indicating her hostage. "He right over there. I ain' gon' let her go till you catch whoever kill Ivory."

Skip glanced at the young man she indicated. She'd once met a confidential informant at a rap concert given by the CI's brother, who she was pretty sure was the victim's "baby." "Hey, is that Ti-Meanness?" she said. "Ti-Meanness, that you?"

The kid slunk back like he'd been slapped. "How you know me?"

"Oh, I know you." When all eyes went to the rapper, she signaled the man next to her to move his chair enough for her to enter the circle. But she didn't go in yet.

She thought of saying, "I'm your fan," but feared that might set Maxine off. "I know your brother," she said instead. "Met you at a concert once. Ms. Maxine, I know this whole family. That's a fine woman you got there. I bet y'all'd be friends if you met somewhere like the Walmart. Or your children's school. How you doin', Ms. Thurlow?" The other woman nodded, to show she heard, but the smile she tried to muster registered only as fear—a slight turning up of the lips, naked terror on the rest of her face. In fact, Skip's words seemed to have given her some sort of permission to let herself feel what she was going through. Tears slid from her eyes and glistened against her grayish skin.

"That's okay," Skip said. "It's okay to cry." She said it for Maxine's benefit, since Maxine couldn't see her hostage's face. Skip was betting she was no psychopath, that she'd feel bad for the other woman.

"You got some girls too, don't you?" Skip continued. "Maxine, you don't want to hurt this lady. What are her children going to do without her?"

"No one care about my chir'ren," Maxine said sullenly.

"Oh, no, that's where you're wrong. I care about your children. Didn't I already take care of Billy when I didn't even know him? I'd have done the same for Ivory too." She had to cross her fingers on that one. She didn't know anything about Ivory. "Dr. Bordelon cares. She cares very deeply. Y'all do too, don't you?" She gave them the "let's-hear-it" sign and miraculously, they began to answer individually.

"Sure we care."

"Care a lot."

"Miss Maxine, you know we do!"

While Maxine's eyes sought out the owners of the voices,

Skip took the opportunity to inch herself ever so slowly into the circle of chairs.

One of them, a young white woman holding a teddy bear, was even crying. Mrs. Thurlow's boy Alonzo, aka Ti-Meanness, was crying too, but presumably not for Ivory.

"Look at that, Maxine. They care so much they're crying. We all care, you believe me?"

She didn't give Maxine time to answer. "I care and I'm going to give you whatever you want to ease your pain. I know you're not yourself right now, you're grieving so hard for your boy, but I'm here to help you, just like Billy told you I'd be."

She could see Maxine relaxing her grip on Danielle Thurlow. Now would be a good time to take her down, but Skip didn't have the heart. She gave Billy's mom time to speak. "All I want is justice." Now *she* was starting to cry. "For my boy. Promise me you'll get whoever kill my Ivory."

Kill? Somebody'd killed him in the hospital? Unlikely as that seemed, Skip nodded solemnly, agreeing to the far-fetched terms, took a step forward, and raised the ante. "I promise you that. I'll get him and I'll make damn sure he goes to prison for the rest of his life."

"Thank you. Thank you." Maxine dropped her weapon —a scalpel or small knife, it looked like. Skip grabbed her up in a hug rather than restraining her. She could afford to be compassionate right now. Ms. Maxine wasn't going anywhere. She left it to Peele the rookie to try to put Mrs. Thurlow back together, but now the whole group was erupting. Ti-Meanness was hugging his mama and everyone else was trying to hug her too.

"I didn't mean nothing," Maxine said to Skip. "I wouldn't have hurt that lady."

Skip knew she might have, though. She was crazy as a

spinning top. But no way she was going to jail for this. For one thing there was no jail. For another... everybody was nuts right now and some things were going to fall through the cracks. Maxine Polite as hostage-taker was probably going to be one of those things.

Skip was good with that.

Kathy Bordelon was hovering, along with a shiny-headed nurse holding a syringe of something Skip cordially hoped was powerful enough to last awhile. She eased Maxine over to the doctor and nurse. "I'll do my best for you, Ms. Maxine."

Suddenly it dawned on her that, like the rapper, Billy should have been hugging his mama by now. With the sinking feeling she'd missed something important, she looked around for him.

15

B illy sneaked out behind a hospital cop on a break. Some of the others yelled at him, but no one chased him. Why would they? If he was outside the hospital, he was no longer their responsibility.

Plenty of people were outside, desperately trying to get in, but no way. The hospital cops kept telling people they were on lockdown—whatever that meant. He wasn't even sure why Dr. Bordelon had let him in. But somehow all those gangbangers had gotten in too. Seemed pretty loose around there, but maybe that was yesterday. Things might be getting back to normal today.

He looked behind him, making sure he was going to get away from the hospital cops, and only when he turned back around did he register his surroundings, other than the little crowd outside. Where he was, on the ER ramp it was dry— at least partially. But now he could see that even part of the ramp was submerged. Other than the spot where he stood, all he saw was water. He was in the middle of a lake, a lake in the middle of the city.

What was up with that? Yesterday, when he'd come in

with his broken wrist, it was perfectly dry. What the hell was this? How did you get all this water when the goddam hurricane was two days ago? He almost stopped and asked the cop on break before he stopped himself.

Instead he rolled up his jeans, waded in, and turned toward Canal Street, not having any idea what he was going to find. He wondered if the French Quarter was flooded, and his own house in Treme.

People were wading and swimming towards the hospital, some holding or leading children, some carrying boxes, suitcases, backpacks. Every now and then he saw a little boat, out there skimming along like it was taking someone fishing.

But no one looked as if they were going fishing. Everyone looked terrified, or dazed, or sad. A lot of people were crying. Looking around like he was, too confused to pay attention to where he was going, he bumped smack into a large woman balancing a straw basket on her head like an African woman in a documentary, except that, probably having no experience at basket-balancing, she had to hold the receptacle in place. Billy hit her just hard enough to unbalance her, causing her to fall backwards and the basket to tumble over, dumping a tiny white dog into the drink.

The dog began paddling furiously, away from Billy and its owner. The woman came up sputtering and yelling at the same time, evidently unable to decide between fury at Billy and fear for the dog. "Goddam you, whathefuck, ROMEO! Get Romeo, you stupid little shit! My baaaaaybeeee!" Assuming Romeo was the dog, Billy was already on it. In fact, he'd already grabbed Romeo twice, only to have him wriggle away. With only one working arm, he was no match for a terrified poodle.

"Let me have the basket!"

"Why I give you my goddam basket?"

There really wasn't time to explain. With one swoop, he twisted it out of her hand, scooped up the squirming animal, and replaced it in her arms. Woman and dog were so excited to be reunited that once again, Romeo wriggled away, and had to be scooped up and returned. Billy couldn't help it, it was so ridiculous he started laughing. Finally seeing the humor, Romeo's mom joined in. "I sure thank you for saving my baby," she said. "I'm sorry I was evil. I'm just... you know... I'm..."

"Yeah," Billy said. "I know. Y'all gon' be all right?"

The woman nodded, jutting her jaw out almost comically. "We damn sure are," she said, and replaced the basket on her head, Romeo and all. "*Damn* sure are."

She started walking again, but Billy wasn't ready to let her go. "Wait, can I ax you something? Where'd all this water come from?"

She blinked at him, evidently trying to figure out what he was getting at.

"Storm was two days ago," he said.

A look of comprehension and wonder at the same time replaced the confusion. "Chile, where you been?"

He showed her his splint. "In the hospital."

"Oh, law! I don't want to be the one to tell you."

He stared her down. "I gotta know sometime, don't I?" But his heart was pounding. She was making it sound like Armageddon.

"Oh, baby, the levee broke!" The moment the words passed her lips, her face broke too. Great heaving sobs poured out of her. "Whole city's under water. Whole. Fuckin'. City."

Billy felt his jaw open and drop. He kept staring,

knowing it was his turn to say something, but unable to form words.

The woman turned away from him, her makeshift puppy crate back on her head, one hand clutching it. As she began once more to slosh her way through the flood waters, brown and slick in places with oil, he heard her say once more, "*Damn sure* gon' be okay!"

Numb, he kept heading downriver, to Canal, and when he got closer, he couldn't believe what he saw—on the other side, the French Quarter, evidently on higher ground, was dry. He almost burst into tears. Hotels were open, he could see that. Probably people hadn't been able to leave, or they'd "vertically evacuated". He'd heard of that—it was something rich people did. They checked into hotels, which had generators and dining rooms.

A lot of businesses looked like they'd been looted and he wondered briefly if there was somewhere with a candy bar or something left on its shelves. Now that he thought about it, he was starving. And probably dehydrated. It was *hot* on the streets. He needed water the worst kind of way. But where to find any? Everybody needed something.

He thought longingly of Miss Skip's huge house—her friend's house—and all the supplies there. He knew she would probably help him, but that was just weird. Did he really want to get any more involved with a cop? Especially one who'd just disarmed his own mama.

Ohhhh, Mama! He moaned inwardly as the morning's events replayed themselves in his head. *Mama, what were you thinking? Did you ever think you might be going to jail?*

But then he remembered she already thought she was. Was she really so crazy she thought she'd shot Kaynard?

He couldn't go there. He couldn't think about his mama taking a hostage or the fact that his brother was dead. Actually dead this time, not just shot up again. Not just in the "dead to me" sense, the way Billy'd thought about him for so long. He was really never going to see Ivory again, and Ivory was never going to come home and say he'd given up the thug life and he was going to be a real brother again.

Billy couldn't deal with any of that, not until he got something to eat. So much to think about, to worry about. So much, when you got down to it, to do.

It was starting to dawn on him that his Aunt Makayla's husband Paul, Billy's funny, four-hundred-pound football fan diabetic uncle, was probably trapped on the second floor of his house and Aunt Makayla would be going crazy right now. Billy might be able to do something to help her, but how was he going to get there?

Because what he'd seen when he entered the hospital was going to get him killed. He'd realized that when he found out Ivory was dead. There couldn't be any mistake any more. That person he'd seen leaving Charity when he arrived—the one who'd opened the door when he slipped in—that was the Dark Knight's little brother Dalton, whose gang name was Chess Knight. Dalton was so lame everyone called him Knight Lite, even the IBoys. Everybody, that is, except for Petey. The scary-as-shit Dark Knight.

Dalton had a whole world to prove. If it was Petey who shot Ivory—and he knew Petey had a damn good reason— little bro' would probably be stupid enough to make himself a gangster hero and finish the job. Billy could see it laid out like a map. The Chess Knight had a perfect opportunity and he took it. And he'd almost certainly seen Billy enter the hospital as he was leaving, having just murdered Billy's brother. So if the gang hadn't had a hit out on Billy before, they sure did now. They'd be watching Makayla's house as well as Billy's mama's crib in Treme.

16

Kathy knew all about Skip Langdon. Even if Adam hadn't been one of two people (the other being Billy) to recommend her this morning, she'd have recognized his favorite partner anywhere. For one thing she had that weird name. But he'd also done a really good job of describing her, with her six feet of height, unruly mane of curls, and awkward clothing. (Although today she had on shorts and a t-shirt like everyone else.)

She felt like she knew Skip, but when she mentioned Adam, the other woman had said, "You know Abasolo?" So evidently they weren't yet a public item. She'd backtracked quickly, giving Skip a sly smile. "He's brought me quite a few patients. Seems to come in contact quite a bit with..." she made an inclusive gesture... "my kind of people."

Skip smiled. She didn't say, "You mean nutballs?" like most people would have, and Kathy liked her for that.

"Although yesterday," she continued, "was a little different. He brought me a baby."

"He told me about the baby. Is he going to be all right?"

Kathy hesitated before she nodded. Best to be positive, she decided. "I'm sure he will." Although she wasn't sure at all. "I only wish..."

"What?"

"They couldn't bring his mother. I wish they'd been able to."

"Oh." Skip's face turned grave and Kathy could see she was having the same thought Kathy was—how in hell were these two going to get reunited? But she moved right along. "Speaking of mothers and children, no luck finding Billy yet."

Skip had sent Peele and his partner on the hunt for him, and Kathy had raised the alarm with the hospital police, but so far, no sign of the kid. "Want to tell me what you know about him?" They were back in Kathy's tiny office, trying to figure out what to do next. At least the cop appeared to be doing that. Kathy was just wishing she'd go.

She had troubles piled on emergencies topped with disasters. Maxine Polite's stunt was minor compared to what was happening to the hospital, what had been happening for hours now, and what was about to happen. Kathy and her patients were trapped, for how long she had no idea. But they were in a world of hurt, and it wasn't going to get any better. It was dark as late afternoon and already hotter than Death Valley.

As if Skip had read her mind, she said, "I know you want me out of your hair, so let me be as quick as I can. Can you take me to the ICU? Or wherever Ivory is?"

"I expect he's in the morgue by now. But there might be a problem seeing him."

"Really? What kind of problem?"

"The... uh... the morgue's flooded."

"Oh, Jesus." She swore in that resigned way people do

when they've had bad news and now they're getting more. "Okay then. I'd like to see his doctor—or nurse."

"Let's go. We need to find Dr. Petrachian. Normally we might be able to call her down here. But..." she shrugged... "not happening today. Also... no elevators." Which meant a climb in the ravaging heat.

They arrived panting, dripping sweat, and in Kathy's case, probably beginning to stink. She'd been in the same clothes for two days, under stress and part of the time with no AC.

Petrachian was happy to talk, clearly had a lot to say and wanted to get it over and done.

Kathy couldn't help thinking, once she saw her with Skip, that the cop would have made two of the other doctor, who was about the size of a large-size doll and just as pretty under normal circumstances. Right now she looked like she needed medical attention herself, at the very least a good night's sleep. She'd developed dark under-eye circles, blotchy skin, and limp, bedraggled hair that had long since escaped the clips and combs that had probably once held it in a neat twist.

"Detective," she said, "glad you're here. I've been needing to talk to someone. Meaning someone official. Whatever happened here shouldn't have."

For a moment, Kathy wasn't sure the doctor was completely in control. Nothing that had happened in two days should have.

"Someone got in here. I don't know who or how it happened, but there was someone here who shouldn't have been."

Kathy kept to herself the entire roomful of thugs they'd had to deal with the night before.

Not to mention the huge patient upheaval in the early

morning hours. "I guess," she said, "that under the circumstances the security system isn't perfect."

"When Nurse Bladen called me in here this morning,
Ivory was already gone."

"You mean dead?" the cop asked.

Petrachian looked at Skip as if she was missing some
marbles. "Yeah. Dead. Deceased. Passed away."

Skip shrugged, gave her an encouraging smile. "There's
more than one way of being gone."

Petrachian looked embarrassed. "Oh, shit! I'm so tired I
can't even think. Of course there is."

"Let's find a place to sit down."

They ended up in Ivory's room, perched gingerly on two
empty beds.

"We stripped the bed," Petrachian said, "but I left that
there." She pointed to a pillow on the floor.

Kathy couldn't follow, but Skip said, "And that's
unusual? A pillow on the floor?"

"Oh, yes. The beds have rails, so they hardly ever fall. So
how would it get there?" She paused, but no one answered.
"Someone dropped it. Or threw it."

Evidently impatient, Skip asked crisply, "How did Ivory
die, Doctor? His mother seemed to think he was murdered."

"Oh, don't you know? I thought everyone in the hospital
knew by now. We think he died of suffocation."

"Oh." The penny dropped. Kathy pointed at the pillow.
"And you think that's the murder weapon?"

Petrachian turned to Skip. "What do you think,
Detective?"

"I'm wondering what makes you think he died of suffocation. I've seen people who did, and there isn't much
that shows."

"Someone saw something."

Kathy watched the detective perk up. If she'd been a German shepherd, her pointy ears would have stood at attention. "Who?" she asked. "Can I talk to them?"

The doctor suddenly seemed to lose confidence. "We don't know who. One of the nurses said someone she didn't recognize—a patient she thought—reported seeing something 'weird' going on in Ivory's room. He said..." she paused to think, obviously uncomfortable... "He said it looked like someone was sitting on a patient's head."

"And?"

"And she couldn't go right away. You have to understand, it was a crazy night. Patients were being moved and everything was getting changed around. Everybody was exhausted. She was doing some other thing and she didn't get there for a few minutes."

Kathy and Skip nodded together.

"Then when she got around to it, Ivory was dead."

"What's her name?" Skip asked. "Can I talk to her?"

Slowly, as if she couldn't believe it herself, Petrachian shook her head. "She left. Talked to her son this morning— her husband had a stroke."

Kathy gasped. "She just walked off the job?"

The doctor nodded. "Do you believe that? Just... left. Left us with all this! And a murder to boot."

Kathy could believe it, all right. *Thanks for nothing, Hubie Julian.* And besides, her husband had a *stroke*? She wasn't going to be much good under those conditions, anyway.

Skip took her name. "And did you see anyone suspicious on the floor?"

Petrachian shrugged. "All kinds of people were here, moving patients around. And patients who could walk were milling around too. So anyhow..."

She evidently wasn't finished with her story. "When they

found Ivory dead, they called me in. And I saw the pillow on the floor, like somebody had just thrown it down there. I was too late for Ivory—I already knew that—but I was suspicious about that pillow. Even before the nurse said that thing about someone sitting on his head. So you know what I did?"

She seemed proud of herself. "I checked his mouth for fibers." She withdrew a plastic bag containing, so far as Skip could see, practically nothing. "I found some. And some hair. Like he'd been sleeping on the pillow and then it ended up in his mouth."

Skip made a face. Kathy laughed. "I see cops aren't as inured to yucky stuff as we are."

"I don't know," she said, "if you ever get used to it."

"That's good," Kathy said. "I mean we do, but it's just part of..." she hesitated.

"The life cycle?" Skip said. "Yes. Crimes are outside that. A homicide cop who gets used to seeing people murdered is a burnout. She'd lose her drive to help the victim."

"An interesting phrase," Petrachian said, "considering the victim's dead."

"They still need justice," Skip said, and just when Kathy was about to judge her on grounds of pretension, she smiled. "Omigod, that sounds so cornball. Forget I said it. But I've gotta have *some* reason to get up in the morning."

She left with the pillow, stuffed in a plastic garbage bag, and the little bag of fibers, but Kathy thought that was mostly to humor Dr. Petrachian. She hadn't seemed too impressed.

Kathy had to admit she was quite a woman. Adam had said he saw some of Skip in Kathy, but who knew what that meant? Kathy was a tall strong babe too—did they all look alike?

Now she was flattered. She didn't think it was about appearance at all, and that drew her to him all the more.

WHEN SHE RETURNED to the third floor, Norm took one look at her and commanded: "Go lie down."

"What?" Lying down seemed unthinkable.

"You need to wind down from that Jacobean melodrama and so do the patients. Norm's hereby declaring quiet time."

"I can't, I..."

"Kathy. I got this. Take half an hour."

Suddenly realizing he did, and he was serious, he could spare her for half an hour practically brought tears to her eyes. "I'm outta here—before you change your mind."

She desperately needed time to process the last few hours—and a shower. Who knew when she might get the opportunity again? The power was already gone. Water pressure was likely next.

When she'd last seen Abasolo, she'd said good-bye to him at the emergency room ramp. All was dry.

She'd heard his words about the levee break and the flooding, but somehow it hadn't registered that he meant the entire city was imperiled, not just certain neighborhoods. She was sure that, as soon as the city's power came back on and the water had receded in the flooded neighborhood, all would return to normal. It was dawning on her that that wasn't going to happen. The flooded neighborhoods were everywhere.

And Adam lived right on the lake—he'd almost certainly lost his house—funny, she'd forgotten to ask him yesterday. Too many other things were happening.

When she went to bed the night before, the hospital was

stirring, restless. On Monday, during the storm, windows had popped out of the hospital. The whole hospital went black for a few seconds when the power went out and the emergency generators kicked in. Patients arrived from nursing homes, and some who should have been sent to other hospitals were re-routed to Charity.

No one knew what to make of it.

Monday afternoon, Nurse Brenda went out for a walk. When she came back to report, all the windows were out in the nearby Hyatt Hotel; it looked like at least a layer of the Superdome roof was gone; and, ominously, water was rushing down Gravier Street, she had no idea why. But the emergency generators were working and all seemed snug enough.

Norm woke Kathy sometime in the early hours. "There's water in the stairwell."

She was groggy. "What? What stairwell?" They were on the third floor.

"Not here. The basement."

"Oh, Jesus." The generators were in the basement. Whose bright idea was that? The morgue was there too.

He told her what she'd already guessed: "We've lost electricity."

"Christ! That's why it's so hot in here." She held her sweaty hair off her neck. And then it occurred to her how big a deal this was. "What about the patients on ventilators?"

"They're hand-bagging them."

"Who is?"

He shrugged. "Nurses. Doctors."

Doctors, people used to giving orders and running things, and nurses, masters of multi-tasking, were standing over their patients, squeezing a plastic device so they could breathe. She tried to fathom how much effort that would take. "How long can they even do that?"

He shrugged again. "As long as it takes?"

She tried to pull herself together. Obviously, Norm was much further along than she was in the reality department. She still hadn't pieced it all together.

"But... what's happening, Norm? The storm was yesterday."

"We think another levee must have broken—out by the lake. Maybe more than one. Listen, we need your help. Everybody's got to be moved to the second floor."

That made no sense to Kathy. "Wait! Why would we move downstairs?"

"I don't mean us. I mean the emergency room. Everybody's going to the second floor auditorium."

The enormity of it struck her. "How many people are we talking about?" She knew it had to be dozens.

"I already have a count. There are fifty-five patients and seventy-five people in the waiting room."

"You're kidding me! How would we even do that?" She left unsaid what they both knew: in the dark. With no elevators.

Norm grinned at her. "Maybe we could get some of those little miners' lights. You know, on headbands?"

"Good thing," she grumbled, finally getting off her air mattress, "that *somebody's* still got a sense of humor."

How they did it was this way: The patients who couldn't walk were strapped to stretchers and carried up the dark stairwells, illuminated only by flashlights, six people to a stretcher.

And in the midst of all that, crazy Maxine decided to

take a hostage. Well, at least Kathy'd had time to get breakfast first—canned mixed vegetables and sliced peaches,
served in a Styrofoam cup.

17

"This is it!" Conrad hollered. "The one with the cop on the roof."

They'd found the cop they were supposed to save the day after the storm. It was the culmination of a day and a half of effort.

Adam high-fived him, marveling at Conrad's pure joy of accomplishment. And maybe helping people. According to Skip, it couldn't be that, but Adam had seen him put his own life on the line. He didn't believe her.

Still, much as he admired his de facto partner, much as he was proud to be doing the work he was doing, he was finding himself depressed in a way he could barely remember. There was so much misery here. So much to be done that wasn't going to get done. So many lives he wouldn't be able to save. And a disastrous failure nagging at him. He couldn't forget Serena Thompson's face as she cried for her baby. Whathehell had he been thinking?

He wanted to give himself the lecture he'd have given Conrad had it been the younger man who'd slipped into despair. To tell himself to think of the good he *was* doing;

the lives he was saving. The people whose lives would be forever changed because he was there to save their kid or their mom or their husband. He wanted to be able to look at the positive side like he usually could, like you had to, to do this work. But he knew this feeling. He was starting to recognize that he'd left "one day at a time" somewhere back at his last meeting and replaced it with "hello, darkness, my old friend." He desperately needed a meeting *right now,* and there was no way he was getting one.

There was no time, no energy (if he wasn't pulling someone off a roof, he was sacked out), and probably no meeting. Although Johnny White's Bar was open.

They got the cop and his family into the boat with many hugs of gratitude and a few tears, some of them Conrad's, some even Adam's. It was an occasion for joyful crying, for those few appropriate tears, but Adam didn't feel joyful. His throat was a vise, his chest literally sore with the effort of holding back the wracking sobs he could feel building up. If he gave into that, he had a good chance of getting kicked out of the department.

No wonder Conrad's so cheerful, he thought. *He's drinking as much beer as water.* That was new. Conrad had brought only water yesterday. Adam wondered if the job was getting to him too.

The irony was, they were getting better at it. At first, they hadn't had a clue what to do. But this morning Adam and Cappello had set up a sort of relay team with his buddy Jake, the one who'd become obsessed with saving Mrs. Laura Roberts from the humiliation of lying dead in the street.

Jake would park his now-disinfected car near a place the boat could access and convey the newly rescued to a freeway onramp to be picked up by buses. The onramps were hardly better than the roofs—hot, exposed, hopeless—but it was a step on the way to safety. Kind of like the Second Circle of Hell, Adam thought. Or the Eighth if they were working backward. The bus would be its own form of hell, then the Astrodome in Houston, then the struggle to find their relatives...

Oh hell, that was no path to be on. He tried to shut off his mind, busying himself with getting water for the family and learning their names—Ed, Shoshana, and their autistic son Albert. He handed out the water and listened to their story: They'd stayed because of Albert, who was prone to meltdowns when he got overwhelmed. They wanted to spare him the stress of evacuation. "You know how many times I've kicked myself?" Ed said with a wry half-grin.

They had an axe ready near the folding attic stairs, and they had the stairs pulled down, but the water came so fast they lost the axe. They barely had time to scramble up, and later Ed had to go down and dive for the axe. The good news was, Albert had been a champ—not a single meltdown in the whole two days.

"I was shaking, though," Albert chimed in. "It was boiling hot and I was still shaking." Everyone had a story. They'd be telling it over and over for the next few months, maybe for the rest of their lives.

Adam was struck by the strength it had to have taken for Albert to hold it together—in fact, for the whole family. If they could do it, he could do it. But it would sure be easier with one of Conrad's beers.

Helping the family out of the boat, Jake suddenly realized he was looking at a fellow cop, someone he'd worked with, side-by-side in the same district. Adam was willing to bet he hadn't even known Ed was stranded, but now he fell on his neck like Ed was his own brother. "Eddie Barr. Oh, man! Eddie Barr. Oh, Man! Goddam!" Ed was hugging back just as hard. Tears again. Both men were crying.

At first, Adam thought, most of the cops and volunteers —the Cajun Navy, as they were starting to be called—had been too much in shock to be able to feel much other than horror. That and the elation of each small victory. They were still trying to grasp the grim reality of their task. Today, it was coming home to them in their minds, in their bodies, penetrating their cells. And there was still so far to go.

How the hell was he going to keep doing it?

Conrad said, "Hey, man, you ready to go?"

"Can you give me five? I've gotta make a phone call." He'd called his sponsor half a dozen times, but either her phone was out, or she just didn't have it in her right now to deal with someone else's problems. Adam could understand that.

Or maybe she couldn't answer. Maybe she was up on her own roof, or roof analogue. Those were the kinds of things he didn't want to think about.

He called his former sponsor, someone with whom he'd had a massive falling-out. Truthfully, he couldn't even remember why. The guy had stood by him for years. What had he done to piss Adam off? He actually had no idea. He hoped to hell the guy would take his call.

Baldy answered on the first ring. "Adam. Been worried about you."

"Yeah? Just today, or for the last eight years?"

"Today, you idiot. This week. Eight years would make me codependent as hell."

It was starting to come back to Adam—something about being codependent. "You on the job?"

Baldwin Devillier was an ex-cop, one of the reasons he'd

been such a great sponsor for Adam. "Yeah. Where are you?"

"Retired to the bayou." He was from Thibodaux in Lafourche Parish.

"Oh, shit. You got damage?"

"Could be worse." Adam could see him shrugging as he spoke. Baldy was a big guy with massive arms. And he really was bald. "Worst thing's no power. But the gas stations still have gas. So we can charge our phones. How'd you do?"

Adam kept his voice steady. "No idea. No way to get home."

"Fuck! You moved to a boathouse, didn't you?"

"Yeah. Out at the yacht harbor."

"Oh, shit! So you lost your house."

"I guess so. There might be a chance..."

"You really think so?"

Adam thought about it. Maybe he was in denial—clinging to a false hope to get himself through. He said, "Whatever keeps me sober."

"Is that why you're calling? Anything else—everyone safe? What you got for me?"

That was what he'd always said when Adam called in distress. This kind of distress. The why-not-have-a-beer-can't-hurt kind.

They both knew perfectly well that if Adam had a beer he'd have every beer in Louisiana before he stopped. He'd lose his job and his fifteen years' sobriety, and his self-respect and everybody else's respect. Hell, he'd probably kill himself if the booze didn't get there first.

"Baldy, you got no idea what this is like. I'm watching people die right in front of me. It's so overwhelming. Massive. There's just no way...I can't...sorry. I can't get hold of my sponsor and I can't..."

"You sayin' you can't solve this thing by yourself? This afternoon?"

Adam heard himself making a weird noise. Oh, yeah. That was a laugh. A self-conscious chuckle. "The army and the navy put together couldn't solve it. This is a fuck-up of such major proportions..."

"You're not talking about the storm, right? What you mean exactly?"

"Nobody was prepared for this! It's like... we've been hearing about the bowl filling up for years, but it's like everybody just shrugged and said, 'oh, well'. Nobody made any emergency plans. Nobody had a clue. I mean... seems like they still don't. People are dying. Little kids are baking in the hot sun. Families are getting separated..."

"Look, what can you really do? If you could change one thing, what would it be?"

Adam saw where he was going with this. Baldy knew better than to try to talk to Adam about praying. But the serenity prayer was more like a mantra, maybe even a way of life. Adam didn't mind admitting he pretty much lived by it, and he wasn't much of a prayer guy. But it made too much sense to stand on rhetorical fine points. It was pure pragmatism, all about having *the serenity to accept the things I cannot change, the courage to change the things I can...*

The man was a great sponsor. He'd zeroed in on the feeling of failure that had simmered inside him ever since Conrad had dived for the baby. Adam hadn't wanted to admit it, even to himself, but there was sure as hell something he wanted to change. He wished he'd figured out a way to get Serena Thompson in the boat with her kid. They'd panicked, they'd been working too fast...they had no idea in hell what they were doing. He wanted a do-over.

But he wasn't going to get that. There was a chance he

could find Serena Thompson, though. What he had to do if he wanted any peace of mind was track Nathan's progress, figure out where he was, and find Serena and get her there.

To that, Baldy said. "Huh. I was kind of thinking about pulling some half-drowning guy into your boat. Must be a supply of those out there."

"That's the thing. There's always another one. I can pull them in, but I'm still thinking about that kid and his mom."

"Adam, you ever notice the end of the Serenity Prayer?"

Adam waited, not sure what he was getting at.

He quoted the words he meant: *"...and the wisdom to know the difference.* You *know* you're not sure you can change what happens to those two people."

"I can change my attitude about it. See, it's eating me up. I have to have a goal. Out here in Atlantis..."

"What's that you just said?"

"I said Atlantis. The Lost City that was sunk by the gods."

"What gods?"

"For God's sake, Baldy! It's just a story about a sunken city, and New Orleans is a sunken city. Out here I've got a negative attitude because I can't make everything right again. And I need to turn that around."

"Okay, you do *that* then. Whatever works, you know?"

Adam thanked him, thinking he needed to develop a plan. He was pretty sure he could get through the day without drinking if he could just start working on a couple of things. One was to start accepting what he couldn't change—he needed to find out for sure what had happened to his house. And the other was Serena Thompson.

"Hey, Conrad," he said, as he put away his phone. "Got an idea."

"Okay. But you gotta talk to me about something first. I

was talking to Jake while you were on the phone and there's the weirdest rumor going around."

"I wouldn't pay much attention to it. This kind of thing's bound to spawn rumors."

"Well, I've heard this one three times and it's really disturbing."

His face was all scrunched up, troubled in a way Adam hadn't seen it. "Tell me."

"You're a straight shooter, right?"

Adam nodded, reflecting that if he weren't, he wouldn't admit to it.

"Skippy always said you were. So I'm gonna take a chance here. Are the cops rounding up criminals—like drug dealers they know, what you might call the usual suspects—and assassinating them?"

"Whaaaat?"

It was so preposterous Adam was too shocked even to laugh. "Do I look like an assassin to you?"

"Jesus! I know it's not you. When would you do it?" He eked out a rueful chuckle. "But is there some kind of order... like if you see anybody you think needs to be removed from the streets, somebody the city would just be better off without... you just..."

"You just what?" He was starting to get mad.

Conrad backed off, literally took a step backward. Maybe he was listening to himself. He said, "Never mind. I knew it was stupid."

"Conrad, look at me. No. No, there's no such order. Cops are not assassinating citizens. The rule of law is still in force. The forces of chaos and evil have not been unleashed..." He surveyed the damage around him. "...despite appearances to the contrary."

"You mean," Conrad said, "they haven't *yet* been unleashed."

Adam hoped to hell this guy, seemingly the most sanguine of rescue workers, wasn't starting to come apart. He decided not to be a smartass for once. "Look, buddy, do me a favor and don't go there, okay? I need you to keep it together."

"Aw, I was just messing around. We can do this! Let's get back out there." He climbed back in the boat, and Adam followed.

"That's the spirit! But mind if I ask you something?"

"Oh, yeah. You said you had an idea—before I went off on that crazy tangent."

"Yeah, well, we've been existing in a vacuum here, you know? Just kind of..."

"Living in the moment? Hey, now I see why it's recommended. Nothing like it!" He threw up his hands like a touchdown Jesus. This was obviously a completely different experience for him than it was for Adam.

"I think we might need a little grounding—at least one of us might."

Conrad looked at him seriously. "Me, you mean? Am I acting weird?"

Maybe, A.A. thought. He literally wasn't sure. What was appropriate behavior in Atlantis? He said, "No, man, I meant me. I'm the one who needs it. I gotta ask you a favor. Tell me something—did your parents stay? I forgot to ask Skip."

"Oh, God, no. They went to Jackson. Why?"

"Have you checked their house?"

"Oh, goddam! I've been meaning to do that. Christ! What's wrong with me?"

"You've been kind of busy, dude. Come on, let's go do it now."

18

Skip left the hospital thinking, *Who the hell is Dr. Kathy Bordelon?* Clearly, she and A.A. had something going, but whether it was personal or professional Skip couldn't tell. He dated her friend Cindy Lou off and on, and Skip wouldn't want to be disloyal, but Cindy Lou wasn't a mate-for-life swan and Adam really needed one of those. Whether he knew it or not.

Skip thought he could do a lot worse than Dr. Kathy. But if he was dating her, why hadn't he told Skip?

She'd decided to take home Dr. Petrachian's pillow and bag of fibers before she hit the streets again. So here she was, wading, holding the pillow over her head, and feeling like an idiot. What kind of chain of evidence was ever going to be attached to this? She didn't see how this or the piece of tissue she'd collected at Billy's house was ever going to make it into court, but it wouldn't improve either case—should it ever come into existence—*not* to have them.

The piece of tissue was on the small bit of ice she had left and would soon shrink to nothing, but there might be some DNA left if it was ever needed. She could label the pillow and fibers and save those in her own apartment, which she hadn't even visited in two days.

Plus, she'd left without taking care of Angel, who needed to be fed and walked—and probably wet down so she didn't have heatstroke.

As soon as she got to her car—which was more a liability than otherwise at the moment, except for charging purposes—she plugged in her phone and called her landlord while she drove home.

He surprised her by not answering in his typical mock-drama fashion, sort of uber-campy and supremely self-aware, a delicately balanced performance that he'd honed to perfection. She expected something like, "Margaret Mega-Star, keeper of the house and protector of the pooch! If you tell me you're dead, I'll have to kill you." For some reason, he loved to call her by her given name.

Instead she got, "Skip, for God's sake—tell me you're all right."

"What? I talked to you yesterday. Why wouldn't I be?"

"Is the house flooded?"

"No, but *I'm* wet as hell. Is everything okay with you guys?"

"We're fine. Mind telling me where you are?"

"In the car driving home from Charity Hospital. Had to wade most of the way, but the French Quarter's dry. What are you so worried about?"

"You don't know, do you? Eighty per cent of the city's under water."

Her stomach flipped. Come to think of it, there *was* a lot more water this morning than there'd been the day before —and with no electricity, she had no easy access to news. "What are you talking about?"

"The Seventeenth St. Levee broke." She had no idea where that was, but he anticipated her. "Out by Lake Pontchartrain. The water's coming from the lake, not the river."

She could have guessed that if she'd thought about it. The whole French Quarter could have been ten or twenty feet underwater if the river's levees had breached. But they were sturdy hill-like structures. Some of the Industrial Canal levees were more like dams—seawalls sunk into the ground. Skip had never thought they looked as if they could hold the lake back.

So... the French Quarter was dry, but... almost everything else wasn't? It was starting to sink in. "Dee-Dee? Did you just tell me the whole city's fucked?"

"Oh, don't be such an alarmist. Only eighty per cent of it is." That was vintage Dee-Dee. Always the joker, but in a weirdly reassuring way.

"That's why you're such a good father," she said.

"Excuse me? Is that a non sequitur or are you having a simultaneous conversation with someone who's a good father?"

She laughed. "I meant you make people laugh when they should be crying."

"Speaking of crying, Sheila's inconsolable." His niece and adopted daughter. "Could you..."

Skip sighed. "Could I do it later? Really, really sorry, but kind of need to conserve energy here."

"Damn, I wish I could be there! Both the kids are chomping at the bit—we just want to get there and... *do* something!"

Skip couldn't help sighing. "Fight that impulse! You realize we're still evacuating people, right? Have to get everyone out of here before we can even secure the city.

Meanwhile, no power, very iffy water, less and less food and gas every day. Trust me, you don't want to be here."

"We just feel so helpless."

"I know. I really do get it. But for now, can you just tell the kids the Quarter's fine, the house is fine, and Angel's protecting the palace?"

"Angel's good?"

"Hungry as hell, I bet. On my way to feed her now. Just been out to a hostage situation."

She didn't say, "and hospital murder." Some things they didn't need to know.

She parked the district car in front of the house. Why not? It wasn't like there was traffic.

Sitting on Dee-Dee's front stoop was a small, dark, thoroughly soaked hunk of human misery, one she recognized. "Bill*lee!*" she hollered. "What the hell happened to you?"

His face was wet, as if he'd been crying. "I'm sorry I bailed. I just needed to get out of there." She was pretty sure there was more.

"You had somewhere to go?"

He stood up and faced her down, as he'd done two nights ago. He was one ballsy kid.

His forehead wrinkled and the space between his eyes folded into a perfect eleven. "I wonder if you could... there's something I..."

He couldn't seem to spit it out. "Come on in. I was just going to feed Angel. You hungry?"

"No, I'm good."

"I know you didn't get breakfast this morning. Or if you did, it wasn't more than a couple of bites—I saw what they were handing out at Charity. How about a peanut butter sandwich?"

His face relaxed into a grateful grin. "Peanut butter'd be good."

"Angel, shut up," she said, as she pushed open the door. The dog was making an outraged racket. Nobody'd ever ignored her for hours. "Hey, go on out and pee. There's no cars coming, you'll be fine."

"I'll take her." Billy grabbed her leash off its hook. He'd clearly scoped out where it was during his stay the other night.

This kid could be helpful, she remembered. Now that Skip had met Maxine, she understood why. He was probably used to taking care of her and whoever she was in charge of taking care of.

"Can you make your own sandwich? I've got to take care of something out back. There's a pantry with everything, but you know what? There's some stuff in the fridge that might still be cold enough. Better to eat that first if you feel like it. And would you mind feeding Angel? Her food's in the pantry too."

The "out back" she mentioned was her own apartment, the slave quarters she rented from Jimmy Dee. She hadn't been there in two days, and needed to check it out. But, more important, she wanted to find a safe place for the pillow and other evidence—if she could really call it that—that she'd collected.

Who knew? Eventually someone might be arrested and go to trial, and a judge might conceivably rule that under the circumstances, the piece of tissue Skip had found, and the fibers and pillow so meticulously saved by Dr. Petrachian, might be admitted into evidence. That would probably be happening, she estimated, about the time hell froze over, but she was damn sure going to do her part just in case. She wished she'd gotten a formal statement from

Petrachian, but Skip could see the doctor had what Cappello would describe as bigger fish to fry.

When she got back, Angel was scarfing her late breakfast and Billy was rummaging around the refrigerator. She looked at her watch. Seemed like she'd been gone about fifteen minutes—was he having a second helping or what? "Long walk?" she said.

He pulled his head out of the refrigerator, "Huh?"

She waved at the dog. "Did you and Angel just get back?"

"Oh. Uh. Yeah. She had to poop and I had to find something to clean it up." He made a face. "Finally found a go-cup in the gutter."

She almost laughed. He was concerned about a little dog poop when it was going to take months to make the city presentable again? Was any kid really that conscientious? Well, if so, maybe they could help each other out. He'd already indicated he wanted something. And she was worried about taking care of Angel, given that her job had now become a dawn-to-dark deal. Maybe he could help her with feeding and walking in exchange for whatever it was he needed.

He'd now found the rest of the cold cuts and begun inhaling Jimmy Dee's fancy deli items without even bothering to make a sandwich. Poor kid must be starving.

"So when I got here," she said, "weren't you about to ask for a favor? What do you need, babe?"

19

What did he need? Was he dreaming? Did anyone ever say that to anyone else? Well, where to start?

I need the Dark Knight behind bars along with every member of his murdering, thieving gang. If you can't manage bars, dead'll do fine.

I need a sane mama. Or failing that, at least one who takes her meds. I also need her not to go to jail for that stunt she pulled.

I need my brother back, but never mind. You might be as tall as a goddess, but you ain't God.

I need to know what happened to fuckin' Kaynard and if he's still alive, I need him dead too.

I need to figure out what to do with a mother of a secret I'm carryin' around before it gets me killed.

That was pretty much the bucket list. But as he was ticking it off in his head, a bigger dilemma hit him. *Hey! I'm goddam homeless. I got no place to stay! And no money and no way to get any.*

Well, later for that. And later for wiping out the IBoys.

He had an emergency. He chose his words carefully. "I wouldn't ask," he said, "but I don't know nobody else."

She nodded, looking like somebody's big sister, just sitting on a kitchen stool like she was.

"You saw my mama, right? Well, I ain't got no daddy. And now I got no brother..."

She grinned at him. He hadn't expected that. "Come on, you can tell me. I'm a cop, remember? I'm supposed to help people."

"I got two more living relatives and that's it. All I got in the world. My Aunt Makayla and Uncle Paul. And they're stranded, up in the Iberville."

"It's not flooded that bad, is it?"

"Well, my Uncle Paul's got the sugar, you know?"

"Diabetes?"

He smiled. "Yeah. The sugar's what Aunt Kayla calls it. And he's got this complication—makes his legs all red and... you know... infected."

"Cellulitis?"

"Yeah, that's it. He can't get it wet, see? I mean, wet's not the problem, it's, you know, more infection. He can't get in that nasty water out there."

Skip nodded.

"He can barely walk, tell you the truth. Weighs about four hundred pounds. Is there... like... anything you can..."

She stood up from her kitchen stool and said, "They need a rescue, huh?"

He nodded.

"Yeah, so does half the city."

Fuck! He'd been so sure she was going to help. "Yeah, I know," he said, "I just thought I'd try."

"Well, I might have a connection. I know a couple of

guys on search and rescue. But it's gonna take a few hours. We might not even be able to get 'em till tomorrow."

"I'd just be grateful for anything." He'd probably never said anything like that in his life. But his mama had taught him right; he knew he had decent manners. He just didn't usually have much occasion to haul them out.

"Okay, tell me their address."

She took it and asked, "Anybody there got a cell phone?"

"Kayla does. Don't know if she can charge it, though."

"Give the number, anyhow."

He reeled it off.

"You got a phone?"

"No'm."

"Okay, then. You go stay with your aunt and uncle till you hear from me."

"Yes, ma'am."

"Come on, let's go. I've got to get back out there." And then, as he left, she said, "You'll hear from me, baby. Don't worry, we're gonna get your aunt and uncle out of there."

He said, "I know you will," and half believed it.

He headed toward Rampart, not knowing what else to do. That was the street people were taking to get... where? Wherever they were going to get rescued. On his way back from the hospital he'd heard rumors about what was happening. The whole city was going to be evacuated. People were going to the Convention Center, where buses were going to pick them up. That was what he'd heard. He sure hoped it was true.

Maybe Petey and his lame brother-killing little brother Dalton were there. *Ha!* That almost made him laugh. Mandatory evacuation, hell. When did gangsters do what the law told them to do? Never, probably. He figured the IBoys would stick around to loot and pillage whatever they could. And that included Kaynard's stash. They'd probably already taken it out of the house. But there was a problem with that, and it could get Billy hosed. He had a piece of valuable information. The kind people killed for.

Thing was, he didn't know if Kaynard was dead or alive. If he was alive, Billy was the first person he was going to take out. But if he was dead, Billy could work with that. *Yeah.*

A plan began to form in his head. If he could get the word to the right person, he might be able to pull off one of those martial arts moves where you use your opponent's strength against him.

He was pretty sure he knew who the right person was, too—Zion, Kaynard's best friend from high school. He was a Corner Boy, and the Corner Boys hated the IBoys. The more he thought about it, the more he liked it.

But how was he going to find Zion? He always saw him at Kaynard's house. He searched his mind for any kind of clue, just a little tidbit... and it came to him. Zion's boo was a lady used to live next door to him and his mama. Brianna. Brianna from the Bywater. That's what Maxine called her when she moved. Maybe she still lived there.

He felt like he just got a reason to live.

The Bywater was below the French Quarter, and also on the river. So it was on the right part of Rampart/St. Claude, which was really one street with two names. Maybe it hadn't flooded. Anyhow, it gave him a direction to go.

He was glad he'd thought of Brianna. She used to babysit him and Ivory when they were kids, and she'd always been really nice to him. Maybe she'd let him stay with her, even if Zion wasn't there. It was a real good thought.

He was almost at her house, feeling so good about seeing her he let down his guard; forgot to watch himself.

He heard footsteps a split second before someone grabbed him from behind and spun him backwards against the nearest house, pinning his hands at the shoulder.

Before he could stop himself, Billy screamed like a wounded animal. "Zion. Let up, goddammit. My arm's broken."

The other man only increased the pressure, "What you doin' here, fool?"

He hadn't intended it to happen this way. He was going to spy at the windows, figure out if Kaynard was there before he tried to talk to Zion. But now he had to brazen it out.

"I'm lookin' for Kaynard," he said.

"Well, now, ain't that a coincidence. Kaynard's looking for you too. Yes, *sir*." Zion had started speaking very slowly, his features taking on a wolfish look, like he was enjoying this. "Kaynard wants to find you real bad. He's real pissed about you shootin' him in the head."

"Oh, *man*. He's okay? My mama's 'bout goin' crazy."

Zion laughed and it was an ugly thing to hear. "Son, your mama's already crazy as a runover cat. Ain't no *goin'* about it."

"Seriously. Kaynard's okay? Gimme a break, bro'. Would I be here if I shot him?"

"Well, I know he's after you, so what do *you* think? Why don't we go see him, awright?"

With one hand, he spun Billy back out in front of him—in time to see two white guys in ball caps walking down the street, wearing those heavy utility belts cops wear, all fitted out with handcuffs, guns, the whole thing.

One of them drew his gun and hollered, "Freeze!"

Shit! This day wasn't getting any better. And then the cop said, "Hello, Zion. Been looking for you and your buddy Kaynard." He pointed to Billy. "Let the kid go."

When Zion dropped Billy's wrists, the cop nodded at him. "Get the fuck out of here."

Billy took off running and didn't stop till his lungs burned and his stomach rebelled. He bent over gagging and trying to breathe at the same time, thinking, *so much for the big plan.* His idea was to transfer the IBoys' attention to Zion, but if Zion and Kaynard were busted, the IBoys weren't going to go look for them at OPP. (If the parish prison had even survived.)

Still, he had his piece. Maybe he should just go knock off Petey and Dalton before they nailed him.

20

Conrad stopped what he was doing, which was trying to get the boat started again, and stared at Adam as if he'd suddenly started speaking Chinese. "You want to go by my parents' house? That's the favor?"

"Part of it. Because normally I'd do it for Skip, since I'm staying Uptown right now and she's been stuck in the Eighth. But I wouldn't be able to go in and you've got a key, I bet."

"Yeah. Yeah, I should have done it already." He seemed shocked sober, like a drunk driver who almost sideswipes somebody and suddenly realizes he's out of control. But it wasn't only Conrad, Adam realized—Skip hadn't asked him to check, which was odd in itself. Evidently, they were all riding an adrenaline high. "What's the other part of the favor?"

"I want you to go with me to check my house."

"You're not in your own house?"

Adam shook his head. And, to fend off further questions, he said, "I live at the West End."

Conrad didn't speak for a minute, evidently taking in what that meant. Finally, he said, "Awwww shit, man! Why didn't you tell me?"

Adam almost laughed. He was trying to decide between a sarcastic and a serious answer when Conrad said, "Awww *fuck*, man! I feel like a grade-A dick. I don't think I even thought to ask. What the fuck is wrong with me?"

"It's not you, dude. It's everything. I didn't want you to know where my house is. Because then it would have been all about me. And that's the last thing I want."

Conrad nodded. *No doubt recognizing my wisdom*, Adam thought, and felt the corners of his mouth turn up automatically. But he stopped the sardonic smile before it could really get started. He wanted to keep this real.

"We're all living on adrenaline, that's all. You are, I am; you can bet Skip is. It's how we're getting through. But I hit a wall today. You know I'm an alcoholic, right?"

Conrad shrugged. "Sure. Yeah. Your nickname and everything."

"I called my sponsor just now and came to a realization. I need to see my house."

Conrad looked like he'd lost his last friend. He didn't speak for a moment, finally saying softly, "It's gotta be gone, man. You know that, right?"

"I need to see it. Don't make me talk about it, just take me there, okay?" He heard the desperation in his own voice.

"I'm not... sure we can even get there."

"Let's just try it, okay? We can go see your parents' first, and talk on the way. Maybe we can develop a plan."

"What about search and rescue?" The younger man looked disoriented.

Adam had never felt more like a drink in his life. "Conrad," he said, unable to keep his teeth from clenching. "I need a little me time. Can you help me or not?" He could barely control his voice.

Maybe it was the word "help", more likely that Adam's desperation was showing—but whatever clicked with him, finally Conrad seemed to understand that this wasn't something that could wait. "Sure thing, man." He started the motor.

"Shall we go there first?"

"No, let's go see your parents' house first." It seemed only decent, since Conrad was doing him a favor.

They followed the system they'd developed—tied up the boat where Conrad had left his car, and drove on the non-flooded streets. "They're calling it the sliver by the river—have you heard that?" Conrad said. "The part that didn't flood."

Adam hadn't and thought it told an ominous story—the word "sliver" said it all. It made his stomach hurt, thinking about the damage, the loss, the impossibility of recreating the cultural life of the city... Once again, he found himself going in a direction he wanted to avoid.

Best to live in the moment, as Conrad had so blithely suggested. It had sounded naïve to his cynical ears, but right now it wasn't such a bad idea.

"Hadn't heard that. Where do your parents live?"

"State Street."

"Pretty fancy. You worried about looting?"

"Damn! I never thought of that."

"Well, don't start now! There are much easier targets."

"Here we are."

They pulled up to a more-or-less mansion, an enormous house he absolutely couldn't imagine Langdon living in, with tree limbs littering the lawn.

"Jesus," Conrad said. "One of those could have hit the roof."

"Let's pile them up in the street, make it look like somebody's home."

They did that and then they went in to check for damage. Predictably, some shingles had probably come off the roof, causing leaks on the second floor, in one of the bedrooms and a dark green, beautifully appointed office, clearly an upscale man-cave. Conrad said, "Damn! Dad's not going to be happy about this. Missed his computer, though. Guess that's the main thing. You know what? This is Skippy's old room."

"Wish you hadn't said that," Adam said. "Makes me feel like a voyeur."

Conrad laughed. "She probably sneaked out of that window three times a week."

"She was a hellion? I'd expect no less."

"Depends on who you ask, I guess. Never could please Mom—now *there* are two people who couldn't be more different. She was pretty nice to me, though."

"Who? Skip or your mom?"

That made him laugh again.

"My mom's not nice to anyone unless they can get her on a board or in a club."

"Ah. That kind of mom." It explained a lot about how an ex-deb from an Uptown family happened to become a cop —and, truth to tell, pretty much of an outlaw as well. "No wonder she's a rebel."

"Yeah," Conrad said. "She was always the black sheep. Till she started getting all those headlines. Then she was suddenly teacher's pet."

"So now you're the black sheep?"

"Oh, hell, no. I'm the boy and I work in finance. I can't do anything wrong."

"Got that white male privilege thing going, huh?"

He looked thoughtful for a moment, assessing the idea. "Yeah, I guess. Never thought of it like that, but now that I think of it, I can guarantee you Skippy did."

They both laughed. "That would be Skip," Adam said. He didn't mention "spoiled brat", "Uptown twit" or any of her other colorful nicknames for him. Conrad beat him to the punch: "She pretty much thinks I'm some kind of white punk on dope."

"Naaah. She just thinks you're a dope."

"She's not wrong, my man. She's not wrong." Conrad gave him a rueful half-smile.

"Hey, she never said you were so self-aware." Conrad faked a punch at him, and they cleaned up as best they could, leaving after turning on the alarm, though it was worthless so long as the power was off. But it was something they could do.

"Okay, now your house," Conrad said. "Sure you want to do this?"

"Absolutely. Been thinking about how to do it." He'd had pretty much nothing else on his mind, despite all the brotherly banter. "Got a kayak, by any chance?"

"A kayak. Now there's an idea whose time has come. The answer is, 'no, but I can get one.'"

"Who do we have to kill?"

"Couple of pit bulls, probably. Maybe a neighbor with an AK-47."

"Piece of cake. Let's go get it."

"Your phone working?"

"Sure." Adam handed it over and waited, leaning on

Conrad's car and surveying the trashed-out yards around him, while Conrad tried to get his kayak-owning friend.

He handed the phone back, shrugging. "Didn't answer. Let's go jack it."

"Oww. Do you have to be so blunt? I'm a cop."

"Oh, yeah, you are. Let's think of it, not as stealing, but improvisation."

"Much better. Let's go improvise us a boat." But inwardly, he balked. He knew this was the way it was going to go for a while. He and the whole department and the whole city were going to be improvising their lives—and not incidentally their laws—for weeks to come. Maybe months or years. The thought didn't cheer him up.

It was actually pretty easy to get to Adam's house, once they picked their way to I-10. They were able to get reasonably close, and it was easy to carry the kayak, which they'd secured to the top of Conrad's car. Adam's heart was in his throat as they approached the West End and, when he actually saw it, so were the contents of his stomach. Only by swallowing hard was he able to avoid making his own contribution to the Katrina stew they floated on.

Every restaurant was gone. Bruning's. Sid-Mar's. Jaeger's...

But Conrad was looking in a different direction. "Holy shit! The Southern Yacht Club's gone. It looks like... can't be!"

Adam strained to see. "It looks like it burned down."

"In the middle of a hurricane?" Conrad seemed affronted.

"Afterwards, maybe? Funny we haven't heard." But it wasn't, really. Nobody knew anything. He had a thought. "Are you a member?"

"Yeah," Conrad said. "Yeah, I am."

"You mean... you had a boat?" Adam dreaded hearing the answer.

"Other than the motherducker, not right now. And I don't mean because I just lost one. Fortunately, I'm a little low on vessels at the moment. Although I just doubled my navy." He nodded at the liberated kayak.

At Adam's confused expression, he said, "Motherducker's what I call my duckboat. Informally, *of course*. How immature do you think I am?"

"Pleading the Fifth," Adam said, but he was only half listening. He was trying to take in what he was seeing. His brain literally couldn't fathom dozens of boats—dozens and dozens of boats, and large boats at that—piled upon one another like giant toys, turned sideways and leaning on each other, capsized on land, masts splintered into pick-up sticks, all that and then a big old open space where the restaurants used to be. He kept going over and over the same material, trying to comprehend it, to work it into his notion of reality.

"The lighthouse is still standing," he said, apropos of nothing. "Why would that be?"

"No idea. Not its best moment, though. Missing that topknot thingie..."

"Cupola?"

"Yeah. Cupola. Hey, old buddy, I'm not feeling too good."

"I can relate. I almost lost my lunch a minute ago."

They'd already been through hell, seen people die in hell, rescued people from hell, and nothing had hit Adam like this. Conrad too, apparently. He thought it had to do with the sheer size of the panorama; the deeply personal feeling of profound dinkiness, of knowing in your cells you're a micro-dot in the face of such immense power. It was harrowing in a way that even the life-and-death horrors they'd already seen couldn't be—because it was personal this time: it was a real-life sighting of the bogeyman you knew was coming for you.

Conrad said, "You sure you want to go through with this?"

Adam couldn't find words to answer, not even "yes." He nodded.

Gingerly, they left the harbor side of the park opposite the yacht harbor offices and picked their way to the other side of the block of buildings, the side where the boathouses were.

Adam's neighborhood, if you could call it that, consisted of about a hundred of the boathouses, in a neat row behind the two-story harbor offices. As soon as they rounded the corner of the row of two-story buildings, Adam knew what he needed to know. The boathouses were shells, if they were standing at all. All the dockboxes from the slips were gone as well. The boats were splinters.

Conrad gasped and set his jaw tightly, evidently preparing himself to see this thing through, to Adam's satisfaction. "Which one's yours, buddy?" His voice sounded thick.

Adam came to a sudden realization. "You know what? This is good enough. Think I've got the picture."

"You sure?"

Adam nodded again, this time with more conviction. "Yup. There's no way mine was the only one that survived. It's just gonna break my heart to see my neighbors' lives hanging out in the open like that." He meant that the facades were gone; you could sometimes see the interior of a house, on display like a dollhouse.

Conrad nodded in return, as if he understood, and maybe he did.

Adam shrugged. "I found out what I wanted to know. I'm

officially..." He paused, making sure he could say the word "...homeless." He set his eyes on the horizon, not wanting to risk the possibility of eye contact.

Conrad was quiet, clearly giving him auditory space, and Adam appreciated it. He didn't want to talk, didn't want sympathy, just wanted the time to absorb what he knew. As the realization settled, he felt oddly lighter, relieved of a burden. The doubt and fear were gone. Not the sadness, but he was going to have that for a long time anyhow, on every kind of account.

He hadn't lost that much. It wasn't even his house—he had a lease with the harbor. He didn't own anything valuable. The most he'd lost, he reflected, was a view.

That and a dream.

But the hell with it, he could get another dream. Maybe one that included Kathy Bordelon.

"You okay?" Conrad asked, finally.

"I am more than okay. I am better. I am movin' on."

"Like...leaving New Orleans, or..."

"Oh, nothing like that. I just mean I'm done here—at the West End. Living in a boathouse was awesome. Beyond awesome. But you know what? I've done that. I'm going to do something else now."

Conrad stared at him. "Just like that?"

"Just like that. You know what's worse than knowing your house is gone?"

"Not knowing," they said together.

"Thanks for bringing me, buddy. I really appreciate it."

"Sure thing."

Adam smiled, noticing they'd started calling each other "buddy". *Guess we've bonded*, he thought. *Langdon's just going to have to live with it.*

21

"Look, I promised this kid. His uncle's got an infection and can't... you know... be exposed to all the chemicals and crap in the water..."

Skip could almost see Adam wincing. "Yeah. I heard that."

After a day in the hell of St. Claude Avenue, she just had this one last thing to do before walking Angel and collapsing. She was on the phone, pleading with Abasolo and Conrad to go get Billy's aunt and uncle before they quit for the day. They had to be exhausted. She knew it was way too much to ask and it was stressing her out to argue with them.

Things had gotten hotter and nastier and more stressful on the streets, with the massive task of evacuating everyone who was left in the city and feeding them in the meantime. The National Guard had started to move in. Buses commandeered by the governor from all over the state were scheduled to move thousands of people out, but so far few seemed to be rolling yet. The roar of hundreds of Coast Guard helicopters plucking people off rooftops was both ominous and hopeful—as well as irritating as hell. Everyone was hungry, thirsty, hot, scared, and worst of all, mad.

They thought they'd been deserted by the government and they were losing hope that help was coming. The early panic when they'd realized their predicament had given way to despair and, in many cases, aggression.

She'd had her hands full all day and so had every cop who bothered to come to work. She hated doing this to A.A. and Conrad, but if you couldn't help a friend, what was the point of being a cop?

Adam said, "How do you even know this kid?" And she realized she hadn't even seen him since the storm except for breakfast with Conrad. How had she managed not to tell them her Katrina-night adventures?

She told him now, just hitting the high spots, with heavy emphasis on Billy and also Ollie, whom he knew and liked, with a little about the animals, especially Iggy's attempt to maim Breesy. She was pretty sure that was good for a laugh.

"So the kid ran out on you, and then turned up again begging for help? Huh? Everybody needs help! Why'd you make a promise to him?"

"He's a good kid, Adam. He helped me all night, even when Ollie went to sleep. Hey, you know about him! He's the one whose mama took a hostage over at Charity. He's had it rough, and I feel bad for him."

"Dr. Bordelon was very impressed with him."

"Ummm. Dr. Bordelon..."

She let it hang there, waiting for him to answer, while she continued pacing, the way she was getting through this call, wandering aimlessly from one room to another, straightening obsessively as she went. She'd already rearranged the cheerful throw pillows on Jimmy Dee's leather sofa, all the while nagging as hard as she could.

Turning to the desk, which had three dirty glasses on it, she happened to notice the drawer was slightly open—the drawer where she'd put everyone's gun the night of the storm.

"That little shit!" she said aloud, and pulled it open, already knowing what she was going to find.

Sure enough, there were only two guns and a knife.

"What's going on?" Abasolo sounded alarmed.

"The little shit broke into Jimmy Dee's desk drawer. Fuck! I went back to my house for a minute—what was I thinking?" She'd been thinking he was a good kid she could trust, that was what.

"Billy you mean? The good kid? He steal anything?"

"Yeah, he did. I took everybody's gun the night of the storm. He retrieved his. He's a minor, goddammit. He can't be out on those streets with a gun."

"You telling me he stole his own gun? With every predator in New Orleans out there running wild? Why, that little shit! How dare he try to protect himself! So we can abort this mission, right? 'Cause he's a hooligan whose uncle and aunt don't deserved to be saved?"

"Hooligan?" Skip laughed, realizing that, some way or another, she had no idea how, she'd managed to win this one. "Can we do it first thing in the morning?"

Later that night, having freshly charged her phone in her car, Skip told the story to Steve Steinman, her boy friend in California, who'd discovered that even when phones didn't work—even when the towers were down—you could still send text messages. Phones with the New Orleans area code couldn't reach each other, but Steve still had his California number, so they could talk too. But he'd also been texting her almost every hour on the hour. Silly ones: "So a priest, a rabbi, and a minister got caught in a hurricane..."

Inspirational ones: "Five Cities That Were Destroyed and Completely Rebuilt".

But mostly sweet ones. He missed her. He'd give anything to be there with her. He was thinking about her every second. He only wished he were there, he was itching to *do* something.

And there were a whole lot of questions. He was watching the news about New Orleans almost non-stop, and of course Skip hadn't seen any at all. What he was seeing was people waiting on rooftops to be rescued; forlorn dogs stranded in trees; and people looting. What he was hearing was that looters were shooting at rescue choppers and people were killing and raping in the Superdome. He wanted the inside story.

"You know more than I do," she protested, and told the Billy anecdote to distract him.

"How," he responded, "are you going to get a four-hundred-pound man into a duck boat without getting him wet?"

"Carefully, of course. Did I ever mention I love you?"

"Sounds like you're signing off."

"Can't keep my eyes open."

It seemed like only seconds before she was awakened by a heavy pounding. Hoping it was Abasolo and Conrad bringing breakfast, she staggered to the door.

It was only one of them, and he was empty-handed.

"Team A reporting in," Conrad said, "A.A. can't make it. The mayor's called the cops off search and rescue."

"You're kidding!"

"Nope. There's a lot going on today. Soldiers and medical teams moving in. The evacuation's really speeding up."

She let him in. "Well, thanks for coming, Conrad. Let me get some clothes on. Make yourself some coffee."

He'd left his boat with a buddy and walked into the Quarter to get her—to do her a favor.

Maybe A.A. was right—she was going to have to reassess her opinion of him as a layabout wastrel. Some people, she thought, are at their best in a crisis. Maybe Conrad was one.

The buddy was only babysitting the boat, so it was just the two of them on the mission. But they'd have Billy at the other end to help.

Or so she thought.

Nobody could have been more surprised to see her than Aunt Makayla. Billy didn't seem to have mentioned the impending rescue. Couldn't have, as it turned out. "I ain't seen him since Monday morning," his aunt said. "He okay?"

"Last I saw him he was, except for an arm injury." She didn't want to worry his aunt by saying his arm was broken.

Makayla seemed not to believe what was happening. "Paul and me, we didn't expect no rescue."

"Well. I promised Billy. So here we are."

"I don't know how he got y'all to come, but we sure are grateful." She paused, evidently trying to take in her good fortune. "He's such a *good* boy! Nothing like that big brother of his. Just the other day, I watched him get shot by some gangbangers he was messing with."

Skip wondered if she should deliver the news about Ivory's death, but decided that was definitely not her department.

"Let me go get Paul together," she said. "And me too. Won't be a minute. I know y'all got more important things to do than cart around a couple of ol' black people."

Ow, Skip thought, not sure how to answer that.

Conrad didn't miss a beat. "No, we don't. It's our honor to help y'all today."

Whathehell? Once Makayla was out of sight, she blurted, "Conrad, you got religion or something?" She realized she'd kind of snapped it out. It sounded hostile, when she didn't feel that way at all. On the other hand, she was a bit annoyed to find herself in the company of a stranger in her brother's body.

"No, I have not got religion or something." He sounded petulant as a junior high brat. Now that was the brother she knew. And then he went into a pretty decent Oxford don thing. "I have merely been taught proper manners and values in the Langdon household. Lessons that apparently did not take in every case."

Skip had to laugh. "Okay, you got me. I don't know who the hell you are any more."

He looked her in the eye, his own eyes a little too shiny. "Whoever you thought I was? You were probably about fifty per cent right. But I've got to tell you something. This is a very meaningful thing for me."

He *had* gotten religion. In a sense. The person she thought he was was something of a parasite. A spoiled Uptown brat who didn't have to work very hard and didn't want to. Drank too much and didn't care who knew. And worst of all, was smug as a pampered pooch about his own good fortune. The kind of person for whom people did things, not someone whose honor it was to save other people's asses.

She should know. She'd had enough requests from him to fix parking tickets. (Which she paid instead.)

Sometime this week he'd evidently gone to bed as a poodle and waked up as a St. Bernard. She tried to match

awoke

his sincerity. "Okay," she said, "I'm going to take you at your word. It's just going to take some getting used to."

"Well, don't try too hard. When this is all over, I'll probably go back to my usual worthless self." He was trying for a laugh, but even the glib pleasantry showed a self-knowledge she didn't know he possessed.

All she said was "I don't doubt it," but she gave him a warm smile and met his eye in a new way, a way meant to say that if this was really happening, she was in.

Once Makayla got herself together, Skip could see she was a handsome woman with her own distinct African-Wise-Woman style. Colorful yet commanding. And she was smart too. Despite being flustered, she packed carefully— even with so little time—grabbing water and medical supplies, some crackers and peanut butter. Skip saw she was already keeping Paul's insulin in a traveling cooler bag, which she added to her backpack. Along with some family photos.

Why photos? And then she realized that Makayla suspected what Skip hadn't even thought of—that she'd never be back here again. That everything she was leaving behind was lost, that this was her only chance to choose what she wanted to keep. Skip was willing to bet she had her jewelry in that pack too.

She said, "Better get hats for both of y'all. It's boiling hot out there."

"Where we going?"

That was the million-dollar question. When Makayla went to get Paul, Skip said to Conrad, "Any ideas? We really going to take these people out to some freeway overpass to bake?"

"Yeah, I already talked to Adam about that. He actually

has a place where they might be able to stay—" He looked sheepish. "Guess we all do. But Mr. Paul's got health issues and all the hospitals are locked down. No telling when any kind of medical care's going to be available here. So A.A. had an idea. They're setting up a medical unit at the airport. We thought if we got there early enough, maybe these guys have a chance of getting out on one of the first transport planes."

"You can get them there?"

Conrad nodded. "Already arranged."

"Let's go for it." She didn't have a lot of faith in the idea, but it beat any alternative she could see.

"Here they come," Conrad said, although the noise coming from the staircase was anything but the easy rhythm of one step after another. It was more of a scuffling and banging, accompanied by cursing.

"Goddammit, lean on me. You want to break your fool neck?"

"If I fall on you, I'm gonna kill you, honey-pumpkin."

Brother and sister stared at each other. "Honey-pumpkin?" Skip whispered. They both giggled. There was something so touching about it—these desperate circumstances, this desperately ill man, and the sweet way he spoke to his wife—that it deserved to be noted.

Skip moved towards them, seeing Paul for the first time. He was a fine figure of a man—a Creole with carefully combed silky black hair. Four hundred pounds, sure, but dressed impeccably in perfectly ironed khaki shorts and a khaki guayabera shirt, surely not what he'd been wearing when they arrived. He looked like a prince about to go on safari.

Conrad was faster than Skip, bounding up the stairs, and offering his shoulder. "Hey, let me. You Mr. Paul?"

"Reverend Paul," the man said. "Pastor of the Star of Judah First Evangelical Baptist Church."

Conrad grabbed the reverend's arm. "Okay, Reverend, can you put your weight on me?"

"I'm gon' kill you if I do."

"Not if you pray for me."

Skip had found a way to brace Makayla, so that the three of them formed a solid juggernaut for the Reverend Paul to lean on.

"Tell you what I'm gon' do instead. I'm gonna sing us down these stairs." Skip braced for that too, and well she should have. The man had a voice to match his build, and a rousing song to go with it.

The Battle Hymn Of The Republic poured from his mouth like honey. "Mine eyes have seen the glory of the coming of the Lord..."

At this point Makayla joined in, "He is stamping out the vintage where the grapes of wrath are stored..."

It was irresistible. Skip and Conrad were right there for "He hath loosed the fateful lightning..." and by the time they got to the first "Glory! Hallelujah!" they were all on the first floor. But nothing was going to stop them finishing the verse. They belted it with the joy of angels in their own pride parade, Skip and Conrad facing the other two, so they could all see into each other's eyes.

Skip had to leave on the pretext of checking on the boat so no one would see her crying. It was one of the most beautiful moments of her life.

22

I t was still earlier than her usual starting time once they got Paul in the boat and Skip had wished him and Makayla good luck.

Seeing Dee-Dee's rifled desk drawer had reminded her that she still had everyone's weapons from Sunday night. She didn't feel all that good about returning Dickie Horvath's, but it *was* his property, and, considering the chaos of the moment, he might need to defend himself.

In any case, she needed to get Ollie's gun back to her. Being a single woman living alone, she'd feel more comfortable knowing she had protection. And Skip needed to check on her anyway—she was capable as hell, but crazy enough to do some quixotic thing, probably involving Iggy, that could put her in danger. So now or never, she thought.

They all lived in the Marigny, the neighborhood immediately downriver from the French Quarter, about a ten-minute walk from Jimmy Dee's. Hardly anyone was out on Frenchmen St., but to her surprise, she ran smack into Dickie. Happy to see a familiar face, even his, Skip gave him a big hello. "Hey, Dickie! How'd y'all do?" The question everyone was asking everyone else. It meant, "What's the damage to your house?"

His answer took her aback: "What the hell do you people think you're doing? Huh? Don't think we don't know about it. Everyone knows. Tell me: How many African-Americans have you murdered today, Miss Cop?"

"It certainly is true about no good deed," she snapped.

"Huh?"

"Shelter. Remember? Your dog peed on the rug. You drank a whole bottle of bourbon and passed out. You didn't help with the leaks, you even added some—by not bothering to dispose of your damn Depends! And instead of thank you I get accused of murder? Whathehell is wrong with you?"

Whathehell was wrong with her as well? That was probably the least professional speech she'd ever given.

"You can run but you can't hide, pig!"

She should have let it go, but she couldn't. "Dickie, what's gotten into you?"

"Cops are out there killing people and I'm not supposed to say anything?"

"What cops? What the *fuck* are you talking about?"

She watched his face change from furious to mildly surprised... and a bit sly.

"You really don't know, do you? Word on the street's you're a girl scout. Maybe it's even true."

She was about over this conversation. "If you've got something to say, say it."

"Maybe you'd like to be the one clean cop, the cop who cracked the case. Huh? Huh? What would that do for your career?" She waited. "How much is it worth to you?"

"Wait! First you accuse me of murder, and now you're

offering to be a confidential informant?" She was almost amused.

"Hell, no! I'm no snitch. I'm offering to sell you information that'll make you chief of police." She couldn't help it—she burst out laughing.

The stress was getting to her; and it had obviously gotten to Dickie. Or else Dawn had beaten him with a crazy stick. She didn't even know if it was safe to return his weapons.

"Nice talking to you, Dickie." She moved on. And then thought: *What if something happens and he doesn't have his gun?*

She turned around and called to him. "Hey, Dickie, got something for you."

"I don't take gifts from pigs."

Thinking how right she was about good deeds, she sighed and caught up with him. "It's not a gift." She turned over the gun and knife without a word. The man was beyond unbearable.

Music was coming from a balcony at Frenchmen and Chartres, someone playing a saxophone. And then a voice. "This is Radio Marigny reporting from Atlantis. The bitch Katrina blew through Monday and now we're sunk. Also fucked. But we're dry in the Marigny and the Quarter! Everywhere else is underwater. The water's still rising, folks —where it stops, nobody knows.

"But never fear, *we* are here! This is your neighborhood bulletin board. Here are the latest headlines:

"There's a working phone at Jo Ellen Hughes' house on Dauphine St. and she's lending it out to anyone who needs it. You don't need the address—you'll know it by the line waiting outside.

"Mayor Nagin has once again ordered the entire city evacuated. He has also imposed a curfew. Everyone in the Marigny will be observing it. *Snarfle*. That means YOU! But not me. Johnny White's Sports Bar remains open. *Fuck* the curfew.

"Buses will be leaving from the Superdome as soon as they're loaded. Better hurry, you don't want to be the last one left in the Sea of Orleans. Oh, us? Hell, no, we won't go!

"All NOPD police have been pulled off search and rescue to...you know...stop looters. And fight crime and all.

"This concludes your Radio Marigny update. See y'all at Johnny White's as soon as we can all get there."

The broadcast, if you could call it that, made Skip laugh. It was so innocent, so upbeat, so much like the old days when the aftermath of a hurricane involved only a quick clean-up and drinking a toast to dodging a bullet. They might have made a few errors—she hoped the water wasn't still rising—but she had to give these guys A for effort. Despite the horror all around her, the incongruous levity lifted her spirits for a moment.

She found Ollie trying to lift a tree that had fallen in her yard. Without a word, Skip picked up the near end and they carried it out to the street, where someone had already started a neat pile of debris. "You do all right?" she said when they'd completed their task.

"My house is fine except for that tree. And Ignatius is thrilled with all the new toys—branches and sticks and hidey-holes. Thanks for the help, by the way. Have you cleaned out Jimmy Dee's refrigerator?"

Skip snapped her fingers. "Oh, hell. No. Meant to do it last night, but I was so beat I just fell into bed. Well...after a phone call with Steve."

"Bet he wishes he was here."

Skip was a bit taken aback. "He does, but...what would

make you say that? I'd think most people would want to be anywhere else."

"Are you kidding? This is where the action is."

"You're some kind of a nut—you know that?" Skip pulled out Ollie's Ruger and handed it over. "Here. In case you run into too much action, God forbid."

"I don't believe in God."

"Well, who do you believe in?"

"Ignatius Reilly."

"You mean Iggy the cat?"

"No, the real Ignatius." Skip filed that one. It cleared up a long-running argument she had going with Jimmy Dee about whether she'd named the cat after the character in *Confederacy Of Dunces*.

"In Ignatius we trust," she said.

"So...the refrigerator. Things getting nasty? Want me to do it? I'll do yours too."

"You have no idea how much I'd appreciate that! Take anything that looks edible. I think I've got some eggs— they'll be ok at room temp."

She gave Ollie a hard look and noticed deep circles under her eyes, a pinching-up of her features. "Hey, you okay? You look like you haven't been sleeping."

"It's just all the gunshots and things." Skip had heard them too. "And the noise from the neutral ground on Rampart and St. Claude. People are camping there."

"Yeah. They walked from the Ninth Ward. But they're not hurting anybody."

"You know developers have already divided up the Ninth Ward now that it's like, destroyed, right? You know that guy owns half the town, has that little coffee place near your house? Right there's where they did it. They met in his apartment above the coffee joint and they figured out how to build high-rises for rich white people on Bayou Bienville. Know what this whole place is gonna become? A fancy vacation spot for retirees." She paused, disgusted.

Ollie did love her neighborhood rumors and the post-Katrina chaos was proving to be a fertile source of them.

"Well, hell, everybody's getting killed, anyhow. The cops are looting along with everyone else. You know that too, right?"

The Ninth Ward story was ridiculous—nobody could buy up anything—all the deeds were likely underwater and the owners were still in shock in Houston or somewhere. Nobody was even being allowed to enter the city right now.

But Skip had no doubt cops really were looting. Everything was up for grabs and nobody was watching. A perfect set-up for certain of her brother cops.

But she lifted an eyebrow in protest. "Not all of us."

"Well, one good thing. At least y'all are getting rid of the gangs."

"I wish!"

"Seriously, Skip. How can you be so far out of the loop? They're not messing around. They're systematically rounding up the usual suspects. And gutting them."

"Whoa! *Gutting* them?" This was going pretty far, even for Ollie.

"Yeah. *You* know. So they'll sink. They just throw them in the river and nobody's the wiser. Neat, huh?"

Skip shrugged, not giving it much thought. "Aside from being mass murder, sure. That would be a great way to get rid of gangs! If it weren't illegal, immoral, plain wrong, bad karma, punishable by death..."

"I don't care, they're doing it. It's all over the street. Why don't you know about it?"

Oho. So that was what was up with Dickie.

"Wait a minute. Did Dickie tell you about this? Because I can hardly think of a less reliable source."

"Oh, hell no! Not Dickie. That guy Trent, you know him? Lives across the park from Kenneth Holditch. Curly-haired dude."

"You mean on Elysian Fields?"

"Just off it—one of those shotguns. Not sure which."

"Did Trent actually see anything, or was he just repeating rumors?"

"If you saw something like that, would you go around telling people?"

That made Skip's scalp prickle. Crazy as it sounded, there was a piece of her that knew that, this week, on these lawless streets, anything was possible.

Well, hell. She had, as Cappello would have it, more sizeable fish to sauté than chasing down rumors. But Washington Square was a pretty small park. It wouldn't take a minute to see if Trent was home.

"Ollie, you have enough food? Get some when you clean the fridges, okay?" As an afterthought, she said. "Better yet, you should evacuate. You know everyone's been ordered out of the city, right?"

"Are you *kidding* me? I just went through a Category Three hurricane for a cat! You think I'm leaving him now?"

⁓

SKIP HAD to knock on a few doors, but it wasn't too hard to find Trent. Neighbors—and, despite the evacuation order, quite a few were still around—either loved or hated him right now. As she got closer, she could see why. She'd been given two ways to find him—look for the house with the fence; and don't worry, you'll know by the smell. Or the noise.

Inside the fence were dogs—maybe twenty of them, some in crates, some ranging about, and Trent wasn't doing the greatest job of poop patrol. Also, the dogs probably barked every time anyone passed. They staged a lively concert as soon as they sensed her presence.

She let herself in the metal gate, hoping the pooches were friendly. A couple were, but most just seemed too dispirited to even get up and give her a sniff.

"Hey, anybody home?"

"Yeah, I'm here." A harried-looking guy in filthy khaki shorts and no shirt stood up from behind one of the crates. His tanned chest was covered with tattoos, and his hair hung to his collarbone in tight curls. It looked as if he was finally catching up with his neglected poop patrol, scooping odoriferous piles into a plastic garbage bag. But the joke was on him. Garbage collection was *so* not happening. Unless he figured out a place to dump the bag, it was just going to stick around and stink anyhow.

"You Trent? I heard you were rescuing dogs."

"Yeah, I've got a generator, so I've still got Internet. Been watching news reports showing all those sad little furry faces... so I've been going into the flood zone and pulling them out. You ever seen such a mess?"

She didn't know if he meant his yard or the whole city. She decided on the mega-meaning. "I don't see how it could get worse. Jeez! The things I've heard." She glided quickly over that for the moment. "Hey, listen, I lost my furbaby yesterday. You don't have a long-haired Chihuahua in there, do you? Little male, white and brown?"

"Oh, no! You lost your *baby*? Awww. I sure wish I had him. What's his name?"

She gave him the name of her boy friend's long-lost German shepherd. "Napoleon. He's quite the little dictator."

"Well, I'll sure keep a lookout for him. There's nothing worse than losing your best friend."

"And he's so much protection! I mean, he's little, but he warns me if someone's coming. I keep my gun with me all the time these days. You know how dicey things are right now. Gangs out there killin' people, think they can do anything they want with so few cops on the streets."

"Well, they might get a rude awakening. No way the cops are gonna take that kinda action lying down."

"Hope you're right."

"Well, let me put it this way. This is an opportunity they ain't never gon' get again."

Skip played dumb. "Opportunity? What kind of opportunity?"

Trent shrugged. "To clean house, you know? A lot of bad actors are taking long walks off short piers."

She tilted her head, as if she couldn't be more fascinated. "Why do I get the feeling you mean that literally?"

"Because I do. I've seen it."

"You mean... you've seen cops... ummm... *killing* people?"

"Not people. They're animals. Worse than that. They're pond scum."

She decided not to push her luck any further. "Woo." She shimmied a little, as if shivering. "Remind me to be on my good behavior."

"Yeah, it's a jungle, for sure. We just gotta get you your baby back."

"Sure appreciate you keeping an eye out."

She gave him a comradely salute and left, closing the gate behind her. But she'd gone only a few steps when she heard someone coming, setting off a new canine concert, and then she heard the gate open again. "Oh, Treeee-ent! Daddy's home!"

The voice was a little raspy, rough somehow. Kind of a redneck voice. But she had the weirdest sense she knew it. She didn't dare look back till she was far down the street. And by that time, Trent's gentleman caller had disappeared.

There was definitely something going down, and she cordially wished she'd never heard of it. She was obligated to do something if cops were killing people. But what? She just couldn't wrap her brain around the concept.

23

Tuesday had probably been the second worst day of Kathy's life, she thought (the first being the day she lost Alyssa). After Maxine's hostage stunt (and Kathy's enforced cool-down), the morning meeting was almost relaxing—and had also brought the fantastic news that FEMA was on its way to evacuate the hospital.

But at noon, Norm came into Kathy's office to announce, "We. Are. So. Fucked."

She had to smile, if a bit wryly. "So what else is new?"

"The governor just announced Charity's been evacuated."

Kathy could almost feel her face go white. "So... nobody knows anything. I mean... even the *governor*?"

"Well, like you said, what else is new?" He gave her his million dollar smile and wiped his brow. He was sweating profusely, as was she, she realized. "God, it's hot in here!"

She'd been sitting at her desk, tying to make some patient notes, but suddenly she leapt up with a huge surge of energy. "Goddammit! We can't wait for them. We're going to get through this by ourselves."

She was too terrified to sit still, thinking of the nurses and docs hand-bagging in the AIDS unit and the ICU, wondering how long they could hold out—how long they could all hold out—and what a staff breakdown would mean for the patients.

Almost as if he'd followed her thoughts, Norm said, "Oh, by the way, we had a casualty this morning."

"Damn! I thought we were going to get out of here with a 100 per cent record."

"Well, it kind of evened out. Somebody was born, too."

That made her think of Nathan, the baby Adam had brought in, which made her simultaneously happy and anxious. She'd discovered her mind wandering to him much more often than she'd have imagined, wanting to check on him, make sure he was all right, to reassure herself he'd be reunited with his family. "Cross your fingers we don't lose anybody else."

"Yeah, well, we're going to if this heat keeps up."

"Yeah." She rubbed her temples, trying to think how to improve the comfort level on the third floor. "Let's call a patient meeting."

Norm looked surprised. "Okay. What for?"

"Let's see if we can think of some morale-builders."

He gave her a sly, slightly wolfish grin. "You know Joe? My sweetie?" She nodded, not at all sure she did. Norm had so many sweeties. "He gave me a little Katrina present to get me through this."

She inclined her head. "Yeah?"

"Box of pralines. Whaddaya think?"

"You kidding? Let's ditch the meeting and eat them ourselves."

They didn't have enough pralines to go around, so they broke them into tiny pieces and passed them daintily on a plate—to people who had had no more than a few spoonfuls in two days. Kathy could hear the sound going round the room—*mm-mm-mm*, as each person got a little piece of the world as it used to be. Some people sucked on theirs to make it last.

Kathy noticed that not only the patients but their family members had come to the meeting. Nurse Brenda was assiduously fanning eighty-year-old Eileen Fisk, Kathy's neighbor who'd gotten admitted under the pretext of being a Venusian. Alonzo ("Ti-Meanness") Thurlow was lovingly fanning his mama, Darlene.

She couldn't help being moved by it.

Mrs. Thurlow had one of her kittens in her lap and the other was getting its chin scratched by Lisa, the baby hooker with the teddy bear. The one who'd claimed to have ailurophobia. What she actually had, Kathy knew from experience, was a notable flair for the dramatic; but she also had a good heart.

Rafe Joseph, never one to hide his feelings, boomed out, "Pshew! Hotter'n the devil's dick in here. These walls are *sweatin'*." To illustrate, he passed his hand over one and shook up a drop or two. "Hey, Doc, why don't you let me knock out a few of these windows?"

Norm laughed. "Rafe, you on your meds?"

When he wasn't, he was one of their scariest patients. He was huge, strong as a Sumo wrestler, and given to the kind of destructive rages that could get downright homicidal. Rafe laughed right back. "I'm feelin' just as sweet as one of Miz Thurlow's little therapy kittens."

Therapy kittens! That was an idea. Kathy filed it.

Norm raised an eyebrow at her. "What would you need?" Kathy said to Rafe.

He got up and examined the window. "Oh, I reckon I

could take 'em out by swingin' one of these chairs." That got a laugh.

"Seriously."

He shrugged. "Looks like you could just bang 'em out with a hammer."

"Okay, I'm gonna get you one. Tell you what. We're going to set up a schedule so everyone gets a chance to go to the bathroom..."

"Yeeech. These commodes gettin' *nasty!*"

"I know. But this is a big hospital. We're going to find fresh ones for you, okay? That's what the schedule's all about."

"Well, somebody been peein' in them stairways. Wooooo...eeeee!"

They made everyone laugh. Kathy said, "I'm gonna ask everyone not to do that, okay?"

Mrs. Thurlow sat up straight like the mama she was, passed the stinkeye around the circle, and spoke like a schoolteacher. "You people are all adults. I catch you actin' like chir'ren', there gon' be *consequences.*"

Nobody laughed at that one. Kathy figured it scared everyone else as much as it did her.

The patient sitting next to Lisa was trying to pet her borrowed kitten, but couldn't quite reach it. "Lisa, can you let Mrs. Handler hold the kitty for a while? I think Rafe was right—these are therapy kittens. You feel like sharing? You got enough love for now?"

Lisa smiled shyly. "Could I...maybe...fan somebody now?"

"Sure. Who wants to be fanned?"

After a near-unanimous show of hands, Lisa got a fannee and lots of other people got buddy-system fanners. While Kathy was assigning fan buddies, Norm chased down a hammer, and they all whooped as Rafe demolished the window. "Damn, that was fun!" he pronounced. The air that flowed in was probably no cooler than the stale air inside, but it felt like progress.

"Mission accomplished," Kathy said to herself. "Patient morale improved." She was about to high-five Norm when a young resident, a guy who looked young enough to be her kid, came in with red-rimmed eyes as big as moons, shot through with more red from lack of sleep.

"I'm Dr. Scofield," he said, and then seemed to realize how pretentious that was under the circumstances. He blushed. "Scott. I think I need your help," he whispered. "Can we talk in the hall?"

She followed him out.

"One of our ICU nurses is freaking out. Can you come?"

It was a woman in her thirties, white, with a doughy face that Kathy suspected would be quite pretty in other circumstances—when it wasn't creased and scrunched with worry, red and splotched from crying, and framed by greasy, lank hair. "This is Nurse Tara," the resident said, "Tara Ferraro."

The nurse was sitting on a bed, rocking herself, shaking like she was freezing, sobbing her lungs out. "God help me, Jesus save me, Mary, Mother of God, save my babies," she kept saying, repeating the same phrase over and over.

Kathy looked at the resident. "How long has she been like this?"

"It's been building. She's been crying a long time, but she could still do her job. She's only been non-functional for about half an hour."

Kathy raised her right eyebrow. "Half an hour! Well, that's it, then. I don't think Jesus is going to show up." She hoped the resident wasn't offended.

He looked shocked, then broke into a grin. "He's taking his sweet time, anyhow."

"I've got something faster—if we can get her to the third floor."

"Tara," Kathy said, "can you walk?"

The woman stared at her, apparently unhearing, continuing her chanting.

"Let's see if we can walk her."

Each of them sat down, lifted one of her arms and put it over their shoulders, but standing up was a problem. Kathy had hoped she'd just go with the momentum, but she didn't budge. "She really needs to be with us, where I can watch her." Kathy said, "We could medicate her here, but then it'll take six people to carry her down. Has she got a special friend in the unit?"

He thought for a minute. "Let me go get Dallas."

When he was gone, she put an arm around Tara and stroked her lightly, murmuring the kinds of things you say to a crying child, "You're okay. Everything's going to be okay. Your babies are fine."

At that she seemed to snap out of it a moment. "My babies? You saw them?"

"I want to. Can you tell me where they are?"

As if suddenly realizing how useless Kathy was, she resumed rocking and chanting.

After what seemed about a week and a half, young Dr. Scofield came back with Dallas, who wasn't the middle-aged white woman the name suggested to Kathy, but someone who reminded her of Norm. He was smaller, bossier, and a lot more Nellie, but just as handsome. Also, he had hair. He probably identified as African-American, but Kathy thought he might have been half-Hispanic—there was something about the way he moved that reminded her of really excellent salsa dancers. He swept into the room like a pint-sized dervish, all twists, turns, whirls, and you-better-mind-me compassion: "Ohhhhh, *guuuurl,* what are you doing to yourself?" He sat down beside Tara and laid her head on his shoulder, at the same time turning on Scott and Kathy as if they were the enemy. "Why didn't y'all call Dallas sooner?" His eyes blazed with rage, either real or feigned for Tara's benefit, Kathy couldn't tell which. "Just look at the state my baby's got herself in! That's right, baby, you just let Dallas take care of you. Now don't you worry about a damn thing. I got this." Tara settled deeper and deeper onto Dallas' diminutive shoulder and he wrapped sinewy arms around her, rocking her like one of her own kids until she seemed almost asleep. Finally, he said, "Tell you what. We gon' find you a real nice place to lie down. You know what, baby? You just been working too hard. Let's go have a nap downstairs, okay?"

"Dallas," Tara said "Dallas, I'm so worried about my babies."

"You know what, my darlin'? You just got to let God take care of that." Tara nodded. "We gon' take care of *you.*"

Scott Scofield stepped forward. "Let me help." And together they got her to the third floor, Dallas proving himself as strong as he was persuasive.

Kathy said, "We could use you in emergency psych," and Dallas answered, "Last thing y'all need. You got enough crazy people down here."

He turned Kathy over to Norm and Brenda, leaving Kathy feeling as if she'd just had a visitation from some sort of benevolent elf.

"Who *was* that masked man?" Norm asked.

"I'm not too sure, but I just tried to hire him."

Norm laughed.

"He could be a patient for all I know," she said, realizing it could easily be true. Roles were reversing all over the hospital as patients bagged other patients, helped them to bathrooms, fed and fanned them. Kathy wished she had someone to fan her.

"You look like shit," Norm said.

She gave him a grin, "Bite me."

"That's my girl!"

24

Ollie'd cleaned out Skip's refrigerator as well as Jimmy Dee's, so Skip had moved herself and Angel back to her slave quarters. The Big House was just too big with no one in it but the two of them. Angel kept walking around sniffing, trying to find her missing companions.

She was off the street now, but she still couldn't miss the racket—or Angel couldn't, anyhow. Alarmed barking was her first clue that she had an early-morning visitor. Pulling a pair of baggy shorts over her sleeping outfit—underwear and T-shirt—and slipping into a pair of flip-flops, she padded to the courtyard gate and stepped onto the sidewalk to find Dawn Horvath pounding on Jimmy Dee's door and shouting for Skip. It was six a.m., she'd worked far into the night, and Dawn was the last person she wanted to see.

"What is it, Dawn?"

"Somebody killed Dickie!"

"What? Are you *kidding* me?"

Dawn's too-curly dark hair looked as if it had been deliberately teased so that it stood up around her head in a monster mane. She'd flung on some kind of raggedy muu-muu garment to negotiate the streets and she also wore a pair of red-framed glasses but no make-up, showing a face nearly as red as her glasses. She'd never been Skip's idea of a poster child for sanity, but at the moment she looked like the Madwoman of Chaillot.

"Hell no, I'm not kidding! He went out for a walk and didn't come back."

"Dawn, you're just upset. That doesn't mean he's dead."

"Somebody found him."

Oh, shit! Skip's first impulse had been to get Dawn inside and settle her down, but this was bad. She figured if Dickie wasn't dead, he sure as hell needed help.

"You've seen him?"

Dawn nodded, tears finally starting, fogging her glasses, making her face even redder.

"Let's go. I just need to get some shoes."

Dawn took her to a flooded area of the Bywater where Dickie lay in the street in curb-deep water, under a blanket someone had tossed over him. "I covered him up," Dawn muttered, her eyes leaking tears. "I had to."

A cursory peek at his face told Skip he was dead. *No wonder people think ghosts are white*, she thought, grimacing. He was as white as one and as cold as a catfish.

"You mind if I look?" She wanted to give Dawn time to look away if she wanted to. Evidently, she didn't. She shook her head, but kept staring as Skip removed the now-sodden blanket, and had a look at Dickie in death. There were no obvious holes in him, and with the flooding, any blood could have been washed away...but there was a trace, it looked like. His belly still protruded above his jeans, and his T-shirt, as luck would have it, was red. But she saw a small, very even tear surrounded by a darker red at the bottom right of the mound. She thought it was a stab wound.

"Dawn? What happened here?"

Dawn backed away from the body, shaking her head and holding her hands palms out in front of her chest, as if to ward off an attack if Dickie proved to be Undead. "I don't know, I don't know. Oh, God, I don't know."

Quickly, Skip threw the blanket back over the body. "Ok, ok, let me take you home." She meant she'd walk her home. Some streets were now clear, but you never knew, going into a strange neighborhood.

"I'll just be a minute. Can you turn the other way?" Quickly, and with severe revulsion, Skip reached into Dickie's sodden pockets, coming up with a sad, shrunken wallet.

Dawn had told her, walking over, that Dickie didn't come home the night before. He'd gone out to find some necessities, she said. *Loot some Depends*, Skip translated. That really was a necessity, and no one was selling them, so who was she to judge?

Well, that made sense, now that she put it all together. Rumor had it that Robert's, at the corner of Elysian Fields and St. Claude, was "open for business", meaning just open. That's where he'd most likely have gone, and Robert's was close. She decided to tackle it head-on.

"Was he going to Robert's, Dawn?"

"Probably," she said. "He didn't say and I didn't want to ask. He took his gun with him, by the way. He was holding it when I found him. I didn't think I should leave it there so I brought it home."

So he might have been trying to defend himself.

"How did you find out what happened to him?"

"I don't *know* what happened to him."

Skip took a breath, trying to be patient. "Let me rephrase. How did you know where his body was?"

"Oh. Arnold Acrobat told me. That little dude with the man-bun. You know...the one who calls everybody 'mega-babe'."

Skip hadn't had that pleasure, but she was pretty sure she knew who Dawn meant. "Hangs with the circus punks?" Gutterpunks who practiced circus routines in Washington Square Park. Or maybe they just looked like gutterpunks—dirty, hairy, and accompanied by a pack of snoozing canines.

The "little dude" she was thinking of liked to fluff out his short ponytail so it looked like a bun and he took off his shirt as often as he could. Despite his shrimpy stature, he had a studly build on him, and he was quite the athlete. She'd seen him walk on his hands halfway across the park. Probably, now that Skip thought of it, he managed to score a decent contingent of mega-babes.

"That's the one."

"He's a neighborhood guy, right? Not a gutterpunk?"

"Oh, yeah. Dickie did a little business with him some-times." A little illegal business, Skip figured, but who really cared? She did a certain amount of illegal business herself—or Jimmy Dee did, and shared his pot with her.

"He was all freaked out," Dawn continued. "He dropped by and pounded till I opened the door. Said he'd seen Dickie lying in the street. And he said he was sorry to have to tell me, but Dickie was a gone pecan." Her eyes flashed outrage. "You believe that? That was how he told me."

Skip just shook her head in sympathy. Arnold had never struck her as Mr. Sensitive, but he was probably loaded on his own wares. "He took you to Dickie?"

"No, he wouldn't do it. He said he was too freaked out to go back. He just told me where he was."

Poor Dawn. She'd had to "discover" the body herself.

"You can get Dickie picked up, right? He can't just *lie* there!"

"Oh. Yeah, I'll try. I'll call it in right away." It was so weird to be saying that. In normal times, she'd have called it in from the scene and waited there with Dawn, till district officers arrived; and then homicide and the coroner. But she hadn't bothered because she knew she wasn't going to get any action. Dickie, like Abasolo's buddy's dead lady, was just one of dozens, maybe hundreds of dead people lying in the streets, not to mention the many more victims dead in houses and nursing homes, the unlucky people in places they couldn't escape from.

There was a plan in place for the bodies—a temporary morgue in St. Gabriel—but Dickie would have to wait his turn to be collected.

Skip called it in now, with Dawn listening, so the wife in her could at least have that satisfaction.

"Maybe he was robbed," Dawn said.

Skip produced the wallet. "I found this on him. And they didn't take the gun. Did he take any money with him?"

Dawn took the wallet and opened it. "We only had fifteen dollars left—with no ATMs working. I gave him five dollars just in case." She pulled out a sopping five-dollar bill. "It's still here." Under the circumstances—chain of evidence be damned—Skip was glad she'd rescued a third of the Horvaths' minuscule fortune.

"Well, it wasn't robbery. Any idea who'd do this to him?"

Dawn just shook her head. And Skip found herself remembering the weird conversation she'd had with Dickie —the one in which he'd offered to sell her information.

A creepy-crawliness wriggled up her spine. She'd felt the same thing at Trent's.

"Can I call someone to come stay with you?" Exactly how she was going to do that she wasn't sure.

But Dawn shook her head. "Everyone we know here evacuated."

"Listen, you've got to get out of here. I can get you on one of the buses."

She shook her hear violently. "I couldn't leave Dickie."

Skip went next door to get Ollie to babysit her. She was going to owe her big-time, but it had to be done.

"Arnold Acrobat was here," Ollie said. "He told me Dickie's a gone pecan."

"So I hear. Sensitive dude."

"I wonder if we're all gone pecans. The whole city's a gone pecan." Ollie's voice had taken on a slight edge of desperation.

That was all Skip needed. Ollie had been her rock throughout the ordeal. She needed her to keep it together. "Ollie, you okay?"

"Running out of meds," she said. "Only taking half a dose."

"Aren't there any 'open' drugstores?"

Ollie shrugged. "Yeah, but you can imagine…"

"Right. Stripped. You know what? You've got to get out of here."

"Yeah, you keep sayin' that."

"Seriously."

"They'll have to carry me out in a box. Like all those people on the barges."

"Uh-oh. Is that the Rumor Of The Day?"

"You didn't know about that? That's what they're doing with the bodies. Just loading them on barges and shipping them out. God knows where they'll end up. In the river probably. With all those gangsters."

"Well, I guess they have to clean up the city fast—for all those high-rises going in in the Lower Nine."

"You makin' fun of me?"

"Only a little. Could you go see what you can do for Dawn?"

She'd expected something along the lines of "Are you *kidding* me?" followed by a lengthy negotiation. But Ollie just said, "Sure," and stood up to go next door.

25

A t first Adam was pissed as hell to be taken off search-and-rescue, but, making an effort to regain a nugget of serenity, he thought it through and realized that might make some kind of sense to someone. The pros were moving in, so there might not be that much need for cops to be doing it anymore, and there was plenty of other policing to do. That would be the rationale anyhow. It might look different on the streets—or canals, to be more realistic—but he had no choice but to go with it.

The silver lining was, the reassignment was a great opportunity to look for Serena Thompson. She had to be at the Superdome or the Convention Center, didn't she? Where else was there to be?

Plenty of places. She could somehow have been evacuated. She could be with relatives, or sleeping under a tarp somewhere. She could even be dead. But looking in the most highly populated places was playing the odds. That was good enough for now.

He wished he had a megaphone. How was he going to ask around—just walk into the Superdome and beat on a glass with a spoon? But once he had the idea of making an announcement, it was only a short step from there to a sign. A sign would be good! But not good for a cop to be carrying. He was supposed to be breaking up fights and helping people in trouble, which, when he thought about it, was just about everybody. Everybody needed something.

The sign was a thought, but he needed help.

He tried calling Langdon. "Hey. You okay?"

"Depends on your definition. Got waked up by a neighbor who found her husband dead. And there's this heinous rumor going around."

"The one about the cop assassins? I mean 'executioners'. Have you dispatched your quota today? I might be up one or two—I could give you a couple if you need them."

"It's not funny, A.A. It's really bugging me."

"Hey! Don't let it get to you. A rumor's *all* it is—just a bunch of angels dancing on a few million neurotransmitters. It'll be forgotten just as soon as any other rumor."

"Oh, I guess so. I'm just a little done in by everything. But enough about me. How're you?"

He didn't speak for a moment, fighting a sudden impulse to tell her everything.

"Adam?" She sounded slightly alarmed. "You okay?"

He stopped fighting the impulse. "You mind talking for a minute? I can't get hold of my sponsor and all the best meetings are in Baton Rouge right now." He snorted.

"Sure," she said, and repeated it. "Sure. You know I'm always here for you. You want to come over?"

"Naaah, just a sympathetic ear."

"Tell me everything."

It sounded so out-of-context he almost laughed. It was what she usually said when she wanted gossip. "Let's see, where to start? Ok, how about this: I'm Adam and I'm an alcoholic. Having kind of a hard week here; you know, one thing and another; lot of people dying, lot of people crying; saved a few folks, made a new friend."

She snickered. "Quit trying to make me laugh."

"Your brother, incidentally. He's the new friend. Good guy. Oh, yeah and my house got blown away."

He heard her loud breath intake. "Adam, I'm so sorry."

"Quit calling me Adam, for God's sake. You never call me that."

"I do when things get serious. It's completely gone?"

"Not a stick left. Conrad took me out to the lake. We didn't get up close, but all the boathouses were smithereens."

"Oh, Christ. I'd forgotten you moved to a boathouse."

"Well, I thought that would make me feel better—to know one way or another. And it actually did, for a bit. But there's this other thing bothering me. Nasty little piece of unfinished business."

She spoke cautiously. "Something...to do with that doctor at Charity? Kathy something?"

He was taken aback. "Why would you say that?"

"It just seemed like...she kept talking about you. Like she knows you real well."

He hadn't seen this coming and didn't want it at the forefront of his consciousness. He wished she hadn't brought it up. "Okay, that's something I need to talk about, but not now, okay? This is about that baby I brought in—you know, the one Conrad dived for?"

"Sure, I remember. Do we know how he's doing?"

"No, I don't even know if he's still at Charity. But here's what's bugging me—we didn't take his mother with him."

"You couldn't, right?"

"It seemed like that at the time, but we could have. We

should have. We were just too overwhelmed to think straight, and Nathan—the baby—almost drowned, so we didn't think there was a second to waste. But we should have taken a minute. Now I can't get that poor woman out of my mind."

"It wasn't...you couldn't..."

He cut her off. She was trying to console him in all the ineffective ways people who weren't in the program did. "Wait. Just listen for a minute, okay? Pretend you're in the program."

"Oh, right, I forgot." He knew she knew plenty about it —she'd once gone undercover in Codependents Anonymous.

"So I called my old sponsor—ex-cop named Baldwin Devillier..."

"Oh, yeah, I remember him—got in big trouble with Public Integrity." The NOPD's name for "Internal Affairs".

"Baldy gave me a great piece of advice. To forget about the things I can't change and work on the things I can."

"Isn't that the serenity prayer?"

"Yeah—a version of it. So look...I can't change the fact that I left that woman crying for her baby, but maybe I can change the outcome."

He waited a while for Skip to figure out what he meant, but she didn't answer. Finally he said, "I have her name. I need to see if I can find her."

She didn't hesitate. "How can I help?"

"Ever clever Langdon. You figured out I need more than a shoulder to cry on."

This time there was a long pause. "Uh-uh, A.A. You've got it backwards. Of course you can have anything you want from me. But if you just wanted something, you'd have asked for that thing first. I take very seriously the fact that you told me you needed a meeting. I want you to know I'll listen to you any time you need me to."

"Thanks, I appreciate that." He was aware that his voice was a little thick. "Okay, here's what I need. That kid Billy."

"Oh, the little shit who stole his gun back. Well, I might have an idea."

~

BILLY HAD TAKEN NOT ONLY his piece from the cop's house, but as much food as he could stuff in his clothes. Fortunately, he knew from shoplifting how to make stuff invisible. His piece was giving him confidence, but when all was said and done, not enough to go looking for Petey and Dalton. For all he knew, there was an IBoys spy on every corner.

He could tell, even from across the street, that there were still lots of people in the Iberville Projects. There was water there, but only a couple, maybe three feet, and most of the doors didn't open right on the ground. The buildings had steps with stoops, so he figured mostly people were dry inside, just kind of stuck there unless they didn't mind wading. But a little water sure wasn't going to stop the IBoys.

The thing that taunted him was he could actually see Aunt Makayla's crib from Basin St. He wished like hell he could work up the nerve to go over there, but every time it seemed like he was going to, he saw someone who looked like Petey.

He ended up crashing on the neutral ground on Rampart with a bunch of other people, figuring nobody was going to come looking for him in the dark and if they did, he was just another body in jeans and a T-shirt.

No way you were sleeping late that way, so he was up at sunrise. He dozed a little more, but as soon as the sun was all the way up, everything heated up like you flipped a switch. He was hot and dirty and not in the mood to eat the week-old banana that was all he had left. He removed it from his pocket and offered it to a little kid, who took one look at it and burst into tears. Some other time, Billy would have laughed. He didn't this morning. He knew too much about how the kid felt. He thought maybe dawn was a good time to try to make it over to Kayla's and hadn't gone far when he saw the boat, a little flat-bottomed one, maybe a duck boat, with two people in it, making straight for Kayla and Paul's.

Holy shit! He couldn't believe the two eyes peering out of his head. It was Skip Langdon herself and one of her white po-lice buddies, probably. She said she'd come for them and she was doing it—*what the fuck*! That was twice she hadn't fucked him over—what was this, an alternate universe? Well, he'd asked her—at some level, he must have thought she might do it. But maybe not; maybe he thought he just had to try. He couldn't get over it.

He wondered if he should go over there and help, but then what? Was she going to take him in again? That could be good, but he doubted it. And who was the other guy? He was afraid they'd make him go with Kayla and Paul. He wondered if that would be a bad thing. Maybe he could help with Paul. But then he'd have to leave his mama. He wasn't ready for that. He didn't think they'd let him back in the hospital, but he needed to be ready to follow if she got evacuated. No way he could just leave her alone.

Standing there, watching those cops go in the house, he hatched an idea. He could walk over there right now, and hang out around a corner somewhere where they couldn't see him. If he got attacked, he'd holler real loud—or start shooting—and maybe they'd help him. Then when they left, he'd be close enough to make a run for Kayla and Paul's.

He thought about it while the cops tied up the boat, gaining confidence by the second. It was way too early for gangstas, he knew that from knowing his brother and Kaynard. And right now he'd be more or less covered anyway. So, yeah. It was his best shot.

Yeah.

Paul walked out on the stoop, propped up by the three others, but he was still walking, looking like a senator or something. Granted, a fat senator, but a handsome, dignified man, a man who had it all together and who was going out in the world looking his best. And Makayla looked like an African singer with that turban and stuff. Sure enough, just like the mama she was, she had a pack full of stuff, probably for Paul.

Hold it here—it looked like...all their mouths were moving at once, and he could hear it, ever so faintly. They were *singing*. All four of them. He shouldn't have been surprised. Paul had a great voice. Before he became a minister, he'd sung in the choir and sometimes even a band. And here he was, singing again, as he left for who-knew-where. Billy'd heard they were taking people to overpasses to wait for rescue helicopters, maybe buses too. Had to be scorching misery out there. He didn't even know if Makayla and Paul knew that much, trapped like they were. But here they were, all dressed up and ready for anything. Singing all the way.

He felt tears spring up—who asked for *that*? He couldn't help it, he just felt so proud of his aunt and uncle. He tried to get used to the sensation—he'd never felt proud of his family before. He had to fight to hold his mama together and Kaynard was sure nothing to be proud of, and Makayla was more or less the mama he didn't really have, he didn't think about her any other way...*oh, wait!* He'd been proud of one person. Ivory. And then Ivory had shattered all that by becoming a gangsta. He could feel his forehead wrinkling at the memory.

He put Ivory out of his mind and sneaked across the street, up behind Paul and Makayla's building like he'd planned, and watched. They stopped singing when they got to the boat.

It was quite a trick wrestling Paul from the stoop to the boat, and took all three of the others. But Paul was making jokes the whole time, Billy could hear him, and Skip and the other cop were treating him so gently. Makayla was rougher, but funny. "Come on, Fats Domino, you better find some way to get in this boat, or it's gon' be *Ain't That A Shame* 'stead of *Blueberry Hill.*"

That made him laugh and bust out with a chorus of *Blueberry Hill.* And it got him in the boat, which rocked like it was going to capsize, but it held. And then it put-putted away, leaving Billy feeling bereft.

But now he could sneak into their crib. He had a key, but it didn't even matter—they'd forgotten to lock the door. He didn't, though. Once inside, he felt safe for the first time since the night his mama turfed him out.

The place stank. Three days with no toilets flushing, one person sick, no refrigerator, and no garbage pick-up had set up a tropical reek that made him so sad and miserable the first thing he did was clean the place up. Even before he foraged for food. He even worked up the nerve to put the garbage out on the stoop. Even if the IBoys saw it, they'd think Makayla had done it. He hoped.

After he did that, he found some peanut butter and moldy bread that tasted like a banquet. And then he went to sleep—a real sleep this time, not a jittery outdoor nap with a thousand other people, half of them crying, the other half walking around and stepping over him whenever they felt like it.

He woke up and ate some more and went back to sleep. He should have been bored as hell, but mostly he just couldn't seem to stay awake. He had a whole day and night of peace and quiet, not being scared, not being homeless, and having enough to eat before the cop came for him.

26

F or an emergency psychiatrist, Kathy was spending a
lot of time in the maternity unit. There being no
Pediatrics facility, they'd housed Nathan with the
other babies. Nutty as she knew it to be, she couldn't bring
herself to stop obsessively checking on Nathan. It was kind
of a running medical joke about psychiatrists being the
craziest people around, and right now she felt as if she was
doing her part for the mythology.

Try as she might, and as much as she needed to, she
couldn't seem to stay in the present, couldn't keep her mind
off that moment nearly two years ago when she'd destroyed
her own life and ended her child's. It was at a kid's birthday
party, one of those contemporary extravaganzas for the
extended family and all the kid's friends and all the friends'
parents. Whatever happened, she'd often wondered, to cake,
ice cream, and presents? Period. This one involved a bouncy
house, a magician, a face painter, a truckload of barbecue,
and an ocean of booze for the grown-ups. And a swimming
pool.

All it took was a second. Another kid fell down, Kathy

turned to help, and for a minute, maybe two—couldn't have
been more than five—with twenty-five moms and twenty-
two dads in attendance, three-year-old Alyssa, paddling
happily in the pool, was without her own personal life-
guard. Nobody saw her go under, nobody knew what
happened. All Kathy knew was that by the time she'd examined the kid who'd fallen for breaks and sprains, the person
she loved most in the world, the one who depended on her
most in the world, had drowned. On her own mom's watch.

Her dad was a sperm donor. So no one, no one in the
world, bore responsibility but Kathy.

How did you get over something like that? She'd asked
her own shrink the question and been assured that Kathy
would. Kathy didn't think so.

She'd remain depressed and angry at herself, and utterly
without self-worth and stark raving mad the rest of her life.
She even hated herself for the only good thing that had
happened to her since Alyssa's death—her relationship with
Adam. A good man was not only hard to find, he was damn
near non-existent, and Adam was the genuine article. That
was why she'd let herself have the pleasure of his company,
something she should never have done, because now he'd
been drawn into the desperate miasma she called a life. He
didn't deserve that. What was she thinking?

She'd deceived him, in a way, like failing to let him know
she had an STD or something. "Baggage" usually meant
relatives or illnesses, but there was psychic baggage too.
Kathy hadn't disclosed hers.

She felt bad about that, and she was still torn in shreds
over Alyssa's death. If Nathan didn't get out of this alive, she
wasn't sure she was going to make it either. He'd had
bronchial problems after nearly drowning, but there were
babies in worse shape. Brand new ones. A couple had been

evacuated by some civilian guys in boats who'd been taught to hand-bag them on the spot. They were airlifted to hospitals in Houston, but there was only room for two—meaning two caregivers to hold the babies—and Nathan wasn't in quite as much danger as the smaller ones. But he *was* in danger, Kathy could see it. He was getting better, his doctor said, Kathy shouldn't worry so much, but the doctor didn't get it, Kathy *had* to save this kid. To make up for Alyssa. Or something.

Well, that was too pat—kind of a layman's analysis. It was more complicated—it was just that, having done such a disastrous thing to a child, she had to see this almost-drowned child to safety.

He was a sweet little thing too. She could pick him up and play with him and he'd coo and giggle just like a little kid leading a normal life. That was killing her. It was really messing her up, wondering if he'd ever get back to his family. She wanted to take him with her, when they were all evacuated, to personally track down his mom and return him, but she knew it wasn't going to happen that way. She couldn't leave her patients. She was going to have to see them to safety and someone else—maybe the doctor who said he was getting better—was probably going to escort Nathan to the next way station. And leave him there.

Kathy knew she would never leave him.

When she got Adam's text, it was an answered prayer—almost as if he'd read her mind. "Looking for Nathan's mother," he said. "Serena Thompson. Pin a note to him just in case." They had his mother's name—had gotten it from Adam when they checked the baby in—but it meant so much to her that he was actively looking. If he was doing something, maybe she could relax her vigilance a little.

You know what? she told herself. *You are really around the bend.* But was it so bad to feel a little better?

Norm came storming into her office. "Reporting in," he said, and feigned a salute. "Armed gangsters have *not* broken into our pharmacy and stolen all our drugs."

Kathy could feel her forehead wrinkle as she tried to figure it out. "And that's news why?" she finally asked.

"Yesterday we'd been evacuated, today we've been robbed. Except not. Just thought you'd want to know."

"Oh. Radio again?"

"To be fair, I believe it was a different station. Now observe." He hauled out a bit of equipment. "This is my demonstration for the day. All the toilets are officially out of commission, so this is ~~what~~ how we will henceforth separate ourselves from our four-legged friends." He lined a bucket with a plastic bag, added bleach, and deftly tied the top. "I think you know what goes in after the bleach."

"Oh, goody. Something new to amuse the patients. Let's call a meeting and pass out pails and bags. They'll get a kick out of it. And also be happy to avoid those disgusting toilets."

"On it." He stood up to go.

"But one question. Then what?"

He looked confused. While she waited for him to figure it out, she realized for the first time that even he was showing signs of wear. Bags had developed under his eyes, and his skin looked slightly rough and grayish. His hair was growing in, but that couldn't be avoided, nor could his beard be halted. The resulting fuzziness was a slightly out-of-focus look that unnerved her. He looked less than alert, and Norm was the most alert person in the hospital—if he went fuzzy on her, it was over. She tried to shake it, thinking she couldn't lose it, worrying about Norm losing it. There were just too many ways to find yourself swimming upstream around here, and she didn't mean on Gravier River, as they'd taken to calling the street outside.

"You mean after the bag has...uh... served its purpose?"

"Yes. Do we have a disposal plan?"

His impish look, one of her favorite Norm expressions, molded itself to his features. "Well...guess we can thank Rafe for knocking those windows out."

She couldn't help it, she let out a delighted hoot.

"You're really gonna tell a hundred crazy people to throw poop bombs out the window?"

As the thought took hold, the imp turned into an evil genie. "Mwhahahaha!" he bellowed, practically dancing out of the room.

Well, okay, then, he could handle the meeting—it looked like he was going to have the time of his life. That meant she had time to locate sign-making materials. Somebody had some, somewhere, because signs had begun to appear in the windows: "God help Us Get the Fuck Out of Here." And "A Thousand People Still Here! Don't Forget Us!"

Or we'll poop-bomb you, Kathy added mentally.

But that wasn't the sign she intended to make. Her sign had a very specific purpose.

I need some crayons, she thought, telling herself that that was the one and only reason she was once again headed for the maternity unit, where supplies were kept for visiting siblings.

She used purple to outline six-inch yellow letters that spelled out "SERENA THOMPSON, NATHAN IS SAFE! TEXT Dr. KATHY BORDELON!" She added her own cell number, thinking that, at least at the moment, she was in no danger of crank calls.

ADAM ARRIVED at Billy's aunt's apartment dressed for wading and armed with a megaphone. He tried knocking politely, to no avail. Then he tried some scary police knocks, accompanied by "Open up in there." Finally, sighing, he resorted to the megaphone.

"Billy Polite, this is the police." He was going to follow that up with a nice threatening little speech about busting down the door, but it was flung open almost the minute he'd said Billy's name.

"You gon' get me killed." The kid's eyes were pie plates, his body battle-ready, but Adam was pleased to see his hands were properly in place over his head.

"Hi, Billy, I'm Adam. Mind if I come in?" Not waiting for an answer, he stepped over the threshold, noting a gun on a nearby table. Casually, he picked it up and stuck it in his waistband. "You can put your hands down. This is a friendly visit."

Now the kid was furious. "Fuckin' white po-lice! What you think you doin', come to my house like this?"

"Your house? Somehow, I thought that was over in Treme. Isn't this more like your aunt and uncle's house? You break in or what?"

"I got a key. How come you know me?"

"Friends with Skip Langdon. You know...white po-lice keeps savin' your skinny ass?"

He ignored the dig. "You don't know nothin'. What you think you doin', come over here like this? My ass is on the line, man."

"Yeah, let's talk about that. Mind if we sit down?" He marched into the living room, made himself comfortable, and kept talking. "I came to offer you a job, tell you the truth. Need a little help with something. But it looks like you need help yourself, son. What are you so afraid of?"

The kid sulked for a while, finally decided he might as well get the conversation over with. "You mighta heard—they got gangs in these projects."

"Yeah, right. This seems a little personal."

"You just let the IBoys know where I am."

"And why would the dreaded IBoys care about a nerd like you?"

"I ain't no nerd."

"Yes you are." Adam picked up a book Billy'd left open on the sofa. "First of all, you're reading a book when you don't even have to."

"No TV and no Internet. You mighta heard about that too."

"Second of all, it's by Toni Morrison. Pretty classy stuff."

He shrugged. "Just somethin' my aunt had lyin' around."

"Beloved," Adam said. "You know what? That's my favorite book in the world. How you like it so far?"

"Hey, man! You come over here for a book report? What the hell's up with you?"

"Langdon says you're a nice kid. She's real mad at you for taking the gun—"

"It was *my* fuckin' gun!"

"Yeah, that's what I told her. I thought, you being so young and all, it might even come in handy." He handed it back. "Here you go."

Billy took it, unloaded it, and sat back in his chair, looking a lot more relaxed. "So... uh... was that even legal? What you just did?"

"You mean giving a minor a gun?" He grinned at the kid. "Not too sure, to tell you the truth—since it's yours and all I did was return it. But it's damn sure illegal for you to have it."

"I can't figure you out, man. What the hell do you want?"

"I need a wing man."

The kid was perfectly still, like he was going to miss something important if he made a false move.

"See, I need to find somebody, but I've also got to work. The city's paying me to keep the peace, you know? I can't just quit doing what I'm supposed to and go off on my own."

The kid scoffed. "Hah. That's a new one."

"What? You don't think we got honest cops in this town?" He laughed. "Maybe one or two. Langdon, for instance. You're her guy, so you're my guy. Understand?"

The kid just looked confused. He probably *didn't* understand, but Adam wasn't going to go all Big Brother on him.

"Look, I need you to help me find somebody. Just come with me this morning. Then you can come back here and read your book."

"Can't come back here. You just gave me away."

"You can stay with me."

"Oh, *hell* no. Not stayin' with no faggot po-lice."

That made Adam smile. The kid's mama might be nuts, but at least she'd given the standard warnings. "Langdon then. You like dogs?"

He seemed to perk up, but didn't give away too much. "Yeah, I know Angel."

"Done deal then."

He was going to owe Langdon one.

27

The rumor about cops as executioners was nagging Skip like a backache. She didn't like that Dickie Horvath had claimed to know all about it, had offered to sell the information, and had ended up dead. Who knew who he'd shot off his mouth to?

If Ollie was her neighborhood rock, she had a couple of professional rocks as well—Abasolo, of course, was pretty much Gibraltar. The other was Cappello. If anything un-Kosher was going on, these two wouldn't be involved. But anyone else...especially this week...she just couldn't be sure of.

After a few hours in the Eighth, which was relatively quiet right now, she needed to head to the Convention Center, where a lot of the action had shifted in the last few days. But first, a quick stop at home to change clothes. She'd developed a habit of wearing plain clothes when working in her own neighborhood, but she wanted to wear at least a uniform shirt, no matter how grubby and wrinkled—at the Convention Center and Superdome. In crowds, people had to be able to see she was a cop. But, Lord, it was hot for that!

She looked at her watch. She'd also promised A.A. she'd be home for twenty minutes to let Billy in. She was stuck with him again, thanks to her favorite partner's generosity—not to mention impulsiveness. The conversation had gone like this:

"Bet Angel gets lonely with you having to work all day and all."

"A.A., you need a place to crash for a while? Come on over! Take the Big House. Cuddle up in Jimmy Dee's king-size bed with Angel."

"Well, it's not exactly me. See, my man Billy's been helping me find Serena Thompson. You were right by the way, he was staying at his aunt's. But he claims I messed that up for him by calling him out with the megaphone."

"You didn't! The kid's only fifteen."

"Yeah, I know. If I said I was just trying to see if it was working, you wouldn't believe me, would you?"

"Probably not. But how come that messed it up for him?"

"He says the IBoys are after him."

"Why? What'd he steal from them?"

"Ever the cynic." She could hear him sighing softly. "Tell you the truth, I haven't pried that out of him yet. But he's homeless and it's on me. Besides...he's got a gun to return to you."

As soon as she heard that, she knew it was for Billy's benefit—the kid had to be listening. "Tell him Angel will be receiving between 11:30 and 11:50 a.m. And you owe me one."

"Roger that." He sighed again. "And thanks."

She had her back to the street, with her key in the door leading to her courtyard, when she heard some kind of small noise behind her. Without thinking, she spun around. A fist landed on her jaw. A big, meaty one, judging from the way it felt. She was reeling, trying not to fall, when she heard someone shouting.

"Hey, stop that! Goddammit, leave her alone." She heard someone running towards her as her knees buckled. She broke her fall with her hands, sliding slowly down the door, back still more or less to the street.

Then she heard her assailant running and her rescuer chasing him. It was definitely a "him". She hadn't noticed much else except a ball cap and shades, but he was bigger than Skip, and she stood six feet tall.

It took a few minutes to get her breath back, but as soon as she was breathing right, she scrambled up, turned the key, and tumbled into the courtyard, feeling slightly bad about not giving chase. Because her rescuer was Billy, she was almost sure. But the two of them—Billy and her attacker—could be blocks away by now, and she still needed some time to recover.

She shot the deadbolt and then sat down at Jimmy Dee's glass-topped café table, trying to decide whether any bones were broken. Inside, Angel barked like the Cossacks were coming.

She was still for a few moments, just breathing, waiting for the pain to subside. *It could have been anyone,* she thought. *A mugger, maybe... who knows?*

But she knew in her heart it wasn't any mugger. She'd been targeted.

This week no one was going to miss her if she took a few minutes to try to hide the damage, but she called Cappello anyhow. "Anything urgent? I'm kind of delayed over here."

"What's going on?"

"Nothing bad. Anything I should know?"

Cappello sighed. "Oh, there's always something. This

one's kind of jaw-dropping. We're hearing people are shooting at rescue choppers."

Skip considered. "Oh, sure. And they're taking bodies out on a barge."

Cappello laughed. "Yeah, you right. I don't have any first-hand reports. I do believe the takeaway of the week might be don't believe it if you didn't see it with your own two orbs."

"You're the only person I know who can get 'yeah, you right' and 'orbs' in the same sentence."

"Naaah. A.A. could do it. He's the one who taught me 'orbs'."

Skip said, "God, I miss working with him. Can't we get him back at the Eighth?"

"I wish. But you'll see him today. He's working the Superdome. Bet you can find him there." Skip bet so too. She'd already arranged to meet him.

"Oh, yeah," she said. "Where the roving gangs of thugs are." Another unsubstantiated rumor.

"Girl got killed in the bathroom. Somebody slashed her throat. Or was that the Convention Center? Get out there and restore order, okay?"

Skip laughed and even Cappello managed a chuckle. Gallows humor was the order of the day, a reminder that, as bad as things were, they weren't nearly as bad as the stories out there.

Okay, then. She had her orders, such as they were. She let Angel out to pee, then went into the bathroom to find some make-up. A cop with a big black bruise on her face just didn't inspire confidence.

A quick cover-up and two Advils later she was out the door. She was too antsy to wait any longer for Billy. He'd just have to fend for himself for a while. She hoped like hell he was okay.

She found Abasolo trying to talk sense to some guy from FEMA who'd come to pick up bodies. "What? You're telling me good news is...fake news? I'm not covering anything up. Why the hell would we hide bodies? And the bigger question is: where? In the river?"

Skip felt a prickle at the base of her scalp.

"I got a report you got 200 bodies in there, and I've got a refrigerated truck to take 'em away. Why have you guys got a problem with that? You can't just let 'em rot in there."

"Go get 'em, Rambo. You see me stoppin' you?"

"I've already been in there."

"Yeah—how many bodies you find?'

The FEMA guy looked sheepish. "Six. I know there's gotta be more somewhere. I got a job to do."

"Well, you're looking in the wrong place. We got plenty on the streets. I got a woman to hug." He turned to Skip and caught her up in the mother of all bear hugs. "Whereyat, Langdon? Been missin' you down here. I could use a little sarcasm today."

"You people," the FEMA guy said. "You just can't be serious about anything, can you? What kinda place is it where cops make out in public?"

Skip couldn't help it, the irony of that struck her funny-bone. She and Abasolo were about as much a couple as George Bush and Condoleeza Rice. But they'd needed that hug like a baby needs its mama.

Everything she'd been holding in for days escaped in a giggle. Abasolo caught it, and the next thing you knew they were laughing so helplessly she was afraid someone was going to come along and slap them sober.

The FEMA guy went away muttering about everybody down here being nuts.

"Yeah," said Abasolo. "That's why they call us The Big Crazy."

And that set Skip off again. When she recovered, she said, "He'll be the first one on Bourbon St. tonight. Hollerin' and dancing on tables."

"Bourbon Street's crankin'?"

"Couple places, sure. The strippers love it. Say they look better by candlelight."

"You're making that up. There can't be strippers left around here."

"Yeah, I am. But I wouldn't be surprised."

"Mind if I ask you what's up with the face?"

Skip touched her jaw and winced. "You can see it, huh? I thought I covered it up."

"Sorry to say your make-up job has suffered a meltdown."

"Damn heat! Well, it's a story, and Billy might be involved."

"*Billy* did that?"

"No, of course not. I think he chased away the guy who did. He never showed up to babysit Angel. Actually, I really need to talk. Are you done with the FEMA guy?"

"Totally done! Guy brought four docs and a refrigerated truck to pick up all the bodies he thought he'd find. Know what it boils down to? Looks like only those six people he found died in the Superdome, just about everybody from natural causes. Although one guy did jump..."

"Ooooh!" she covered her ears. "Don't tell me."

"Some tough cop."

"I just hate to think of the *SPLAT*! With all those people in there."

Abasolo guffawed. "Don't get me started again."

"I didn't mean to make fun of it. I mean... you can't blame the guy, can you? But think how much worse that must have made it for everyone else."

A.A. was suddenly serious. "This is hell, girl. Hell squared, truth be told. The other five probably died of fright. Come on, walk with me. I've got to checkout a possible body on Diamond Street."

"Yeah? What's so special about this one—we got bodies littering the landscape."

"Now, now. Cynicism doesn't become you. Got a report it might be a cop. Weird thing. Second time in two days. Although if it is, what we're gonna do about it I have no idea. Maybe notify next of kin if it's someone we know. Probably not much else is gonna happen."

She thought about Dickie. "Yeah. One of my neighbors got killed. He's still lying in the street."

"Hope it wasn't a friend."

"Fortunately, not so much. Asshole, actually. But, God, I hate to see it. It's just not decent."

Abasolo made a sound like a bark. "Yeah. That's what my buddy said when he found that body on Jackson Avenue. Those were the days! Poor naïve soul actually thought the coroner was going to come. You believe how innocent we were a week ago?"

"I've now heard that story about eight more times, mostly from people who didn't believe it. Sounds like just another rumor, right? You sure you really saw it?"

"Saw it and smelled it. Would I make up a thing like that?"

"The way stories are flying around you can't tell what's real and what's not." She paused, seeing an opening. "Which brings me to what I need to talk to you about."

"What, rumors?" He shrugged, then got her drift. "Oh. You mean the cop assassin story. Round up the usual suspects, kill them, and throw them in the river."

"Listen, A.A., I think it might be true. But you're the only person in the entire city I can trust."

"Well, there's Cappello."

"Yeah. But she can't know...at least not yet. This is just between you and me, right?"

"You don't even have to ask."

"What do you know about it?"

"Are you seriously asking me—again—if it's for real?" He was outraged. "Whothehell would give an order like that? Right. No one. And no one, but no one would do it *without an order,* but out of the kindness of their cold, cold heart. Just to clean the city up."

"Well, when you put it like that, I'm pretty reassured. If there's no profit motive, nobody's doing it. Nobody in this department, anyhow."

"Not even the Dirtbaggs." It was their nickname for Elvis and Kirkus Baggs, a couple of cop brothers everybody knew were dirty, but who kept skating, probably because their family was old line cop royalty.

"Well, *maybe* not the Dirtbaggs," she said. "But a few things have happened..."

As they reached Diamond St., he was suddenly distracted. "Wait, here we are. Hey, can we table that for a few? I want to give it my full attention. And right now we gotta start looking for a body."

lready they could see there wasn't one. The street was only a couple of blocks long, divided by a neutral ground as big as a park. But just in case, they strode its length, looking in doorways and behind anything that hadn't been blown away.

Then they walked the other side.

"Officers! Hey, y'all po-lice?" It was a woman's voice, coming from above.

On a third-floor balcony sat an African-American woman who looked to be about seventy-five. Drinking a cup of something at a small table. "You need something?" Skip hollered.

"Yeah. Ran out of water yesterday. Afraid to go out and try to find some." Along with no electricity, there was no available safe drinking water. She held up her cup. "This is warm Coke and it's *nasty*."

"I got an extra bottle," Skip said. "Can you catch?"

She reached into her backpack and threw the bottle. It took several tries to get it to the woman. She wasn't very agile to begin with, and seemed a little groggy. Dehydrated, maybe.

"Hot up there?" Skip asked. The woman was in a loft building of about four stories.

"Not so bad. I got the balcony." She looked slightly gray.

Abasolo said, "What's your name? We're going to get you some water. You got food?"

"I got food. My name's Josie."

"I'm Adam. And this is Skip."

"Skip? That ain' no name for a girl!"

"Look, Josie, we're gonna holler for you when we get back and you can throw us down a key. All right?"

She looked dubious.

"Or you can come down and get the water. We'll try to get you a case."

"Key'll be ok."

Skip said, "Somebody over at the Convention Center's gotta have water." The second big evacuation scene along with the Superdome. It was just around the block.

"Yeah, the military," Abasolo said. "And all the journalists. I've made friends with a few."

Skip just bet he had. Female ones. "Ok, here's a riddle for you. How many cops who have an entire world of chaos to take care of does it take to keep one old lady from dying of thirst?"

"Relax, Langdon. They're loading the last of the buses. Things are better. We're still doing our jobs. Let's just do it in a low-key way for a few while you tell me about the face. You never got to that, you know. That man-bear of yours slip-and-fall on it? Oh, right—he's in L.A."

She laughed. Her man-bear, Steve Steinman, was the gentlest of men. "Right indeed. He doesn't understand why I don't call him three times a day. None of them do. Jimmy Dee, Cindy Lou..."

She stopped, remembering their friend Cindy Lou was his sometime-sweetie. "You talking to Cindy Lou?"

Abasolo sighed. "Yeah, briefly. I just can't..."

"I know. Can't focus on anything but this. And too tired. And don't want to tell the story ten times a day. Am I right?"

"Partly, yeah. But also..."

"The lovely Dr. Bordelon?"

He winced. "Yeah. But later for that. What about the face."

"Well, I kept hearing that rumor—about cops taking out the gangs—and then the first person I heard it from ended up dead. I think he was murdered."

"You mean the asshole you mentioned?"

"Yeah, my neighbor, Dickie."

"How?"

"Stab wound, I think, but pretty hard to say. You know"—she waved an arm—"with all this." And all that was missing too. Like an autopsy. "So I might have asked a few people a few questions."

"Uh-huh."

"And then someone slugged me." She told him how it happened, ending with her unseen rescuer.

"What makes you think it was Billy?"

"Pretty sure it was his voice."

"Yeah, you're good with voices."

"He hasn't got a phone, right?"

"Naaah. Almost nobody has, you know? One of the most goddam frustrating things about this whole..." He opened up his arms, as if to accommodate the universe.

"Cataclysm?"

"Apocalypse?"

He was quiet for a while. She let him contemplate the story until they ran into a reporter he knew (female as predicted), and negotiated a water deal—a case for 30 seconds on camera. He used it to make a plea for information about Serena Thompson.

The reporter was mad. "Hey! I get to ask the questions."

"Sorry," Adam said. "That's my subject. Run it, it's a good story."

"Yeah, no question." She brushed hair out of her eyes. "We probably will."

They got their case of water and headed back. Skip said, "You know that little stand-up's going to infuriate the chief, right?"

"He can go screw himself. Did you know he told Oprah people were raping babies in the Dome?"

Skip gasped.

"And other stuff. Like we confiscated thirty guns from people who fired in the Convention Center. Nobody fired a gun in there. Well, maybe one person—I talked to the SWAT team. Billy and I were there almost all morning." He paused. "Asking everyone in the whole goddam place if they know Serena Thompson."

"Ooooh. That's what the megaphone was for."

He looked dejected. "You couldn't even hear it in that place."

"No luck?"

He shook his head, remaining silent as they walked back to Josie's. They were trading off carrying the water, both wishing they'd brought A.A.'s car. They were on Josie's street, though—almost there. Skip was trying to take the case from him when suddenly he dropped it, causing bottles to scatter all over the sidewalk and prompting them both to look down.

"Jesus, what's that?" A.A. was already reaching for his gun. There was something on the sidewalk about a block away—something that looked like a body.

And there sure as hell hadn't been one on this block half an hour ago. Forgetting all about Josie, they broke into a run. It was a dead man with a bandaged head, but they didn't think a head wound had killed him. He'd been stabbed in the belly. Not exactly gutted, but close enough. It was a long, lethal-looking cut, nasty enough to give rise to the gutting rumor. Which was seeming more and more like reality.

Skip searched the man's pockets and came up with a wallet. She took out the driver's license. "I know this guy!"

She passed it to Abasolo, who whistled. "We just caught a big one. This is Kaynard Cochon."

"You're kidding! You know him too?"

"Yeah, sure. He's a lieutenant in the Corner Boys Gang."

"You're *kidding* me," she repeated, trying to take it in. "They're the biggest wholesalers in the city."

"One of 'em," he agreed. "There's more, but they sure move a lot of crack. How do you know him?'"

"Never actually met him. He's Billy's stepfather. Did I tell you the part about taking him home Monday morning?"

"Not that I recall."

"Pretty sure you'd recall." She told him about finding two pools of blood and a giant stash of crack in Billy's house.

"One of the blood spots had to be from Kaynard. Body's fresh, but he could have gotten the head wound that night. I found a little...uh...organic matter."

"Want to take a ride out there, check the place out? And we better find Billy too—he's got a few blanks to fill in."

"Sure. Soon as we get Josie squared away."

As if on signal, they both looked up at her balcony. She

wasn't there, but something was. It looked like a pile of clothes topped by the blue-and-green muu-muu she was wearing when they met her. "Holy shit," Skip said, and they both started running, yelling her name, Kaynard be damned.

The muu-muu had blood all over it—fresh blood, still red—and the pile didn't move. They stood in the neutral ground, swearing. Finally, Abasolo said, "Are you thinking what I'm thinking?"

"That whoever dumped Kaynard saw her watching and shot her? Doesn't seem like much doubt, does there? These guys don't care who they kill."

"I wonder if I can somehow swing onto the second floor balcony and then, maybe..."

"You could if you were with the Cirque de Soleil."

"Ok. But just as a point of discussion, where do we take her if she's alive?"

Skip grabbed his arm. "A.A.! Look. In the right hand corner."

Peeking out of the balcony's open French door was a tiny head. "Oh, God, it's a kid."

"Hi, baby!" Abasolo hollered. "You can come out. Nobody's going to hurt you now. Those men are gone."

"Hello, darlin'," Skip called. "What's your name, baby?"

Gingerly, the child stepped slightly forward, a little girl, five or six, maybe, in shorts and a pink T-shirt with a white heart on it. "My grandma dead." *Day-ed*, she said.

"Honey, don't think that! I bet she's alive. Can you throw us the key so we can come up and try to wake her up? I see it right there." Josie had a bunch of keys waiting on the café table where they'd seen her sitting, anticipating their arrival with the water.

"I cain' do that. My grandma say don't talk to strangers."

Skip thought about trying the old "a policeman is your friend" gambit, but that was sure not going to work on this kid. "Are you thirsty, baby? Your grandma told us she needed some water."

The kid brightened. "You the water po-lice?"

"We sure are." Evidently Josie had mentioned them. After that, it still took a bit of persuading, but eventually the kid dropped the key and they used their flashlights to climb the two pitch-dark staircases to the third floor. They had to walk the halls and bang on doors, yelling, "Josie? Josie's grandbaby? We're here with the water."

Finally they heard, "We in here."

When they'd found the right key and wrestled with the lock in near total darkness, Skip knelt to hug the girl, but she looked so disappointed Skip was taken aback. "You okay, baby?"

"Where's my water?"

"Oh, Jesus." They'd left it lying on the street.

A.A. said, "Let's see about your grandmother first," and raced over to the body. "Skip, she's breathing!"

Stunned, she stared at him. "Unconscious?"

"Yeah."

"What are we going to do?"

"Well, I'm pretty sure we can't get an ambulance."

"Or even a taxi. We could try the fire department," she said doubtfully.

"Dream on," Abasolo said.

The little girl raced excitedly to Abasolo. "She really alive?"

"She really is! Look, see how her chest is moving? We're gonna get y'all somewhere safe."

Skip sighed, wondering how the hell that was going to

work. She heard Abasolo ask the girl her name again. She spoke loud and clear. "Destiny."

Oh, brother, Skip thought. *You said it.*

"Hey, I've got an idea," Abasolo said. "How about I just go out on the street and recruit a couple of guys? I hate to ask you to babysit, but..."

"No, it's good. I'll look around, maybe make some calls." She pointed with her chin at Josie, hoping he'd know what she meant. "You go. Just throw us up a couple of bottles of water."

She had plans for the few minutes his absence would give her. She checked Josie again, seeing she had a wound to her mid-section, just above the waist, and found some towels to use for pressure. Kneeling by the older woman, she said, "Destiny, come talk to me while I take care of your grandma." The girl knelt too, mesmerized by the rise and fall of her grandmother's chest.

"Y'all live here?"

"No, ma'am. We live on Tennessee Street."

That was ominous. "Just the two of you?"

The girl nodded.

"Does the rest of your family live near you?"

"They stay in Lafayette." She looked at the floor. "All 'cept my mama. Don' know where Mama is."

That was sad for Destiny, but Skip was relieved—if her mama had lived on Tennessee St. there was a good chance she'd be dead. Josie'd been wise to bring her granddaughter here—they lived almost on the banks of the Industrial Canal, which inundated the neighborhood when the levee broke. They were almost certainly homeless now.

She asked if Destiny knew whose condo they were in, but all she said was, "my grandma work here."

"OK, then, I'm going to try to find out. Can you sit here

and hold this towel on your grandma? Hold it real tight now." She figured a task was the best babysitter she had access to.

The condo was a very high-end loft, one of the nicest Skip had seen, with two bedrooms, one of which Josie and Destiny were obviously occupying, and an office. Heading for the office, she rifled drawers until she found household bills addressed to Alice and Hutchinson Campbell. That was a start. She retrieved Josie's purse from the bedroom, where she found a cell phone and a driver's license for Josephine Tompkins. The battery was dead, but somewhere in there, she was willing to bet, was a number for her employers.

She pocketed the phone and took the purse with her to wait for Abasolo, trying to text any locals in her directory who might know a doctor. She struck gold with her brother.

"Skippy, how ya doin'? Hangin' in there? How's my buddy A.A?"

"You busy right now?"

"Working with the Cajun Navy today. Whatcha need? Have boat, will travel." Definitely not the old Conrad.

"Good. Got a situation."

"Need somebody rescued?"

"Gunshot victim, hospitals barricaded."

"Came to the right place. I've been taking people to a doctor in your hood." She'd never known Conrad to sound so confident. He really was having the time of his life. "Guy never left. Running a trauma clinic in his office. Even has a nurse. Brave, huh? Most docs'd worry about getting sued."

She heard noise in the hall, probably Abasolo returning. "Gotta go. Address?"

Abasolo barreled in with three good-sized men, two black and one white, all scruffy and smelling none too great, but Skip was just glad there were three. She was strong, but still not confident she'd be much help—and someone had to wrangle Destiny. The largest one, Harland, was as big as a grizzly bear and twice as confident. "I'm gon' make a stretcher," he said. "Y'all got a screwdriver?"

Someone risked Harland's ridicule by producing one on a Swiss Army Knife, but he took it without comment and proceeded to remove the Campbells' bathroom door, onto which they loaded Josie and, guided by Skip's flashlight, wrestled her downstairs, where Abasolo had lined up a makeshift ambulance—a news van complete with driver. "Got money?" he asked Skip, but Harland looked at Josie, now lying on the floor of the van, as if she were his own grandma. "I don't want no money for helpin' this lady." The others were too intimidated not to follow suit.

After shaking hands with "Dan from CNN," Skip said, "I've got the address of a doctor." It was the corner of Frenchmen and Decatur and the doctor was outside smoking a cigarette.

She couldn't help herself: "I thought doctors didn't smoke."

He stared at the little white stick as if he couldn't figure out what it was. "First cigarette in thirty years. Not that this thing's getting to me. I'm Martin Moreau. And you are?"

"Skip Langdon." She flashed her badge. "Got a lady with a gunshot wound."

He sighed and ground out the cigarette with his foot. "You Conrad's sister? He said you were coming."

By the way he walked, she could see how tired he was.

They stuck around while he looked Josie over. "She needs surgery, but the bleeding's stopped." He shrugged. "Since she's stable, I'm going to have to send her to the airport triage center. Hate to, but I can't do surgery here. Got some drivers shuttling people out there. But..." He waved unobtrusively in Destiny's direction, "What about the little girl?"

Skip and A.A. looked helplessly at each other. What if they sent Destiny with her grandmother and Josie died? What would be her chances of finding her family again? But if they didn't, the same reasoning applied.

Abasolo finally said, "Think what that scene's like," and the mental picture was enough. Yesterday, when it was first opening, it was worth trying for Paul and Makayla. But now that it was up and cranking, she knew A.A. was right. It was going to be bedlam. They couldn't send a kid there. Skip said, "We'll figure something out."

29

Fuckin' white cop had a nerve, comin' over like he own the place and blowin' Billy's safehouse in less time than it took to say his name. *Goddam!* Cop didn't have no clue! No clue at all what Billy was up against. Didn't have no clue what his life might be like and didn't give a fuck.

Right now he wasn't so sure about Skip Langdon either. She was the one ratted him out. According to the cop—name of Adam, he said—she saw the garbage outside on the stoop, figured it had to be him. *Stupid, stupid, stupid!* He damn well knew better than that—he just couldn't stand the smell. Damn cop guilted him too. Said Langdon rescued his aunt and uncle, he could damn well return the favor.

Made him a pretty good offer, though—eighty bucks just to run around with him for a couple of hours, him and his megaphone. Had to know Billy would have done it for fifty. Hell, twenty-five!

Looking back, though, Billy had to admit, once they got over the part about whathehell was he doing outside with a megaphone, everything went okay. Billy was eighty dollars richer, even though no stores were open to buy anything. And he still had his piece. Fuckin' cop actually gave him his piece back. Meant he trusted him. That was something. Something good enough for Billy. For now anyhow.

First he wanted to know if Billy could make a sign.

Billy had to grin. "You come to the right place on that one. See, Kayla's political. She's always makin' signs for something. Bet she's got some we can recycle."

Sure enough, he found some in a closet—something about President Bush. *Whoo!* Makayla didn't like him one bit. The cop helped him remove one of them from its wooden handle and make a different sign on the other side. All it said, in great big Magic Marker letters, was a name: *SERENA THOMPSON.* The lady he was trying to find.

"You know her?" the cop asked.

Billy snorted. "You think all black people know each other?"

Cop didn't even get his feelings hurt, just fired back. "What makes you think she's black?"

"You axed me if I know her."

That made them both laugh. The cop wasn't that bad. He explained about why he wanted the lady and Billy knew he wasn't lying—he'd heard about the baby from Dr. Bordelon. It was decent of him, he decided. Trying to put the family back together.

This was something Billy could be proud of. He didn't know when he'd see his own mama again, but at least he could help this baby find his.

"Why not two signs?" he'd asked. "One for you too."

"You kidding? I'm a cop. I can't be walking the streets with a sign. Everbody's gonna think I'm crazy."

Billy laughed. "I think you're crazy."

Adam grinned at him. "Yeah, you're right."

So they walked all around everywhere, Billy with his sign and the cop with his megaphone, asking everyone they saw if they knew where Ms. Thompson was. Adam would just let loose on the streets with that megaphone or in the Superdome, anywhere: "Serena Thompson, I have your baby." Over and over again.

He thought people were gon' think he was crazy for *carrying a sign*? Fuckin' cop was out of his mind.

That wasn't all they did, though. Billy had to give the guy credit for being good at his job—he was actually working while he looked, helping people find other people, or find the buses they needed, sometimes just talking to them...a lot of people just needed to talk, it seemed like. He never knew cops did stuff like that.

"They're hurting," Adam said. "Aren't you?"

"Who, me?" Billy's felt his eyes flood, heard his voice drop. "Got no time to hurt. Gotta get my bi'ness done."

"Oh? And what *is* your business?"

Billy thought about it. "I guess, right now, I just gotta be here for my mama. Gotta make sure she gon' be all right, and figure out where we gon' live. Stuff like that." There was a whole lot more, but Billy didn't go into that. The main thing was staying alive.

The cop nodded. "Maybe I can help you with that."

"For real?" He almost believed him.

"Sure. Let's keep talking. Let me have your phone number."

For some reason, that had made Billy feel small. "Got no phone right now." He knew he sounded sulky.

"Okay, I'll give you mine." He handed over a business card. It was a few minutes before he spoke again, but Billy knew there was something else the cop wanted to say, and he didn't want to hear it.

Adam didn't disappoint. "Maybe I could help right now. I know you got problems with the Iboys. But you don't seem like a gangster to me. You're not, right?"

"You got that right. I ain't no gangsta." The question upset him so much Billy just started blurting. "Gangstas killed my brother. Right in the hospital."

The cop did that thing you see in cartoons—stopped in his tracks and shook his head to get the cobwebs out. Billy figured it was meant to make him laugh, and it almost did. "Come again? What hospital? I didn't hear anything like that."

"Charity. You know about my mama, right? How she off her meds, took a...ummm...well, she kinda took a hostage..."

Adam nodded. "Oh, yeah. I know all about that."

"Well, that was the day after they killed him. She did it to draw attention to Ivory gettin' murdered, but that didn't work too well. They shot him day before the storm, but he didn't die, so they come right in, kill him there."

The cop pondered that awhile. "I think I might need a few more details."

"I don't know *how* they kill him, but they kill him." Billy hated himself for ever opening the subject. He had to get out of this, fast.

"And you would know that...how?"

Billy wished he could seal himself shut. "Just know. That's all."

"Your brother's name was Ivory?"

"Why you need to know?"

"It's not respectful not to use his name."

Billy appreciated that.

"Why would they want to kill Ivory?"

Billy just shrugged, knowing silence was his best friend. Wishing he'd remembered that a minute earlier.

Adam spun him around and made Billy look him in the eye. "Listen, son. When you're ready to talk about this, I'm here."

Billy pulled away from him quick—because his damn eyes were flowing again. *Goddammit, what was up with that?*

"You've had kind of a hard week," Adam said.

"Leave me alone." Billy headed back to Skip's house. He knew he had to be there at a certain time and he was almost late.

Had to book it. Shouldn't have let the other cop draw him into talk that was none of his damn business.

He was just in time, though, coming down her street the same time she was, saw her and waved, but she was too intent on her own business and didn't see him. He didn't see the other guy till Skip turned to unlock her door.

Whathehell? Did that guy actually hit her?

Billy didn't think about what he was doing, he just started running. And yelling.

Whoever the guy was managed to outdistance him and disappear before Billy could even get out of breath, a good thing, since the asshole was a lot bigger than he was. The lucky part was, he didn't look back to see who was chasing him. He'd have recognized Billy before you could say "Kaynard", and probably killed him. 'Cause Billy knew him. He just couldn't understand why he'd just attacked another cop.

Well, he'd ask Miss Skip. He headed back to make sure she was all right—also to keep his date with Angel—but no luck. Seemed like he'd missed her.

30

Quickly, Skip scribbled a note and put it in Josie's purse: "Destiny's with me. I have your phone and keys." She signed it with her name and phone number, gave the purse to Martin Moreau, and crossed her fingers that these two would see each other again. It reminded her uncomfortably of the way Nathan had been whisked away from his mom.

Skip borrowed Dan's charger while he drove them back to their cars, Destiny a miniature storm cloud in the back. As soon as she was separated from her grandmother, a car-filling aura of darkness had formed around her, landing on the other three like a sodden blanket of calamity. The little girl didn't cry, only shrank into herself and emanated misery.

They were all so disturbed they could barely thank Dan properly when he dropped them. "I want to thank *you*," he said, "for letting me help." Skip understood completely.

This was what was up with Conrad. She heard the other side of it from Jimmy Dee and her boy friend Steve every time she talked to them. "I just feel so helpless!" "I need to *be* there, doing something!" She'd started to call it Conrad Syndrome.

She wondered briefly if Ollie could be persuaded to take Destiny for a few days, to *do* something. But only briefly— Ollie was about as maternal as Harland the grizzly.

She tried Josie's barely-charged phone, and found a number for "Alice", not a 504 number, which could be good —with towers down in New Orleans, people's phones were out even if they were somewhere else.

It was the right Alice, nearly crazy with Conrad Syndrome, and also crazy with worry about Josie and Destiny. It seemed Josie was her housekeeper, whom she'd persuaded to stay in her condo when Josie declined to evacuate: "*She said she had to take care of her Aunt Lou, who can't walk and has 'the sugar'. She didn't bring Aunt Lou with her?*"

"*Only Destiny*" Skip texted back. "*Do you know if they have any relatives here? I need someone to take care of D.*"

Alice replied with confidence, obviously happy to have a task. *"I'll find you somebody."*

As it turned out, she didn't know any of Josie's relatives, but she did know someone with a generator. She was back in five minutes, with instructions to deliver Destiny to a house on St. Charles Avenue with a sign in the window that said, "You loot, we shoot."

Skip gave the kid a big hug and handed her over to the St. Pierres, a handsome couple in their late 50s who in no way looked like they knew what to do with a young child. It was a sad good-bye. The girl clung, and cried when they tried to peel her off.

"Lap of luxury," Abasolo said. "She'll be fine. They'll probably paint her nails for her."

Skip managed a laugh, thinking they probably would.

But she knew he was only trying to make her feel better. It was going to be a long time before Destiny was fine.

"Let's go secure the condo."

"Yeah. And see about Kaynard. He must be missing us."

"Well, he's not gonna get up and walk away. We never did take that ride out to his house. Let's do that first."

Kaynard's house had taken on water, which had now receded, but it smelled like a wet dog, and worse. It already had an X on it, showing that it had been searched. The code the rescue workers used worked like this—whoever searched a house spray-painted an X on it, in each crook of which was written a piece of information—the date, any hazards, number of bodies or animals inside, and searching agency. This one said no people, no animals, and CHP, so that was good. They'd had enough death lately.

But the place had been thoroughly tossed, maybe before the searchers even got there. Everything that could be dropped on the floor had been.

"What do you bet are the odds," Skip said, "that all that crack's missing?"

"That's one bet I wouldn't take."

As predicted, the stash was gone. A quick canvass of the neighbors turned up only one old guy, looked to be about ninety. "Elmo Jones," he said. "Never left for a hurricane. Never will. Beautiful day, isn't it? Always goes back to normal."

You, sir, Skip thought, *are living in la-la land.* "How're you doing now?" she asked. "Do you have everything you need?"

"I could use me some Jim Beam."

"Got food and water?"

"Got a friend who does."

"Okay, then. You know the Polites down the street?" She pointed. "They got a kid named Billy?"

He stepped outside, revealing that he was wearing only jockey shorts. "Which house now?"

Skip pointed.

"Oh. *Those* people. No, I ain' know those people."

And that was as far as they got.

They headed back to Diamond Street, but found it as absent of bodies as the first time they'd searched.

"Guess he did walk away," Skip said.

Abasolo gave her a wry grin. "Why am I not surprised?'

"Yeah. It's the Street of Disappearing Bodies. First we get a report of one and that's wrong and then we find one and now *it's* gone. Know what I'm thinking?"

"Absolutely. You're thinking that first report was right all along. Am I a mind-reader or what?"

"And what else, Uri Geller?"

"Probably what I think—that whoever these guys are, they're working in tandem. Someone dumps a body, somebody else picks it up."

Skip grimaced. "Sure hate that idea." She sighed. "But here's a worse one. Then they gut them and throw them in the river?"

Abasolo winced. "We need to surveil this street."

"That's lot of manpower to use up with so much to do out there."

"Yeah. Okay. Not both at once then." He looked up, assessing. "We could do it from the condo—obviously, Josie could see everything. Need fuel, though. You had lunch?"

"Oh, hell. Lunch. Who eats lunch these days?"

He nodded. "Tell you what. Why don't I go loot us some lunch from the press guys at the Convention Center?" He kicked at one of the bottles of water they'd spilled earlier. "Then we can take turns. Meanwhile, you could gather us up some of this nice water and see if anybody drops off another package."

"Yeah, that'll work—the entrance is on South Peters, so you can get in without anyone seeing you from here."

She picked up some water and walked around the corner, dreading the grim climb in the dark building. The relentless misery and discomfort, along with the heat and long hours, were beginning to take a toll, she supposed. Still, it was good to be here, to be part of the disaster effort. Those who weren't seemed in even worse shape.

By the time Abasolo arrived with a couple of brown bags, she'd set up a nest of pillows on the floor, far enough back that it was out of sight if someone looked up from the street. She'd even rooted around in the office and come up with a pair of binoculars.

He tossed her a bag. "From our buddy Dan. With his compliments."

"Omigod, an apple! It's been days since I've seen anything fresh."

"Yeah, they've got a supply truck, or choppers or something." He unwrapped a sandwich. "Damn! Ham and cheese again. That's all they've had the last two days."

"A.A., there's a car out there." Skip abandoned her lunch and looked through the binocs as someone got out carrying something large and flexible, like a garbage bag. "Holy shit! It's a cop in uniform."

"Are you kidding me?" Abasolo commando-crawled almost to the edge of the balcony. "Whathehell is he carrying? Is that...?"

"Yeah. I think it's a body bag."

The cop pushed open a gate and disappeared behind it. When he came out, he was dragging the body bag. And now it was full. He was walking backwards, grabbing the body around the shoulders. Abasolo said, "That's why he's wearing the uniform. If another cop sees him—or *anyone* sees him—they'll think he's just doing his job. Wish we could see his face."

"I think I can read his plate number. Can you jot it down?"

"Sure." When they had it, they both rolled out of sight.

The cop turned halfway around. Skip said, "Aw, hell. Sunglasses."

He opened the truck and wrangled the body into it.

"Well, the body bag was a nice touch, but a body in the trunk is just downright unprofessional."

"Probably doesn't want the car stinking. Which is what he'd say if anyone came around. This frontier thing leaves a lot of loopholes."

After he'd closed the trunk, the cop turned around again, looking up very deliberately, and then framed his eyes with his hands, as if to bring Josie's body back into view. Evidently, he'd noticed that somebody'd moved it. "Hey," he called. "Y'all all right up there?"

His voice was familiar...maddeningly familiar. Skip knew she knew it. But she couldn't place it.

Getting no response, the cop took off his shades. *Elvis Baggs!* Definitely. But she knew him only by sight. Why was his voice familiar?

When he finally shrugged and left, they shifted back up to sitting. "Was there any doubt in your mind?" A.A. asked.

"Had to be the Dirtbaggs. And I'm damn glad it is. I don't need to know any more crooked cops."

Abasolo seemed surprised. "Think they're working alone?"

She considered. "Maybe not. Why don't we tail them? Each take one?"

"Great idea! But we just missed El."

She stood up. "If the rumors are right, he'd go to the river to dump Kaynard, right?"

"Yeah, but a lot of choices there. They don't call it The *Big* Muddy for nothing."

"It's not about how big it is, it's how accessible. And also the story the rumors tell. People have seen this, supposedly. So it has to be a place where they could."

"The Moon Walk would be really easy. Almost too easy. You know where those steps are?"

"You can practically dangle your toes."

They closed the balcony door and ran down the dark stairway.

They didn't catch El in the act, but, driving back, caught a piece of luck—a glimpse of some cops leaving a hotel, where they'd probably just cadged a free meal. They weren't in uniform, but even without the utility belts, the cocky swagger marked them. One of them looked familiar.

Skip yelled. "Hey, I think that's Kirk. Is that him? Oh, Jesus. What if all those guys are in this?"

"Yeah, definitely Kirk. I'll get out and follow on foot. You circle the block, okay?"

It seemed a dubious plan, but since there were so few cars out, it worked—Kirk had been able to park only half a block away and not only that, had stopped to send a text message before he took off.

He'd split off from the others, who'd all piled into another car.

Quickly, Skip collected Abasolo. "Could be a good sign," she said. "Maybe it's just Kirk and El."

Abasolo said, "Let's go bag us a Baggs."

31

Kathy was eaten up with worry about Nathan. Nathan and...everything. Every. Fucking. Thing. They were going to be here forever, sweating and stinking and trying to save people with no power, no dialysis, no nothing. Well, nothing but some meds and flashlights.

The hospital was a maze of hostile catacombs—dark, hopeless, walls sweating, doctors sweating, patients sweating, everyone's face scrunched and crumpled with the sheer effort of keeping it together. In a way she envied her own patients—at least they had a little chemical help.

She'd have given an organ or two to talk to Adam... even to text. But with no power except what they could steal, she couldn't exactly use the emergency generators to charge her phone. There was a working landline in the hospital, but *only* one, and it could reach only long distance numbers. It couldn't receive calls at all.

Norm had made her laugh with the generator story, the only reason they had any power at all. "See, turned out there *were* emergency generators, in case, you know—the emer-

gency generators gave out—six of them somebody thought
to buy. So a bunch of residents wrestled those damn things
to all the ICUs on all the various floors. But I don't know
why...because, no fuel, naturally."

"Naturally." Kathy smiled at that, thinking *how
Louisiana.*

"One of the docs was so frustrated he kept kicking them,
and this one guy—somebody on staff, respiratory therapist,
maybe? Anyhow, he says, 'Hey, you know what? Let me get
you some fuel. I've got a Mississippi credit card.' Guess what
that turned out to be?"

"Give up."

"Hammer and a screwdriver."

"Huh? Still not getting it."

"Well, turns out you can use 'em to bang off the caps on
diesel vehicles, then you just grab some handy oxygen
tubing for a siphon. Few other guys tried it and now we got
thirty-five gallons of fuel."

She laughed.

"See? I knew you could do that." He left to cheer somebody else up.

That got her through for a while, and then came the
breakthrough news that a helicopter was dropping supplies
on the roof. She hurried up, along with everyone else
hoping to grab what they could for their units.

At first, it was like Christmas—a huge net landed with a
bang that sounded like gunfire.

And then everyone noticed the roof was getting wet. The
water bottles had burst as a result of the impact.

The food supplies were a bust too—boxes and boxes of
Rice-A-Roni, a perfectly good choice—if they'd had any way
to cook it. "Oh, well," Nurse Brenda said, "nothing really
wrong with cold canned ravioli."

"A feast to be savored," Kathy replied. "All three raviolis per meal. With fruit cocktail for dessert."

"Nothing like a starvation diet for dropping some pounds."

Another worry. The kitchen staff was doing great—sending something, however meager, several times a day to every single patient and staff member. But you couldn't subsist on a few hundred calories a day for very long. People definitely were losing weight—and many of the patients couldn't afford to.

In addition, Kathy had two patients who needed routine dialysis—and they were already yellow.

Brenda was still rooting through the dropped supplies. Beaming, she held up a large can of cat food. "Well! Madonna and her kittens aren't gonna starve. Look what I got for Ms. Thurlow!"

The nurse left with her booty, but Kathy stayed awhile, taking in the air. A lot of the staff were sleeping on the roof, finding it more comfortable than inside the tomb the hospital now resembled.

It was peaceful up there, but she had to get back, couldn't afford to think about... well, anything outside. Anything but her patients for now. It was a long walk down those dark stairs, so she took a break with Nathan. How could she not?

Nathan was fussy today, but he seemed hungry, scarfing a graham cracker a nurse gave her to feed him. Hungry was good, considering what he'd been through. He made her smile every time she saw him, but he made her sad too. She couldn't give in to the sad part now—she had to just suck up the sweet and keep it inside her till they got out of this *fucking*... she stopped herself in mid-thought, thinking she couldn't lose it now, just couldn't...had to keep it together...

She was nearly at the staircase door when the command came: "Stop or I'll blow your head off! Hands on your head!"

She froze.

"Do it! Do it! Hands on your head! Now turn around. Slowly."

She managed to move, as though in a dream, vaguely aware that she'd lost control of her bladder. She found herself staring at four armed men in camo and boots—not gangsters intent on stealing narcotics, but National Guardsmen.

She felt a bolt of fury surge her body, but before she could unleash a single swear word, the commander said, "Stand down," and they lowered their weapons, looking sheepish. Clearly, they were surprised to see a woman—Kathy was an unusually tall woman, and she happened to be wearing her now-filthy hair tucked off her sweaty neck under a baseball cap.

They could also see her nametag now, and the stethoscope she wore, having left for the helicopter drop after checking someone's cough.

A small crowd of staff had begun to gather.

As she realized she now had the upper hand, the liquid fury hardened into an icy rage. "Exactly *what* do you Grade-A assholes think you're doing?" she said in a voice she fervently hoped sounded like Dame Maggie Smith's.

"Uh...doctor...we...uh, got a report...uh..."

"Well, take your report, tear it into tiny bits, cram them into your collective...*ears*...and get out of here and get us some help."

The tiny group of spectators erupted in applause, leaving the four would-be heroes backing down the hall like a bunch of teen-agers leaving the principal's office.

Nathan's doctor said, "Dr. Bordelon, I'm ashamed of you. Did you have to be so mean to those poor lost lambs?"

Vanquished, the lost lambs turned and tramped off, boots thudding amid a chorus of hoots and laughter. Even Kathy laughed. "Anybody got a clean pair of scrubs?"

"Already on it." Someone handed her a turquoise pair.

She nodded her approval. "Thanks. They'll go with my eyes."

Somehow or other, she wasn't sure how, she'd just been held at gunpoint, peed herself, and still managed to leave in a good mood. *No question*, she thought, *I'm officially around the bend.*

She stepped into the stairwell, removed her scrubs and underpants, kicked them into a corner, donned the clean ones, and realized her hands were shaking so hard she couldn't even tie the drawstring.

Oh, no. Adrenaline crash.

In a moment, she was shaking all over. She sat down quickly, tears starting, wishing she had the nerve to stretch out—it was going to take a while to recover. But it was just too filthy on the landing. She was alone, though. She could let go. She bawled like it was the end of the world.

They're so young, she thought. *They didn't sign up for this any more than I did. They really are lost lambs.*

32

S kip and Adam watched Kirk Baggs drive to the Iberville Project—the only Project still livable. He parked and strode in, evidently having a destination in mind. A few minutes later he came out lugging a cardboard box, which he loaded into his car. Wiping his brow, he rested a few minutes and drank some water, obviously winded. Finally, he made a call.

"El, betcha anything," Skip said—and waited till someone joined him. But it wasn't Elvis, it was someone else who helped Kirk carry out several more boxes, each time locking them in the trunk. Someone she recognized.

She met Adam's eyes with trepidation. "Is that...uh...who I think it is?"

Adam's jaw was set so hard he could barely move his mouth to talk. "Yeah. Baldwin Devillier, my old sponsor. The guy I talked to a few days ago—when I was about to check into Johnny White's. The one who more or less saved my ass."

Skip tried for levity. "Thought that was me."

"Naah. That was yesterday. Shit! Fuck! Motherfucker!"

She was alarmed. "Hey, you got a right to be pissed as hell. But think they might hear us?"

"Goddammit to fucking hell." He looked as hurt as she'd ever seen him. "Well, he's got a right to..."

"What? Be a criminal?"

"It's an AA thing—'I didn't cause it; I can't cure it; I can't control it.'"

"Huh?"

"You know what? I'd forgotten why Baldy and I fell out in the first place. He was a criminal even then—remember that evidence-planting scandal he was in? I felt all betrayed then too—like he was refusing to be my hero..."

"What's wrong with that? Nobody wants their idols having feet of clay."

"Yeah. Gotta get over that, goddammit. He said he'd moved to Thibodeaux. Wasn't exactly obligated to mention he wasn't there now."

"*That's* what you're so upset about?"

"Naaah, Just the whole damn thing. Don't worry. I'll get over it."

Skip wasn't so sure. But now was no time for an impromptu meeting. "Wonder what that is. That they're loading up. Looks like gold bars, the way they're carrying on."

Abasolo said, "Who are we kidding? Drugs. What else? Especially given the Kaynard experience."

"Yeah. Probably bags of it, packed in the boxes. H kilos, maybe?"

"Or pot bricks."

"Kaynard was peddling crack—these guys must not be specializing."

Skip said, "I wonder if we can find out who they're

ripping off in there? Know any good customers in the Iberville?"

"Got a buddy working narcotics." Abasolo sent a text message while Skip kept watching—in fact, kept watching all the while, as Kirk and Baldwin finished, split up, and drove off in different cars. She followed Baggs, who drove to a secluded spot near Audubon Park, and transferred the boxes to another car, one with Texas plates. They could run those later—though how much later, she had no idea. It was going to take a department with a working computer system to manage that one.

Abasolo finished his text messaging. "Did we get lucky on the timing, or what?"

"I don't know if it was luck. Probably if you tailed one of those guys any time of the day or night, this is what they'd be doing. Did you get any names?"

"Two, with addresses. Samuel Jones—"

"Of Jones Gang fame?"

"Yeah. They're damn near as big as the Corner Boys." He consulted his notes. "And Alden Comeaux. Also of the Jones Gang. Let's go see them."

"Cross your fingers for their continued good health."

They found Samuel Jones in perfect health, but handcuffed to his own bed, nearly naked, somewhat battered, and mad as hell. In fact, too mad to even be scared by two more white po-lice.

"What the *fuck* do y'all think you're doing? Those other pigs gon' get me killed. Y'all come back to finish the job?"

"What job?"

"*You* know what job. Y'all tryin' to jack the rest of my stash? Well, guess what? They got it all, and I'm a fuckin' dead man."

"They say they're coming back for you?" Skip asked.

"Fuck, no, they're done as hell with me. But *you* know who's gon' kill me."

"Your supplier, probably."

"You a regular Einstein."

"You know Alden Comeaux?"

"Yeah. I know Alden. He the one rolled on me."

"Tell you what. You rest here a few minutes, okay? We'll be right back."

Unlike Samuel, Alden Comeaux, far from being hand-cuffed and miserable, was out enjoying the fresh air. Either that, or fleeing the aforementioned supplier—or more likely, fleeing Samuel Jones.

"Or," Skip suggested, "the Dirtbaggs took him out."

Abasolo winced. "Ow. Shall we go see Sam again?"

"Oh, by all means."

"He's gone, Samuel," Abasolo began. "You want to tell us what happened here?"

The thug shrugged his bare scrawny shoulders. "Those two assholes busted in here with their guns out, beat me up, cuffed me, went right to the stash."

"Want to try again, Samuel? We know that isn't what happened."

"Oh, hell, the first one come first. What difference it make?"

"Just testing you," A.A. said. "Anything else?"

"Yeah, they tol' me Alden rolled on me and they let him go. Say they gon' kill us both, I give 'em any crap."

"And there," Skip said, catching her partner's eye, "you have it."

"There you have what?" Jones said, "What the goddam fuck you have? Y'all gon' get me killed."

"*Au contraire*," Abasolo said. "We are going to save your life."

"Oh who?" Jones said.

Skip laughed. "You are such a nerd, A.A. Always with the fancy words."

"You know you love it."

"Actually, I do. You," she said to Jones, "have the right to remain silent. You have the right..."

"Y'all *arrestin'* me? Hey, two pigs just ripped me off. What'd *I* do?"

"That," Abasolo said, "is way too complicated to parse right now."

"Parse. See what I mean?" To Jones, she said, "Trust us. We're saving your life. We're gonna take you where that supplier can't get you."

"Him or any other dirt bag," A.A. said, and winked at Skip.

"Whatchoo chargin' me with? I ain't done nothin'."

"How about resisting arrest?" said Abasolo. The all-purpose grab-bag charge that fit just fine when somebody really hadn't done anything. The dirty-pool he-said-she-said charge. Skip hated cops who hid behind it, but with Elvis and Kirk in the wind, it was Samuel's best chance.

They took him to Camp Greyhound, a collection of open-air cages at the Greyhound Bus Station that was currently serving as Orleans Parish Prison. He'd be shipped out to Angola in a few days and eventually freed.

"Okay," Abasolo said, "that was our good deed for the week. Now let's get into some trouble."

"Something's been nagging at me—you know?"

"And that would be?"

"You know how Elvis yelled when we were in the condo—you know, where we found Josie? I recognized his voice."

"Well, it *is* kind of distinctive in a country-boy, corn

pone, raspy kind of way. But considering we know who he is, how's that going to help us?"

"Remember I told you about that guy with the dogs—Trent? He told me flat out he'd seen cops shooting 'pond scum'. And when I left there, I heard someone else coming to see him. He said something like, 'Honey, I'm home.' Wait! It was '*Daddy's home!*' That was it. In that voice. Elvis'."

"You didn't look to see who it was?"

"I was trying to be low-profile, but evidently it didn't work."

A.A. took a moment to put it together. "You mean you're jumping to conclusions just because they tried to kill you."

She swatted him. "Do you ever stop being funny?"

"You know you love it. Did the guy who hit you look like Elvis?"

"I guess he was about the right height, but I really couldn't tell anything. Elvis *is* gay, right? Isn't he, like, semi-out?"

"I think he's married but...yeah. I don't know if he's any kind of out, but rumors abound, as they say. And the Trent thing would be a hell of a coincidence if it *wasn't* El—gay, voice like El's—yep, that was probably El. Do you like Trent for a Dirtbagg?"

"A witness, anyhow. He sure knows *something*. The main thing is, if Trent's his sweetie, we've now got a way to track Elvis."

"He knows you, so let me handle that. I'll leave you the pleasure of reporting our giant Jones Gang bust to Cappello and covering anything she's got for us."

He texted her around four. "*El back at Trent's 3 p.m. Just rolled out. Where r u?*"

"*Uptown. Ish.*"

Fifteen minutes later: "*Headed ur way.*"

Twenty minutes after that: "*Ripping off some thug like Samuel. All 3 at once. Wanta watch the fun?*" He gave her an address.

Watching in their separate cars, they agreed that when the job was finished, A.A. would take Kirk, because Baldy might recognize him, and Skip would stay with Baldy.

Skip texted, "*Meet at Jimmy Dee's later?*"

33

This was quite civilized, Adam thought—he with his water and Skip with her glass of wine, sipping by candlelight in Jimmy Dee's elegant parlor.

She raised her glass to him: "To better days. Dee-Dee told me to take anything I need—and boy, do I need this wine right now. Guess who was on the doorstep when I got home?"

"Had to be Billy."

"Yeah, where else was he going to go? Said he was worried about me, but he was exhausted—out cold, right on the stoop. I sent him to Kenny's room to continue his nap."

"With Angel, of course."

"Of course. What have you done, A.A.? Did I just adopt a kid?"

He chuckled. "If you did, I pity him. Hey, guess what? I got a lead on Serena Thompson. Somebody left a message for me at the command post at Harrah's. I think they saw me on that little stand-up I did."

"Awright! The suspense is killing me."

"They said she's in Houston."

"Well, that narrows it down."

"Hey, I thought you'd be excited—she's probably at the Astrodome. You know my megaphone trick at the Dome? I could try it there. If we ever get out of here." He sighed. "Oh, by the way, before we get into the substantive stuff, I guess it's time I told you about Kathy Bordelon."

"Ah. The beautiful and mysterious doctor."

"I met her one day when I took someone to the emergency room. And maybe that's the whole story—fell hook, line, and sinker, right there in the hospital."

She straightened up at that. "A.A.! That isn't like you."

"Well, it could be," he said, aware he sounded a little defensive. "If I met the right person."

She stared, sipping wine. She was assessing—he knew her. But there wasn't much to give away. "So. Is Kathy it? The person?"

"I was hoping so, but here's where it gets uncomfortable. I'm staying in her house right now, taking care of her neighbor's dog. And I found all these pictures of her—with a kid. She never told me she had a kid."

"Kind of a big omission."

"Yeah. To be continued. All I can tell you right now is I really care about her."

"I'll try not to be jealous." She smiled like maybe she meant it.

He didn't know if he should say it, but he did: "She reminds me of you." To cover any awkwardness, he took out his notebook. "So...how'd you do with Baldy?"

"I tailed him to a shotgun Uptown on Foucher Street. Don't know if it's his or he's staying with somebody."

"Wait a minute! Remember Mike Weber?"

"Sure. Good guy. Retired last year.

"Well, Mike lives on Foucher Street. I used to give him

rides home sometime. Near Magazine, river side?" When she nodded, he said. "Well, if Weber's involved, that makes it kind of awkward. He's everybody's friend. Retired a hero and all."

She thought about it. "It would be a tough sell to the brass. Cappello's trustworthy, but she'd want to take it higher, and you just don't know who those guys are in bed with."

"And then there's the fact that we don't how many more there are. It's not like we can keep dicking around trying to figure that out. Sure, people are getting hurt, and maybe killed—we had to rescue that wholesaler they ripped off this afternoon—but this is no crazy, misguided attempt to exterminate vermin. These guys are thieves, pure and simple. We know they killed at least one guy—Kaynard—but I bet it's whoever gets in their way, not some concerted effort."

Too late, they heard Billy's steps on the stairs, followed by Angel's soft pads. "Kaynard? Y'all sayin' somebody killed Kaynard?"

Adam stood up. "Hey, Billy." He stuck out a paw for a homie handshake. "Heard you rescued my partner today. Hey, Angel. Long time no see." He roughhoused the dog.

Billy said, "What's that about Kaynard?"

Adam didn't blame the kid for changing the subject. He had a right to know. "Okay, sit down. Listen, I'm real sorry to be the one to tell you. I know he was your stepfather..."

"Naaah. He was just my mama's bad idea. He and my brother were tight, but not me and him." He shook his head for emphasis. "Uh-uh. No. We didn't get along at all."

"Well, glad to hear it's not going to hit you too hard. Yeah, he's dead. We found his body."

"What! *Y'all* two found him? Whaddup with that?"

Adam spread his hands in the who-knows sign. "Somebody dumped his body in the warehouse district. Still had his ID on him." He paused to let Billy assimilate that. "He have any gang affiliations?"

"Oh, yeah. He was a Corner Boy, and my brother Ivory ran with the IBoys. For a long time, Ivory wasn't even allowed in the house. Nice family, huh?" He didn't wait for an answer. "That's not who killed him, though. Gangstas."

Adam and Skip stole a glance at each other. Skip said, "You know who killed him, baby?"

"Thought for a while it was me." He stole sidelong glances at both cops. "Know that blood we found at our old crib, Miss Skip? I shot him—I don't mind telling you now that I know I didn't kill him. He attacked my mama, and I shot him. Thought he was gon' kill her. That's why I was out on the street the night of the storm. My mama threw me out for killin' her man." He smiled. "But he rose from the dead, you know? Rose right up to kill *me*."

Skip cracked a half-smile that said, *Teen-agers! Always with the drama.*

Adam asked, "What are you sayin', man?"

Billy scratched the side of his nose, obscuring his face like he was hiding something. But maybe he just had an itch. "I'm sayin' I ran into this gangsta say Kaynard's looking for me—say he's real mad 'cause I shot him. And then two cops come along, say they lookin' for the gangsta—*and* Kaynard—and they boot me outta there."

"What was the gangster's name?"

"Zion. He a crime partner of Kaynard."

"So maybe Zion killed Kaynard. Why do you say it wasn't gangstas?"

"Cause those cops are dirty, man. Bet you anything they done it."

"And why do you think that?

"One of 'em was the guy I saw beatin' up on Miss Skip. The one I scared away. Now how fucked-up is that?"

"Very," Skip said.

"Extremely," Adam added, regretting they had no access to photos. But he had an idea. "What kind of accent did he have?"

Billy looked puzzled. "Huh? White."

"Think for a minute. He have a New Orleans accent?"

Billy took a minute. "Nope," he said decidedly. "Redneck. Guy was a redneck."

Once again, Skip and Adam shared a glance. This time Billy saw it.

"What?"

"Well... we think you might be right," Skip said. "You mind feeding Angel while we figure out what to do about it? Maybe you could find something for yourself as well?"

He didn't have to be told twice. He stood, called, "Come on, girl," and Angel trotted with him to the kitchen.

"What do you think?" Adam said. "True or false?"

"His story? I believe him. I mean, I *knew* I got attacked to shut me up. And we were already pretty sure the Baggses killed Kaynard. What's not to believe?"

"I don't know. I just feel like there's more there, that's all. We might need to find out more about why the kid shot Kaynard. And something else is funny—Corner Boys don't hang with IBoys. You hear how he said Kaynard and Ivory didn't get along?" He paused for her nod. "And then they did. Something's going on there."

"You mean something was—considering they're both dead."

"Yeah. Maybe for the same reason. You know how Billy's paranoid about the gangs? Maybe for a damn good reason. Maybe he knows something he's not supposed to."

"Hmph. I think you could almost guarantee it. He just admitted he shot Kaynard. Wonder what that fight was really about?"

"Yeah." He shrugged. "Well, that's for later. Meanwhile, we've got some dirty cops to take out."

"Oooh...that sounds so...vigilante!"

"What choice have we got? We can't take this to Cappello and we can't let it continue. But we don't know how big it is. We've got to come up with a plan."

"You know what?" she said. "Three of their guys is all we need to bring them down. 'Cause you *know* the Baggses are running this thing. I've been thinking—you know what we could do?"

What she said shocked him. It wasn't that different from what he was thinking himself, he'd just thought it would be a harder sell, in a way had more or less depended on her to put the brakes on. When she didn't, he said, "You know if this ever comes out, *we're* the dirty cops, right? And that could mean not just disgrace, but..."

"Yeah, prison." All her fear and distaste for the operation showed in her face. "To me," she said carefully. "It's worth it. We can't stand by and let this happen."

He nodded. "Yeah. Desperate times and all that. Okay, I'm in."

34

For four days that seemed like four months, watching the deterioration of everything she thought she knew about how a hospital should work (everything but one, that is), Kathy's spirits had soared with false hope, collapsed in disappointment, and finally dissolved into resignation at least once a day.

The one thing that had worked was the competence and plain *doggedness* of her fellow staff members. Sometimes Norm almost made her cry he tried so hard to keep her from falling apart. "You're the psychiatrist, not me," she'd told him more than once. And he was equally good with the patients.

Outside their unit, it was the same—to Kathy, everyone was a hero.

They withstood the daily disappointments and they moved on.

Help was on the way, they'd be told, and every time they'd get the ICU patients ready, strapped to spine boards, meds for three days, with instructions attached, their histories pinned to them like school kids—Kathy couldn't believe the jobs these nurses and docs had done.

But help wouldn't arrive, or sometimes it would, but the choppers would take the wrong patients, or another hospital's patients...

And the water bottles would break and the food wouldn't be useful.

She knew there were more than 1000 people in the building, probably closer to 1500, and there were probably just as many down the street at Charity-University and Tulane. Sometimes the task of rescue seemed so impossible she couldn't even picture it.

They'd lost eight patients and more were hanging on by their toenails. But by Thursday, ICU patients were starting to get out. Boats came that morning, to pick up patients who'd been taken by truck to a parking level outside.

Then everything stopped when someone started shooting from another building. The National Guard vanquished the sniper, but another fired a few hours later, and the evacuation had to be stopped again.

Kathy went out to watch when they started up the second time, and noticed a group of doctors and nurses cradling a patient, talking to her, patting her and stroking her. Finally, they let her go, and one of the nurses stepped away for a break, tears pouring like sweat. "She was so brave, that lady. Up here for twelve hours maybe, waiting, and finally she just started to fail. We couldn't...do anything. So we just..." she paused for a giant sob, "all we could do was... we made sure she didn't go alone."

But Kathy really needed no explanation. She'd understood exactly what was happening. She was crying herself.

Helicopters roared all night, barely disturbing her sleep. She woke up on her air mattress, starving and sweaty, never thinking this day would be any different from the last five. *Oh, goody*, she thought, *can't wait for breakfast. Love me some string beans and fruit cocktail!*

Norm arrived with something so much better she could have married him. "Want a Frappucino?" He held out a cup of something brownish, which she sipped gingerly. It was like harking back to a different era, one in which security, safety, even a few luxuries were a given. It was like rescue.

"Oooooooh. I can't decide whether to sip slowly till noon, or just up and chug it like I really want to. Whathehell *is* this thing?"

"Secret recipe. But since you're my buddy, I'll let you in on it—it's Ensure with instant coffee. Not bad, huh?"

"Oh, lord. Wars have been fought over less."

"I got something better for you—news. Black Hawks came last night. Almost all the critical patients are gone."

"That's huge!" For a moment she was elated. But she was too used to disappointment. "But there are so many more of us. At this rate, it's gonna take forever..."

He nodded. "I know. I heard somebody say only about 100 are gone. But I wish you could see out the window. Boats out there. Oh, and guess what? The AIDS unit's getting out today. This is the good part—Ross Perot's sending helicopters for them!"

"Ross Perot—you mean the Texas billionaire?"

"Yeah. I got the scoop. Dr. Berggren knew a volunteer from Texas in Haiti. That lady found out what was going on and organized it."

"Whoo! The cavalry's coming for *somebody*."

He patted her shoulder. "They'll be here for us too."

She barely had time not to believe him.

Pretty soon the place was bustling with boats and helicopters. Panicked, she went to check on Nathan, making sure she got contact information for his doctors and nurses. At least, she reasoned, they'd know where their unit ended up.

But where she was going to end up, Kathy had no idea. That afternoon, she and her staff loaded the patients onto a truck bound for the Superdome. There they were put on buses headed for central Louisiana.

For a while, all was silent, everyone in shock, engrossed in looking, for the first time, at the wreck of their city, and trying to take in what had happened to them—six days of hell that were now over.

But when someone timidly asked the driver if they could borrow her cell phone, bedlam broke out. There was also a guard. He and the driver agreed to let each person have one minute with one of their phones, Nurse Brenda to act as the timekeeper.

When it was Kathy's turn, she texted Adam, "*Safe. En route to Pineville, wherever that is. CU soon.*"

She was about to text her brother to come get her when Adam's text came back: "*On the way.*" She was going to tell him, no, don't come, she'd be fine, but her minute was up. Maxine Polite grabbed the phone from her.

35

Skip awoke at sunrise almost refreshed. Quickly, she dressed in shorts, t-shirt, and badge, and went to bang on Ollie's door.

Ollie answered, sporting serious bedhead and holding Ignatius Reilly to her cheek.

"Ollie, why the hell are you still here?"

"Bigger question—why are *you* here in the middle of the night? And by the way, I'm not leaving. The 82nd Airborne was here yesterday. If they couldn't make me, you can't. They pried Dawn out, though. Good thing—I think she was starting to go nuts."

Skip thought Dawn already had a pretty good start on that, but kept it to herself. "I came to ask if you could do me a favor and watch someone for us. But you just gave me a great idea. Is there anyone in Dickie and Dawn's house?"

"Just Breesy."

"Who?"

"She couldn't take the dog. So I'm pet-sitting and watching the house. He stays over there because Iggy bullies him. Why do you want to know?"

"You got a key."

"Sure."

Skip took a breath, reflecting that working on the crooked-cop project was just about the only time she felt normal—thus, she easily rationalized drawing a civilian into it. Quickly she told Ollie the story, holding her breath for her reaction.

Ollie cried, "Oh, God, *thank* you! I've been feeling so damn helpless."

Skip knew the feeling. "Thanks a million, babe."

"I'm here when you need me."

Skip left to get Abasolo and a fancy pocket recorder Jimmy Dee had bought for his nephew Kenny. Abasolo stared at it: "Why does a kid need that?"

She shrugged. "School newspaper, of course. And horsing around."

They stuck together for the first part—waiting at Trent's house for Elvis Baggs to drag his lazy ass out of bed and head out to his car. When he finally did, Abasolo approached him, "Hey, El, remember me?"

Expectantly, the other man turned around. *He's handsome for a thug*, Skip thought. *Probably thinks it's some twinkie who just can't forget him.* But once he saw it was a cop, his hand went for his gun. Abasolo karate-chopped him, causing Baggs to grab his injured wrist, swiveling his head for an escape route. He spun towards their unmarked car. Skip opened the door at that exact second, knocking Elvis into Abasolo's arms. "Nice timing," said Abasolo, planting his knee in the small of the man's back.

"*I* thought so. Nice catch."

Elvis said, "What the fuck?"

"You know exactly what the fuck. You knew it the minute you saw me."

"I shouldn't have let the bitch live." He turned murderous eyes on Skip. "Some goddam kid got in my way. Shoulda killed 'em both."

Abasolo smacked him on the temple. "Don't call the lady rude names."

They wrestled him into the car and into the Horvaths' house, where they were greeted by a furious Breesy. Skip hoped El was afraid of dogs, but if not, there was always Ollie. Half the neighborhood was scared of her.

They cuffed him to the Horvaths' bed—which had evidently been purchased for handcuff compatibility—and went on their way with strict instructions to Ollie: "Shoot him in the balls if he makes any sudden move. Even a tiny one. And don't remove the cuffs for any reason."

"What if he has to pee?"

"Not your problem."

"THE *BALLS*?" Abasolo asked later.

"Uh-huh. It's what I always aim for."

And then they split up, Abasolo to find Kirk, Skip to beard the third guy, Baldwin Devillier, who, with any luck, didn't know she'd been asking questions about crooked cops. One thing, he'd be easy to spot. He was a big, beefy, red-faced clown who fit the stereotype of the corrupt cop far too well for Skip's comfort. He even wore aviator shades and a ball cap.

She'd been at the Foucher Street house almost an hour when he lumbered down the sidewalk, self-importance oozing from every pore, a ceramic mug of coffee clutched in his right hand. That part was excellent. She got out of the car, gun in hand. Startled, he stumbled and spilled coffee all over his clothes, flailing helplessly as the hot liquid hit him.

"You don't have to dance for me."

He straightened up and stared at her, hatred beaming out of his eyes. "Take it easy," she said, "I'm here to help you. Your buddy Adam Abasolo sent me." He relaxed a little. "Said to tell you he's really, really disappointed in you."

"Yeah? He's a grown man. He can tell me himself." But he looked slightly alarmed, his dirty secret clearly out of the bag.

"He couldn't get away today. But you're still his friend, he said. He was real grateful for that advice you gave him the other day. So he wanted you to know you've got a target on your back."

"Whathehell are you talking about?"

She shrugged. "He heard some guys talking about a double-cross. Your partners, maybe. Last thing I want to know is *what* guys. Somebody jumped me just for asking questions in my own hood. So I know something's going down I don't want to know about. I've got my own don't-ask-don't-tell policy. You understand me?" The big man didn't speak, trying to take it in. "We square?"

Slowly, he nodded. Skip got in the car and drove off before he could collect himself and kill her. It was kind of a thin story, she thought. Not nearly as good as it seemed the night before. But it didn't have to be—it only had to be good enough to put him on edge. He'd have to check it out and he couldn't do that without showing his hand.

Abasolo had a better yarn, though. While she was conning Baldy, he was blowing similar smoke at Kirkus Baggs, the twist being that Baldy had already killed Elvis and was now gunning for Kirk. They'd have to wait for Kirk to panic and go looking for his brother, but that was okay. More opportunity to prep for showtime.

Skip parked down the street, stalking Baldy with the binoculars from the Campbells' condo. Once he'd gone back in the house, changed his coffee-stained clothes, and headed out, she settled into a lazy tail, hoping he'd paid a lot more attention to the cop with the gun than to the car she'd exited.

Abasolo texted, *"How'd it go?"*

"Wheels turning slowly."

"Things good here. Maybe trouble w/Baldy before. Kirk just said, 'I'll take care of it.' And rode off like Clint Eastwood."

"You're kiddin' me!"

"Only about Eastwood. I think the recorder got some of it."

"Bodes well for the next part."

Which was the tricky part. The plan was for Skip to keep on Baldy, and A.A. to keep on Baggs till the two thieves met up. Baldy made a few stops, apparently looking for Baggs and not finding him.

She reported to Abasolo. He texted back: *"Baggs went to Trent's, came out loaded for bear. He's texting now."*

"Baldy's reading a text."

"Bingo. Ready?"

"Loaded for bear."

Skip followed Baldy to an isolated area of City Park. There were areas where the park was as woodsy as Golden Gate or Central Park, though much of it had been devastated by Katrina. It was going to take months or years to clean up, and in the meantime tent cities of workers were beginning to spring up there. But it was a huge piece of land, big enough to have a private meeting unnoticed. The Dirtbaggs had chosen well. Skip watched Baldy park and walk deep into the woods.

Abasolo and Kirk Baggs were already there. She followed at a discreet distance.

They'd decided the person who got there first would be point on this, and the other would serve as back-up. Abasolo was ideal, since he had the recorder, and, luck of the draw, it worked that way. She could hear yelling even as she approached.

"Where the fuck is Elvis?" It was Baggs.

She stationed herself behind a bush that still had enough foliage to provide cover. The two men were standing on a narrow path, maybe ten feet apart. Baldy was talking.

"I don't know where your goddam brother is, and I don't give a shit about either one of you dirt bags. I'm sorry I ever got mixed up with this goddam sleazy operation. I'm walkin', okay? I resign. I quit. I am o-u-t out. You understand? You assholes *keep* the money—I'm not doin' this no more."

Baggs's voice was shrill with desperation. "What'd you do with my goddam brother?"

"I didn't do nothin' with him. I'm leavin'." But instead he stood his ground.

"You killed him, you low-life Billy Bob Bubba. Killed him and dumped him in the river."

"I...what? Dumped him in the river? What are you talking about?"

"You think you're smart, don't you? Fakin' me out with the innocent act. You've got the stash in that garage, you're the one with the hotshot connections, you think you can get rid of us now that we got the drugs for you. Well, guess what, douchebag?" He went for his gun even as he talked, and Baldy did the same.

Abasolo shouted, "Drop it, assholes, or I'll blow you all the way to Biloxi!"

And then two quick, deadly pops in quick succession.

Skip thought Baggs shot first, but she couldn't be sure. Maybe the two thugs fired simultaneously, like the men who'd famously dueled in City Park a century ago. But only Baggs went down.

"Drop it," she yelled, but Baldy didn't. She fired, he fired, and so did Abasolo.

Baldy fell like a tree—all six feet of him exploding to the ground at once, making a cracking noise like a fifth shot.

Baggs was still alive, bleeding badly from the shoulder. They tossed him in the back seat of Abasolo's car and Skip applied pressure while they hauled ass to the triage center at the airport. He didn't deserve Dr. Moreau. "Don't bother dying, Baggsy," she whispered. "Your brother's alive and you're both going away for a while."

"Fffffffffff......" was all he said, but she knew what he meant.

They tried to get a crime lab team, but when that failed, settled for documenting the scene as best they could with Skip's little digital camera. Along with the bad-quality, half-assed recordings they had, it might or might not do any good when the case went to court—if it ever did. But nothing was by the book this week. They made up procedure as they went along, piling Baldy into the trunk instead of processing the crime scene. A temporary morgue had been set up in St. Gabriel. They'd have to see that he got there.

And Elvis was just going to have to wait a little longer to pee. Taking their cue from Kirk, they broke into Baldy's garage, but there was no stash there. None in the house, either. Of course he was walking away—he'd already double-crossed the Dirtbaggs and was probably planning to kill them. "You can't make anything up any more," Skip grumbled. "The worst thing you think is probably true."

"Life," noted Abasolo, "imitates art."

The only thing left to do was rescue Elvis and process him into the temporary jail.

Ollie was in the room with him, staring intently, looking as if her eyes could produce lasers that would cut him in two if he tried anything. It was actually pretty scary.

But she was elated once they'd removed Elvis and thanked her. "No. No, *I* need to thank you," she said. "Because now I know I did one thing. Wait, maybe two. I got the 82nd to take Dickie's body somewhere. Anywhere, just out of the street. I don't know where they took him, but they hauled him off.

"This is the worst goddam thing I've even seen—neighbors dying in the street, people on rooftops, everybody looting, no water to shower, Cheetos for dinner, nutcases all around... damn, you should have seen Arnold Acrobat this morning. He egged the 82nd. Said they didn't belong here. God knows where he got the eggs.

"*Everybody's* a nutcase. This has gotta end somewhere. Somewhere it's gotta end. But I'm good now. I can die or anything else. I don't care, I did one thing. Maybe two."

She meant it too. Skip could tell.

"She needs to get out of here," she said on the way to Camp Greyhound.

"Yeah," Adam answered. "Who doesn't?"

36

Adam made up his mind the second he saw Kathy's text—he was going to pick her up and take her wherever she wanted. And they were going to do something together—he was sure she'd feel the same way.

How he was going to get enough gas he wasn't sure. But first he had to get shelter for Darth and Crevette. Permission to go would be good too, but fuck that. He hadn't seen or talked to his lieutenant in three days—he could probably be back before anybody noticed he'd gone. Except Langdon. She'd know and have the National Guard looking for him. Anyway, he needed her.

As soon as he thought she'd be home, he loaded up the animals, drove to her house and banged on the door with a tiny cat in a carrier and a tiny dog on a leash. He gave her his most ingratiating grin. "Company for Angel."

She didn't hesitate: "You moving in?"

"Just these guys—if you can keep them for the weekend. Kathy got out. I'm going to go get her in Pineville."

"Pineville? I didn't even know there was a Pineville. What the hell's she doing there?"

"Mental hospital."

"Oh. Come in." She helped get the animals inside. "Billy's walking Angel. Tell me what's going on while he's gone —they sent the psychiatric patients there?"

"I don't know. Just got a text from a borrowed phone."

"Well, Billy's going to want to go if he finds out where you're going, and I'm sure you don't want that."

"Negative."

"So do me a favor, okay? If Maxine's there, see her if you can, and tell her Billy's okay and we'll get them together ASAP."

He frowned. "Sure that's the best thing for Billy?"

"I'm sure it's what they both want. And honestly? What's the alternative?"

"Since you put it that way. Uh...one more thing. I might need a little gas."

"You and half the city. I don't even think I've got much."

"Okay, make you a deal. Let me siphon enough to get to —oh, Baton Rouge; I know they'll have gas—and I'll bring you back five gallons."

She laughed. "Okay. Deal."

Kathy was waiting for him, wearing shorts and sitting on her duffel. Whatever the outcome of their romance, he was instantly glad he'd come. Seeing her made it seem like everything he'd been through was worth it. If this woman was on Earth, it didn't matter that he'd seen horrors no one should—and become a reluctant vigilante. Didn't even matter if he was tried and convicted of the half a dozen felonies he'd committed that morning. Something about her just made everything better.

After a few heartfelt hugs and kisses, he asked to see Maxine and, truth be told, that was pretty emotional too, although they'd never met. She said she'd never met a white po-lice like Officer Langdon, she'd taken Maxine's son in like he was her own, and she hoped Adam would tell her how grateful Maxine was. And that Officer Langdon had to return her son. ASAP.

So, sure, he promised to get the family back together. It occurred to him only as he was leaving that neither he nor Skip had given a moment's thought to charging Billy with shooting his stepfather. Such was the power of instant civic breakdown. Perhaps in the back of his mind he'd thought they'd deal with it later. But reuniting him with his mama probably required shipping him off somewhere, unhampered by bureaucratic legal maneuvers.

Oh, well, he thought, *maybe a stern talking-to instead. About firearm safety and all.*

As if they'd had fifteen phone calls on the subject, Kathy said, "I just talked to Nathan's doctor. They sent him to Cook Children's in Fort Worth."

"Awesome! I have it on good—yet entirely unconfirmed authority—that Serena's at the Astrodome."

"Same state anyhow." She hesitated...

"You want to stop for anything, or shall we proceed?"

She hugged him. "I showered here. And they fed me. Omigod, I was ravenous!"

"How about a steak when we get to Houston?"

"How soon they forget."

He'd done it again. "Oh, right. You're a vegetarian."

~

SKIP HAD MOVED BACK to the Big House, there being no room for Billy in the slave quarters. She wasn't about to leave him alone. He'd been through enough for any adult, but he was still a minor.

And it struck her dumb to contemplate what he'd suffered in the last week. He'd shot a man; lost a brother and a stepfather; saw his mom go nuts and hold a woman at knifepoint; lost his home; and watched his last relatives leave their home. Not to mention the whole Atlantis thing.

What really bugged her was she sensed there was more, that he was still carrying some private burden. She just didn't know how to find out what it was.

But whatever she could do for him, she was going to.

She'd been offered the weekend off, and had first thought *what's the point*? Her boy friend was in California, her adopted family (Jimmy Dee and company) were in Shreveport, her actual family in Mississippi, she had no gas to go anywhere, and there was nowhere to go in any case. MRE's had become available, so no need to try to scrounge food.

Then it occurred to her that she could rest. She could read a book. Better yet, she could sleep.

She was sleeping upstairs in Sheila's bed when the pounding and shouting started. She pulled on shorts, grabbed her gun, and met Billy in the hall, also armed. She didn't hesitate: "Drop it and get back in your room!"

For a moment she thought he was going to obey, but before he could budge, someone shot the lock off the door. She and Billy both fired.

"Drop it, goddammit!" She'd turned slightly to make her point, so that her gun was half-pointed at him.

Shocked, he did drop it, in fact dropped it right over the railing, causing it to hit the floor below and go off. Whoever was outside hollered, "Hey, Toast! Give it up or you're dead!" and took off running. Skip took off after him, pausing only long enough to shout at Billy to stay put. But the intruder had a head start and a huge incentive to get the hell out.

There was blood all over the sidewalk. When he disappeared at Rampart Street, she came home panting.

Billy was waiting outside, looking frightened for the first time she'd met him.

"Who the fuck was that?" she said. "One of us hit him."

He shrugged. "How the fuck I'd know?"

"Clean up your language, goddammit!" Seeing the absurdity of that, she started laughing, and after a moment, Billy's mouth curved up as well.

"Billy, we gotta have a talk."

"Yes, ma'am."

She sat him in the parlor. "You hear what he said before he left?"

"'Give it up or you're dead.'"

"And he called you a nickname."

He wouldn't meet her eyes, just gave her the turtle-in-shell move. "Must be a mistake. Nobody knows I'm here."

"Yeah, they do. You walked Angel last night, right? You've probably been out other times. Somebody saw you and gave you up to the IBoys. Now why'd they do that?"

He didn't answer, but whatehell? She could wait him out. He was good, though—seemed to have as much practice as she had. In the end, she broke the silence, but only when she judged he'd had plenty of time to think about what might have happened if she hadn't been there.

She said softly, "Come on, baby. Let me help you."

When he finally lifted his head, his face was damp and flushed. Tears were still rolling. "I'm sorry, Miss Skip. I shouldn't'a brought this to your house. I'm gon' leave right away."

"Hell you are. You're gonna tell me what you've got that that thug wants."

He didn't answer.

"Tell me who he is and I'll take him down."

Was that a ray of hope she saw in his eyes? Maybe. Because he started talking. "They call him the Dark Knight, but he ain' no knight. He just Petey. His little bro' Dalton's who killed Ivory. They know I know, need to kill me." He shrugged. "End of story."

"I hear you. Now all I need's the beginning and the middle." When he didn't speak, she said, "Okay, let's work backwards. You mean Dalton shot Ivory or he came in the hospital and killed him?"

"I saw him leave Big Charity that day. Right when I came in. He saw me see him."

"Well, why'd Dalton want to kill Ivory?"

"Keep him quiet. 'Cause Petey shot him—Ivory could rat him out."

"Well, all right then. Now we're getting somewhere. Why would *Petey* want to kill Ivory?"

He looked at his lap again, evidently fighting tears—and himself. Finally, he looked up and blurted, "Miss Skip, this is some nasty gangsta shit. I don't want to get you all up in it."

She almost laughed. "Billy. Did you forget I'm a cop? Nasty gangsta shit's what I do. Why don't you tell me why you really shot Kaynard?"

"I tol' you. He was beatin' up on my mama."

"I can do this all day. Why was he mad at her? What was the fight about?"

He sighed and leaned forward, elbows on his knees. She had the sense he'd come to a decision. "Okay, then, Let's do it. I don't want to get you killed is all."

She was amused. "Seriously? You think maybe I can take care of myself? I'm gonna wipe up the floor with that Petey kid, and his brother Dalton both."

That made him laugh. He didn't realize she was dead serious.

But he must have believed it at some level because the next time he opened his mouth, he didn't close it till he'd told his tale. "See, you gotta know the background. Kaynard was a Corner Boy, see? And Ivory was an IBoy. They hate each other, they s'posed to. But Ivory, he sees a way to rip off his homies and he teams up with Kaynard."

Bingo! Skip thought. *Theory proved.* But she kept her mouth shut.

"So they do that for a while, and then two things get in the way. First of all, the IBoys figure out about Ivory and Kaynard and they shoot Ivory. Then along come the storm. Kaynard's desperate—can't use none of his usual hiding places. So he brings a big ol' stash home—thinks it'll be okay for the weekend 'cause of the storm. But Mama finds it and loses her shit. She didn't know nothin' about none of that, she just happy Ivory's comin' around again. And now her baby's all shot up and she can't believe there's some big ol' stash right in her bathroom.

"She takes after Kaynard and he starts beatin' on her. So I shoot him. What else am I supposed to do?"

She was about to say, *calling 911 would have been good,* but he said, "Couldn't even call the cops, you know? With that storm out there."

Well, hell, how mad can I get? That system doesn't work half the time, anyhow.

"So Mama threw me out and you know the rest."

"Umm...not quite, maybe. The stash is missing, and Petey just said 'give it up.' You've got it, right?"

"No'm. I ain' got it. They must'a took it back. What I got's the money."

SHE AND BILLY boarded up the door and spent the rest of the weekend taking turns keeping watch, Billy unarmed this time—and, if Skip had anything to say about it, unarmed for good. But Petey never returned. She hoped he was dead.

Early Monday, she met Adam at Envie, a little coffee shop a few blocks downriver which had set up a hot plate powered by a marine generator and opened almost immediately after the wind died.

He looked like he'd had a month off.

"Wow. What happened to you? You get engaged?"

"*Au contraire*. Matter of fact she dumped me. But we're good."

"She *what?* That total bitch!"

He patted her hand. "Relax, Langdon, we're good. Seriously. She needs space, you know?"

"Space. The universal kiss-off."

"Uh..." he gestured at their surroundings... "This could be a little different. You know what that woman just went through?"

Skip's cheeks got hot. "Yeah. Sorry, I just felt bad for you."

"Well, don't. We found Serena Thompson and drove her to Fort Worth to pick up Nathan. It was a... well! Dare I say it was a religious experience?"

She nodded. "Yeah, go for it. I know that was your... I don't know, your hot button or something."

He nodded. "Kathy's too. Turned out she lost a little girl to drowning." Skip winced. "I'm no philosopher, but it was almost like we met just to do this one thing together."

She scoffed. "You don't really believe that, right? 'Cause you're right, the Abasolo I know is no philosopher."

"I don't know. Maybe I do believe it. All I know is, it was one of the most gratifying things I ever experienced."

She considered. It was a weighty thing for him to say. "I'm envious. Really."

"You kidding? That was good work we did Friday."

"Yeah, I kind of feel like Ollie. If I never did anything else in my life, I did that. But you know something? There might be something even better we can do. Billy finally opened up."

She told him the story, winding up with Billy's surprise pronouncement about "the money."

"What he meant was, he had the money from Ivory and Kaynard's previous deals—at least the latest ones. Billy watched Ivory pack it in one of those giant plastic boxes, like you get at Walmart to store stuff in."

"Usually not cash, though. Where'd Ivory hide it?"

"Seems the kids—Billy and Ivory—used to play hide and seek and forts and stuff under a neighbor's house—and that happens to be where Billy hid the day after Katrina, when he ran away from me. He found the box while he was there."

"You know what? This coffee's not bad. You've gotta admire a business that improvises like this. Okay, so he found the box—but that was before the flooding, right?"

"Right. No idea whether it's still there or not. But here's the crazy coincidence. Guess who the neighbor is? It's the one person we know in the neighborhood—that old guy we talked to the day we checked the house. You know—the one who wanted us to bring him some bourbon."

"Ha! Elmo Jones, I remember him well. Well, let's go take him some."

Jimmy Dee's liquor cabinet proving sadly lacking in Jim Beam, they looted a bottle of Maker's Mark as a substitute, foregoing the usual paper bag. They wanted to signal their intention loud and clear. Adam was elected gift-bearer, an honor they flipped for, since searching under the house was going to involve muck and slime. Skip peeled off before he climbed the porch steps, but even under the house, she could easily hear the ensuing transaction.

"Hey, Mr. Jones. Remember me?"

"Don't b'lieve I do."

"Oh." Abasolo sounded disappointed. "Didn't you ask for some Jim Beam? I thought you were expecting me to bring it. I'm real sorry I couldn't find you any. Think this might do instead?"

"What's that stuff?" She could almost see him reaching for it.

"Why don't you invite me in and try a taste. You know, to make sure it's up to your standards."

They had a big ol' laugh over that, followed by the closing of the door and then, Skip supposed, a couple of shots on Elmo's part, and some bonding.

As for her part, she cursed herself for losing the toss and Adam for yukking it up with his new buddy while she was scrabbling around in mud. But she didn't have to scrabble for long—the box was big and the space small. The trick was dislodging it from its settled-in state. When she finally broke the suction, thousands of dollars smacked her on the nose, dislodging with a *splat* she worried Elmo Jones might have heard.

But apparently he didn't.

Triumphantly, she conveyed her booty to the car.

"That," said Adam, "was the most fun I've had in a week."

"Yeah, me too."

"Never seen you quite so filthy. But I bet Billy'll be glad to see you anyway."

"Yeah." She was openly gloating. "Can't wait to see the look on his face.

They spent the rest of the trip home planning their entrance.

In the end, it went like this: "*Billy*! Got a little present for you!"

THANKSGIVING 2005

37

"I guess," said Jimmy Dee, who was hosting the feast, "we don't have to do the traditional thing and have everybody say what they're thankful for. I think we'd all say the same thing."

"Just glad to be here," said Cindy Lou Wootten, the police psychologist, who had arrived home only recently.

Skip felt her eyes fill up and Steve Steinman squeeze her hand simultaneously. She looked down so no one would see. It had been a tough few months and the fallout from Katrina was going to last for years. But she was extravagantly grateful for what was left—and to be with these particular people.

The other usual suspects—Steve and the Scoggin-Ritter family—Sheila, Kenny, Jimmy Dee, and Layne—had arrived in early October as soon as the lights went on and it was legal. Skip and Adam had stayed the course, occasionally getting out of town for a day or two.

There was a newcomer for Thanksgiving this year. Adam, with Skip's consent, had invited Conrad.

Everybody'd already heard most of the Katrina stories,

but they were filling Cindy Lou in. They had to leave out the best part—how they took down the Baggs gang—but didn't mind at all bragging about ripping off the IBoys and the Corner Boys with one stroke. With or without the Baggses, the gangs were temporarily dispersed—mostly gone to Houston—and wouldn't be coming around for revenge.

"So how much money was there?" Cindy Lou asked.

"Ninety-two big ones, believe it or not. And soggy! You wouldn't believe. But fortunately, money's very durable, as you know if you've ever left a buck in a pocket and washed your jeans. We cleaned it up and took it to Jimmy Dee in Shreveport."

Jimmy Dee said, "I was bored as hell. Glad to have something to do. I set up a trust fund for Miss Maxine and Billy to live on, to supplement her disability payments, and still have some left if Billy wants to go to college."

"They're in Houston now," Skip said. "Dr. Kathy arranged for Maxine to be sent there and I took Billy to her on that trip to Shreveport."

Cindy Lou said, "Seems like just about everybody ended up in Houston."

Skip nodded. "Almost a quarter of a million people. But Josie didn't—she got sent to Atlanta. She and Destiny are back in Lafayette with their relatives. Serena and Nathan settled in Dallas—thank you, Conrad! Dr. Kathy's in Houston, though—she got a great job at the Menninger Clinic."

"She sold her house?" Cindy Lou asked.

Adam said, "Not yet. Guess who's renting it?"

"You?"

"Yeah, we're neighbors," Conrad said. "Been needin' me a fishing buddy. Kenny, you want to go fishing with us sometime?"

Kenny, unbeknownst to Conrad, hated the idea of killing

animals, but he was more a pleaser than a protester. "Thanks," he managed, but couldn't seem to get another word out.

Jimmy Dee raised a glass. "Hear, hear! Thanks indeed. That's what we're here for."

Kenny grinned. "Yeah. Best Thanksgiving ever."

Tears flowed even as glasses clinked. There wasn't a soul there who didn't agree.

~

EPILOGUE

IT'S BEEN fourteen years since Katrina, and almost everyone from the story's still here, most thriving but none unscathed. Katrina left scars. The year or two after were tough on everyone, some settling into a new city, others left homeless or jobless, some just trying to cope with the enormity of watching an entire city drown. One way or another, just about everyone went a little nuts for a while. Mental health professionals did land office business, including Skip's neighbor and former therapist Boo, whom she found herself consulting for the first time in years. Abasolo, on the other hand, relied on the other AA to get him through.

The crazy settled down, finally, and New Orleans is once again more or less The Big Easy, possibly even a better version of itself. To tell the truth, the first Mardi Gras after Katrina was probably as therapeutic as all the shrinks in town put together.

Here's what happened to everyone in our story—human, canine, and feline alike:

Josie's one of two who's gone, sad to say. She died of compli-
cations from her injuries two years after the storm, but
Destiny's okay—in a manner of speaking. She still lives with
relatives, working part-time as a clerk at a gas station store.
"Doing real good," her aunt says optimistically. She means
Destiny's been off drugs for six months. She's never seemed
her old self after Katrina, but there's still hope.

The Reverend Paul is the other who's passed on. He died in
2010, after five good years with his family in Houston, where
he and Makayla were reunited with Maxine and Billy.
Makayla is an art therapist who's made quite a name for
herself working with children displaced by Katrina. She still
works and, in addition, does very well giving lectures about
how to cope with PTSD caused by natural disasters.

Miss Maxine's doing much better! She's only gone off her
meds once since the storm. Ended up in a hospital, and that
time, she married her nurse—a funny, sweet bald guy who
she said reminded her of the only man she ever loved.
Sometimes, accidentally, she refers to him as "Norm."

After two weeks, the 82nd Airborne finally pried Ollie out of
New Orleans by luring her with transportation on a "pet
bus", which conveyed not only humans, but their animals as
well, to Baton Rouge, where the mother of all animal shel-
ters had been set up on the LSU campus.

She spent the exile in her home state of Maine, where Iggy
was able to roam free and brush up his hunting skills, and
then—to everyone's surprise—she decided to stay. She later
admitted the two weeks after the storm had taken more out

of her than she realized, and she needed a change. In addition to a change, she sought therapy for PTSD.

They wouldn't let Breesy on the bus without a kennel, so Skip said she'd take him for a while. That ended up being almost ten years. Breesy made it to October, 2014, when one day he decided not to wake up for breakfast. "*Everybody*," Skip texted Ollie, "*should go that peacefully.*"

Serena and Nathan came back home! Serena works as a concierge at the Marriott and Nathan, a high school sophomore, wants to be a doctor. He still suffers bronchial issues as a result of his time underwater.

No charges were ever filed against Kirk and Elvis Baggs, since, among other reasons, there were no eyewitnesses to their crimes and, without the stolen drugs, not enough evidence. (The other reasons may have had something to do with a little improvised police procedure on the part of Skip and Abasolo.) But Cappello saw to it that they never returned to New Orleans. Kirk Baggs' injuries prevented him from working, so the NOPD took the opportunity to say good-bye, good riddance, and keep your brother out of town. They fired Elvis, and so far, Kirk has kept his promise.

Kathy Bordelon and Norm both got fired almost immediately. The decision was made to close down Big Charity for the first time since 1736 and build a new University Medical Center. Norm was offered a job there, but he just couldn't do it—it seemed too disloyal to Big Charity. So he's at Ochsner Baptist, another hospital that went through hell after Katrina. He has nightmares, but the same sunny spirit.

Kathy's still in Houston. She married a Cajun chef and had
another baby, but they were divorced in 2017. She and
Abasolo are still friends.

Conrad's still active in the Cajun Navy and continues to find
it the most meaningful thing in his life. Shortly after
Katrina, shell-shocked and giddy with thoughts of what's
really important, he went back to his wife, the lovely
Camille, from whom he'd been separated for nearly a year.
But they needed a fresh start and both were too traumatized
by the storm to start over. They were divorced with no children, but Conrad's by no means given up hope for love.
Meanwhile, hell froze over: he and Skip never lost their
newfound appreciation for each other and remain close to
this day. Although with an edge. Always an edge.

Billy went to Xavier and got a degree in pharmacy. He's
married to a lawyer and works at the Walgreen's in the
Lower Garden District. Every year at Christmas, he brings
Skip a pan of his wife Tanisha's stuffed mirlitons. Unlike
Kenny, he actually does go fishing with Conrad and A.A.

Adam Abasolo moved out of Kathy's Victorian and bought
himself a little house of his own on a canal at Venetian Isles,
right off the lake. It's actually much nicer than the
boathouse and he's still got the lake. He and Crevette are
still together, and he and Cindy Lou are still an off-and-on
item. But he never forgot the brave, brilliant doctor who
powered through the week after Katrina with a hundred
patients and then teamed up with him to reunite Nathan
and Serena.

As promised, Skip mopped the floor with Petey and Dalton, and enjoyed it thoroughly. She and Steve Steinman have been happily cohabiting for years in Steve's Bywater cottage. They were devastated over losing Breesy, but are now the proud parents of a sweet spaniel named Rambla.

Oh, and she got promoted to Sergeant!

THE END

ACKNOWLEDGMENTS

Hurricane Katrina was a milestone in the life of everyone who went through it and all those who are writers eventually must write about it. I feel a bit sheepish that in my case it took fourteen years, but as it turns out, there was quite an up side—that gave other authors time to write some wonderful books that I was able to rely on for my own story.

For instance, Dan Baum's incomparable NINE LIVES. I not only enjoyed it but found it important, and in the end gleaned from it a tidbit that forever will stick in my mind—an action so touching and so telling that it's impossible to forget. A real person actually did it—a fictional character does it here.

Many of the anecdotes I've incorporated are exactly like that —based on real events that I've fictionalized, although perhaps I should mention that the parts about the murder and hostage-taking at Charity Hospital are completely fictional. A similarly shocking event that actually happened was the assault on a doctor by a military team.

My bible for much of the Charity Hospital material was Jim Carrier's remarkable book, CHARITY: THE HEROIC AND HEARTBREAKING STORY OF CHARITY HOSPITAL IN HURRICANE KATRINA. Because I had a good friend who was working at Charity the week after Katrina and because, by pure accident I happened to meet others who were, I knew there was a stunningly heroic story to be told, and Mr. Carrier told it beautifully and movingly. My friend is Dr. Ken White, whose job—and many of whose experiences—I gave to Dr. Kathy Bordelon. Ken, I salute you!

My other informants were Dr. Ruth Berggren and her staff, whom my husband and I met in Dallas right after they were airlifted from Charity. They'd have no idea who I am, but I'll never forget them. Dr. Berggren was the first person to explain hand-bagging to me and when she did, I was incredulous that these doctors and nurses had found the stamina and courage to keep their patients breathing—by hand!—for five straight days. I still don't know how they did it. We were both beyond impressed at their cheerfulness after what many would consider a trauma, and by their passion for their jobs.

Other authors I'd like to thank are Denise Danna and Sandra E. Cordray for NURSING IN THE STORM and Lori Budo for KATRINA THROUGH OUR EYES: STORIES FROM INSIDE BAPTIST HOSPITAL. I hope I haven't forgotten anyone—I've read so many great books about that awful week.

I also hope I've managed to do well by those whose stories were first—I'm especially grateful to Mr. Carrier for giving me a good timeline on events at Charity. I may have manipulated the order of events ever so slightly, but I tried, as much as I could, to be true to the actual sequence. Mr. Carrier, thanks for bringing the Charity story alive and especially for Hurricane Frappuccinos and the unique concept of a Mississippi credit card. So far as I could tell, you scooped everyone on those details.

I was also aided by numerous stories published on nola.com and various other online sources. A thousand thanks to all the authors thereof.

Craig Melancon helped by answering a medical question.

In addition, I owe all kinds of debts to Debra Allen, who may recognize aspects of herself in one of the characters herein and who saved our cats, Cammy and Remy, by holding out for a pet bus. Debbie, thanks so much for heroic cat care, for sharing your stories, and for cleaning out our refrigerator. (Anyone who went through Katrina will understand how heartfelt that last part is.)

I've spent many a delightful evening in the elegant condo in which Josie and Destiny took refuge. Thanks to my dear friends, Allison Stewart and Campbell Hutchinson, for the fictional use of their home. And a special shout-out to Kathy White just for being such a stellar person and spectacular friend.

A word about communications and transportation during the week after Katrina—neither was probably as easy as I've indicated herein. One 504 area code number couldn't call another, but often people don't have cell phones from their own area code, and sometimes you could text. So I gave that ability to many of the characters. As for driving, I actually have no idea how fast certain streets were cleared to make that possible; if I have anything wrong, I plead literary license. But you could walk on the famous "sliver by the river" and in some places you could wade. I tried to keep characters on dry land when I could.

As always, I couldn't do this without my husband Lee Pryor and all the bBn ladies—Stephanie Nilles, Mittie Staininger, and Sarah Holtz. You make it easy and you make me look good. Profound thanks to all! (I hope I say that enough—you are all treasures.)

You can catch up with Skip's latest adventures in
MURDER ON MAGAZINE,
available in bookstores and online.

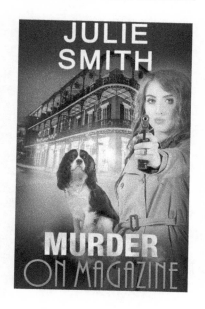

ABOUT THE AUTHOR

JULIE SMITH is a former reporter for the *San Francisco Chronicle* and the New Orleans *Times-Picayune*. NEW ORLEANS MOURNING, her first novel featuring New Orleans cop Skip Langdon, won the Edgar Allan Poe Award for Best Novel, and she has since published nine more highly acclaimed books in the series, plus spun off a second New Orleans series featuring PI and poet Talba Wallis.

She is also the author of the Rebecca Schwartz series and the Paul Mcdonald series (as J. Paul Drew). In addition to her novels, she's written numerous essays and short stories and is the editor of NEW ORLEANS NOIR and NEW ORLEANS NOIR: The Classics.

CPSIA information can be obtained
at www.ICGtesting.com
Printed in the USA
BVHW081315151221
624016BV00006B/294